The
Drowners

A novel by

Ian Galloway

To Wendy

for helping me to swim

Cover illustration: Head of a Drowned Man by Theodore Gericault. Oil on canvas circa 1819.

Saint Louis Art Museum, St. Louis, MO, US, courtesy of WikiArt.

The following text, set in 1996 is inspired by
real events

An eye for an eye will only make the whole world blind

Mahatma Gandhi

CHAPTER ONE

What the fuck had just happened? That was all Mike could think. What the fuck had just happened? He wasn't trying to go any further with it or figure out the answer. He kept repeating the thought over and over, like a tongue teasing an exposed nerve in a tooth. He ran a hand through his waxed hair, exhaled a thin stream of smoke through pursed, dry lips, and finished the last of his pint. Carefully he replaced the glass onto the ring stained dark wood of the table, and took stock of his situation. There was that question again. What the fuck had just happened? Rather than figure it out he strode to the bar and replaced his empty glass with a full one.

Eleven twenty-five on a Monday morning. It takes a certain type of pub to look good at eleven twenty-five on a Monday morning, and The Nag's Head didn't manage it. It didn't come close. It would be a good few hours before it would come into its own. The smell of disinfectant and bleach still hung self-consciously in the air, waiting to be replaced by the more comforting aromas of cigarette smoke and spilt beer. The sound of happy slurred conversation was still some hours away, in its place the steady grumble of traffic and the sporadic electronic fanfare from the fruit machine in the corner. Not for the first time that morning Mike surveyed his surroundings. He was in the lounge, the room given its elevated status due to its floor covering. The carpet was so heavily soiled, that the stain had gone past merely colour and had a texture of its own. There was no doubt the carpet could tell some stories. Huge reams of them, great leather-bound volumes, but none for the particularly discerning reader. They all followed the same theme, misplaced dreams, unrealised hopes and expectations. Any optimism in the prologues and early chapters quickly turned into anxiety and trepidation as the thick nicotine stained pages progressed before in turn turning into despair and occasional sudden, and brutal violence.

The décor was the same as any one of thousands of other pubs in England. He'd been in here with Rachel a couple of weeks ago and had described it as character from a catalogue. That had amused him then, and he'd made a mental note to remember the phrase, and nonchalantly use it in different company. It didn't make him smile this time though and the thought of Rachel, just brought back into focus his current situation. Half a dozen horse brasses adorned the space above the bar, while a seemingly random collection of decorative china plates attempted to give some colour to the far wall facing the windows looking onto the high street. On the wall opposite the bar, a blackboard held centre stage. Written in thick florid writing across the top were the words, "Today's Specials". There was nothing written below. The Nag's Head wasn't a place where anything special happened.

The door opened and the dull grey outside world ejected two more people into the slightly less grey interior. Briefly Mike wondered what brought these two to this pub at quarter to twelve on a Monday, but only briefly. It wasn't much of a diversion. People did tend to have a reason to enter the Nag's, especially before lunchtime when most people – the normal people - started to think about starting drinking. The majority of people came here to escape from something, as opposed to try and find it. The other reason was habit, and that seemed to sum these two up. Mike watched them as they collected their pints and lolled on the bar, then lost interest, focusing instead on the one other customer sat under the blank blackboard. He was probably in his late fifties, with a scruffy stubble and scruffier shirt and jumper. He was concentrating intently on the cigarette he was rolling, his thick yellow fingers squeezing it thinner and thinner. His large forehead - creased in concentration, almost reached to the top of his head, and what hair remained was long and skulked greasily down his neck and onto his shirt collar.

Mike stopped himself staring. It was something Rachel often pulled him up for – along with biting his nails, leaving the TV on, talking with his mouth full, stubbing his cigarettes out in mugs… - but as he would tell her he wasn't being nosy just curious. Just interested in his surroundings. There he was, thinking about Rachel again, and then in turn the events of that morning, and that question. What the fuck had just happened?

After the…, *it* had happened, Mike had automatically chosen to come here. There wasn't really any decision to be made, only which pub, and that was fairly easy. The Nag's did have the knack of making you feel better about yourself. For a while anyway, after a while it turned it on its head and made you feel really shit about yourself, and even shitter for thinking that you were better than those you'd chosen to surround yourself with. It was always exciting to spend a day in the pub when the rest of society, normal five days a weekers, nine to fivers were engaged in toil. It made you appreciate the time, especially seeing them trudge back to work after their diminutive lunch hours. It made you feel different, special that you were bucking the system. A quick glance around though at his fellow rebels, stopped him getting too carried away and proud of himself. There wasn't going to be a revolution in the Nag's Head. Not today anyway.

Lunch hour was marked by the switch to stout and two packets of crisps (prawn cocktail starter followed by beef and mustard), the entertainment provided by two builders playing darts on the board on the wall behind Mike. The cork around the twenty had become swollen from overuse and appeared like a tumour on the black and beige wheel. This was about as sporting as Nags' drinkers got. That and the racing channel on the TV in the bar and the occasional brawl at the weekend. The only other competition seemed to be between the settees and bar stools to see who could show most of their guts. The one Mike had chosen was just winning, by a spring.

The morning had started better than average. He'd had sex with Rachel, and after a hurried breakfast they'd walked to the bus stop together and waited for the number 12 that would take her to the train station. Though he knew he would miss her a lot more than he'd openly admit, even to her, whenever she went away for one of her conferences, there was always a slight excitement of the freedom he'd be given for the coming five days. An excitement he knew would rapidly fade and turn into boredom, as this freedom would materialise in the shape of a poor diet, cheap red wine and masturbation. After waving her off, catching her exaggerated blown kisses and returning a big one of his own; he'd headed off to work, enjoying the forty-minute walk for a change, savouring the memory of Rachel's smile and the touch of her moist full lips on his. His mood was temporarily checked, when after bounding up the steps and into the foyer, his cheerful "Morning" was greeted by a worried looking receptionist informing him he was to go straight into Mr Jackson's office, and that "he looked ready to blow." In the lift on the way up to the 5th floor he had racked his brain for clues of what he could possibly have done to warrant such a meeting at ten to nine on this hitherto fine Monday morning, and especially how his actions of the previous week could have set Jackson off on route to one of his legendary outbursts.

His nine months at the company had been unspectacular but he liked to think that he'd done all that was asked of him and shown an adeptness and willingness to learn. Jackson had a reputation, a hard earned and proudly maintained one at that, for playing hardball. Actually this wasn't strictly true. Jackson liked to think that this was the reputation he had, and regularly told his staff that that was what he was known for, not only inside these four walls but in the industry as a whole. To Mike he seemed to be a parody of every fat police chief he'd ever seen on television and the sad thing was he seemed to actively play up to it, and not in an ironic way. He talked in an almost constant stream of clichés and hackneyed phrases. He was the only Englishman Mike knew who used the word "ass", and was constantly having his busted or chewed and threatening to do the same to everyone else's. That wasn't the only part of the body that he paid attention to either, but so far they had all been idle threats - Mikes balls remained unbroken and his "johnson" was still attached to his torso.

Jackson even used the phrase "kapeesh", leading to the now legendary encounter with Billy Clarke. Billy an old school salesman, while enthusiastic and talented when it came to the hard sell, was equally apathetic and lacking when it came to paperwork and the admin that had come to be an equally large part of the role. They would often come to verbal blows over some paperwork Billy had lost or not filled out, sending volleys of accusations, spittle and counter accusations across the open plan office. In this particular instance - one that was replayed long into the night at the Black Bull by those present - Jackson and Billy were facing each other across Billy's untidy desk. It was late afternoon on the last selling day of the month and as usual Billy hadn't got his figures in on time, nor was he able to get his hands on them when Jackson had emerged from his office after having his ass both chewed and busted by the MD. After five minutes of increasingly loud exchanges both parties were leaning, palms flat on the desk, red faces inches from each other.

"If it's not on my desk by four PM, that's it sunshine. Adios. Good night Vienna. Kapeesh?"

"I've said…."

"Kapeesh?"

"I have no…."

"I said do you kapeesh?"

"Look, where the fuck…?"

"DO YOU FUCKING KAPEESH?"

"YES I FUCKING KAPEESH."

Both these last two sentences were screamed, and they managed to hold eye contact for five, ten almost fifteen seconds afterwards, Jackson underlining the fact that he'd just won, while Billy was equally eager to show that though he'd been forced to back down, he certainly wasn't intimidated.

For once this episode didn't bring a smile to Mike's face as the lift juddered to a halt and after a slight pause and a metallic chime the doors slid open to reveal the sales floor. It was still early, and only a handful of people were visible.

A minute later he was sat in leather chair with an uncomfortably low back in front of Jackson, while the HR manager – an ineffectual ginger haired man in his mid-thirties – sat in ominous attendance to Mike's left.

The meeting had lasted approximately five minutes. Five minutes for Mike to be told that he was in serious trouble; that he was being asked to leave the premises immediately; that a full and thorough investigation was being carried out and until that was completed and an informed decision made he would be kept on full pay. After consulting with their lawyers (their fucking lawyers!) he had been advised to say no more, but if his input was required he would be contacted at home. Twice more Jackson had to state that he had been instructed to say no more and that this was an incredibly serious matter. They were hoping that they would not have to involve the police (at this point he made it very clear that this was because he had no intention of bringing the company's good name into the affair, and not out of loyalty or deference to Mike), but it may be out of his hands.

Mike listened to all this, delivered in the plainest language he'd ever heard Jackson use, in disbelief. In so much disbelief that he took it all without much complaint, and instead just watched Jackson's eyes as they bored into his own, occasionally trying unsuccessfully to find those of his accomplice in HR, before returning to Mike's.

"What the hell am I supposed to have done? Why…what …" He finally managed. He shook his head, his mouth hanging open. "You can't just do this without even telling me what I'm supposed to have done…..for god's sake this is ridiculous." Gradually, incredulation was giving way to anger, and sensing this the HR man stepped in.

"We are doing everything in accordance with our company policy in terms of gross misconduct Mr. Burley (Mr Burley!), as set out in our company handbook which you read and signed when accepting your position, and as Mr Jackson has said we have consulted long and hard with our lawyers on this."

The whole situation was surreal. Thirty minutes earlier mike had had a spring in his step, planning a few pints after work before a Chinese takeaway, now he was being told that he was as good as being sacked for gross misconduct. It was so out of the ordinary that he even considered shouting and demanding to know what he was being accused of, threatening violence. But he didn't. He wasn't an angry person, and certainly not a violent one. It would take a very extraordinary situation to push him to violence, and apparently this wasn't extraordinary enough. Instead he just lowered his head and shook it slowly from side to side.

And that was it. The HR manager checked he had his correct address and telephone number, he was relieved of his pass and was told that they would be in touch. No, they couldn't say when that would be, but they certainly wanted it all put to bed in ten days.

Put to bed. Jesus Christ, Mike thought, after twenty-six unspectacular years, and limited aspirations, his career and hopes for a moderately successful future were being put to bed.

There were tears in his eyes as he left the building. The bewilderment had gone, trampled by the short-lived anger, and the vacuum that left had provided a comfortable home for fear and misery. Common bedfellows they fed off each other, spiralling downwards, taking their host with them. And here he was, scared and miserable. Though they came in the same package they were different by design. Misery was all encompassing, and hung on you like a thick wet coat. Misery was non-specific and seeped into everything you did and tried to do. It wasn't fussy who it touched or where it led you. Fear on the other hand was very different. Under the one banner it came in a myriad of guises, each one giving birth to bastard children, new ones spewing out everywhere you looked, from every place you tried to find shelter and solace.

Mike was scared that he had probably just lost his job. They'd mentioned the bloody police. For god's sake he didn't even know what he'd done and he was half expecting the police to walk into the Nag's Head at any minute and arrest him for it.

He was scared what he was going to tell his mum and dad. Twenty-six years old and still having to make up lies to make up for his failings. He tried to convince himself that it was more for their sakes this time, but this is where the misery came in. With its dark shadow over everything it touched, it was very hard to put a positive spin on anything. After six months he'd managed to de rail his fast track career. And what's even better he didn't even notice he'd done it.

He was scared of not actually having a job. But probably most of all he was scared of telling Rachel. For the first time in his life, he loved someone else. Properly loved someone else. Apart from his parents and his brother, but that was different. You were born to love them, you couldn't help it. From the moment you were born you could do nothing else but love them, and it wasn't until many years later that you actually realised why. Rachel was different though. That was a love that he had developed himself. Born from a small seed of a significant smile here, and a glance and protracted eye contact there, it had developed into an all-encompassing emotion that made him see everything not through his own eyes any more, not even through those of Rachel, but through those of both of them. It was as if he had ceased to be his own individual entity. Everything he did was for both of them, and likewise, everything that was done to him, was inflicted on her. But he didn't shy away from this; he welcomed it with open arms, revelling in it. Every emotion felt was doubled as he thought how he could tell Rachel and let her experience it.

He sort of knew that he wasn't unique, that this was nothing new, and that most people were lucky enough to feel what he felt at least once in their lives. But occasionally, mostly when it was just the two of them, sharing a joke, a bottle of wine or just themselves, there were definitely times when he thought that what they had was unique, was different, and that was one of the best feelings in the world.

And that was what scared him the most. He would have to tell Rachel, admit that he had let them down, that there was a chink in their ideal lives, something from outside had intruded on their happiness, and it was him who had invited it in. And he didn't even know he'd done it. She wouldn't be angry at him, not as such, they'd survive. Bloody hell, he could get another temping job at the drop of a hat, it'd probably mean their first proper holiday together would have to wait another six months, but that wasn't it. In his eyes, she was perfect. Everything she did was perfect, and it wasn't just him looking at her through his rosé (claret, Bordeaux, lager, Guinness) coloured spectacles. Everyone else thought the same too. The people at her work loved her – three promotions within a year. His parents loved her; even the local shopkeepers loved her. And what had happened today was just another thing to add to the long list he was compiling of why he wasn't good enough for her. Of why he didn't deserve her.

It wasn't a lack of self-confidence, and certainly wasn't attention seeking - he'd never tell her his fears – but was the truth as he saw it. He was basically an ordinary twenty-six-year-old Englishman. Averagely good looking, five feet eleven to six foot tall depending on his posture, thick dark brown hair that refused to be teased into any style too fashionable, but on the other side of the coin looked to be in for the long haul. He was occasionally witty, and had a talent for remembering and retelling other people's amusing stories well. If he had to sum himself up in one word, it would probably be solid. Solid or reliable. But solid sounded less boring, more edgy.

Rachel knew he would never lie to, or cheat on her. She knew he would always be there for her, to provide a solid (there was that word again) foundation on which to build her stunning life, knowing that as the inevitable disappointments came he would be there for her, to pick her up, wipe away her tears and smudged mascara, make her smile, give her a hug and send her on her way again. And maybe that's what women wanted. Mike didn't claim to understand women, not even the one he considered his own, but he'd spent hours and hours contemplating this mystery and this was the conclusion he usually ended up with. It did make sense. Of course, solid was ok - some women would strive for solid only to fall short- but it wasn't perfect. Often he told himself that no, he wasn't perfect and never would be but hardly anyone was, and trying to achieve it was always going to end up in failure, disappointment and disillusionment. All this would be OK, if Rachel hadn't done it with apparent ease.

Another thing about this situation worried Mike. Solid so often went hand in hand with boring, and it wasn't just in soap operas and Hollywood that the lure of something, someone, more exciting came along to successfully tempt them away.

The thing Rachel would be most upset about was the fact that he didn't know what had happened, and now that he looked back, he himself found it hard to come to terms with the fact that he had left Jackson's office without a clue as to what had just happened. Or rather why it had just happened. With the benefit of the wisdom of hindsight and the daring donated by the six pints, he could now play out scenarios where he got to the bottom of the whole episode, and had even started dialling the number on his mobile a couple of times to have it out with Jackson. In the end common sense won through and he decided that an angry, drunken conversation now wouldn't achieve anything that a sober level headed one tomorrow morning couldn't.

It was three o'clock, or as near to it as made no difference. That was just one of the relaxing things about spending the day in a pub, especially compared with the office. Only two times really mattered – when it opened and when it shut, and usually if one was an issue, it was unlikely you had the stamina for the other one to come into the reckoning. There weren't deadlines, time limits, targets. Time stretched and shrank in tune with your emotions; no external force could come in and pull the plug or crank the pace up.

Three o'clock and he had a decision to make. A tough one, but admittedly in the scheme of things probably not the most important one he'd have to make in the coming days and weeks. Was he here for the day (to be honest he'd broken the back of the Autumnal day, so the evening or night was probably more apt)? Or did he finish his drink, and do the sensible thing, go home and start as he meant to go on. When he spoke to Rachel, slurring his words probably wasn't going to help the situation. He understood women – his woman – enough to know that. He'd have one more drink to make his decision, no need to rush into anything.

The face that stared back at him, from over the urinal was not totally unfamiliar, but not instantly recognisable. Mike had had some passport photos taken three or four years ago and whenever he pictured himself in his mind's eye, that was the image that came swimming into view. When he met people for the first time, it was that image, that face that he assumed was the one that they would see. To be fair, the face in the photograph wasn't a million miles away from the one he now presented to the world. His hair was a little shorter, but no less dark or thick. The face had thinned slightly, his cheeks slightly less convex, bringing more attention to his full lips, and accentuating his cheekbones. An odd line or two had become etched onto his face as well, on either side of his eyes, and when he smiled - which was often – around his mouth. These were from smiling and not from worry or stress he was quick to point out whenever they were mentioned. This was partly true, over the previous twenty-six years Mike Burley had had a lot more to smile about than to worry about, but if truth be told, the lines probably had more to do with the twenty or so cigarettes he enjoyed a day.

A consequence of carrying this image of himself around in his memory, was that every time he saw a reflection of himself there would be a second or two of readjustment, as his mind would try to work out how he had suddenly aged four years. This wasn't such a big problem at the moment, as for one, these occasions didn't come about that often, and also four years doesn't shape a mid-twenties man's face a great deal. At the back of his mind however Mike was aware that if left unchecked there will come a time when seeing his unbidden reflection would cause distress.

All these thoughts came to his mind as he locked eyes with himself in the toilets of the Nag's Head. He was drunker than he had thought; the cold bleached air in the gents, and the bright, 100-watt light reflected off all six white walls, created an unsympathetic arena and highlighted not only physical imperfections in the bank of mirrors, but exaggerated the effect of the alcohol. In the bar, the dull lights; the tans and browns; the thick, deep, shag-pile shadows; the undercurrent of noise and conversation; the beer smells and smooth, rounded shapes sympathised, and stroked the brow of the slightly incapacitated. Here in the stark, harsh laboratory of the gents where the only sound was the extractor fan whirring on the ceiling above made you long for the womb of the pub proper, just behind the scarred wooden door. He found himself swaying slightly while urinating and to correct this had leaned forward resting his forehead against the cold glass of the mirror. This also served to break eye contact as well. Wearily he leaned back, back into the upright position, his forehead leaving a slight greasy mark on the already greasy mirror. Not bothering to wash his hands, he gratefully left the toilet, zipping up his navy suit trousers as he went.

At the bar his full glass was waiting for him, alongside his change, which he pocketed while taking a long sip. The lounge was quite busy now, solo drinkers and couples having gradually drifted in unnoticed over the last couple of hours. He located his table – his territory marked by his suit jacket on the back of the chair and coat lying on the gut belching settee. He'd reached the table and was in the process of sitting down when he noticed the tape. The black audiotape, in its clear Perspex case lay on the table just in front of the full ashtray. It had been deliberately placed on Mike's table, there was no question about that. It had even been placed so that there *was* no question about that. The circular green ashtray was in the dead centre of the square wooden table (Mike couldn't be sure if that had been moved at all), with the tape just touching it, face down on the table. The edge of the case dissected the ashtray leaving about half a centimetre on either side, so that it was directly in front of him as he sat facing it. Staring at it, as if waiting for it to do something, burst into life and reveal its owner. There was no question that it had been left specifically for him. It had been placed, not dropped, not misplaced or even thrown. And besides, it had his name on it.

CHAPTER TWO

Its eyes constantly moving - always on the lookout for any predator, any hidden danger - the black cat's muscular body described an elongated "S" shape as it prowled along the fence dividing 43 and 45 Beechcroft Road. Three quarters of the way along it came to a halt, its head and upper body lowered, its back hunched, shoulders and hips bulging. Its head scanned the garden to its left for more signs of the thing that had at first woken it from its slumber on the flat garage roof, and then had further tempted it to come and investigate the promise of food being carried on the breeze.

Twelve feet away, sat on a garden chair in the gap between a shed and another fence marking the end of no. 43's territory, a man was hunched forward, his lips pursed making soft welcoming noises, his right hand stretched out in the direction of the cat that was still on the fence, poised, only its nose and whiskers betraying any movement.

"Here puss, come on puss, look what's here." His left hand moved a blue saucer an inch or two; "look what I've got for you... look some fish...come on puss.... lovely fish....here puss...."

Finally persuaded, as if deciding the bland looking man offered no immediate danger, the cat jumped and trotted towards the proffered gift, its gaze on the pink tuna piled on the saucer; now on the figure sat still, leaning forward, his hand still outstretched over the saucer, his thumb and forefinger no longer rubbing; now on the saucer again.

"That's a good boy puss, that's a good boy, are you hungr

With a quick glance back from where it had come, the cat (
towards its last meal, its silver nametag (Jeff) swaying rhythm...ally on
its red collar. Six inches from the saucer he stopped, licking his lips,
sniffing the air, yawning displaying his teeth before licking his lips once
again. Sensing its hesitation, the figure slowly pulled his hand back,
resting it on his knee, soothing noises once more coming from his
pursed lips.

After three, four, five seconds final hesitation Jeff closed in on the
food, gave it a sniff and took a small chunk of the fish that had been
chopped and flattened with the back of a fork and spread to fill almost
all the saucer. He gave a quick look up at the watching figure, one
further lick of his lips, before his taste buds and stomach took over, and
crouching low, began hungrily devouring the food.

"That's a good boy.... there that's nice isn't it...mmmm you like that
don't you... there eat it all up, there's a good boy."

Thirty seconds later and the plate was almost empty, just a small chunk
nearest to the figure remained and another that had been knocked onto
the grass by his eagerness to gobble down all the food. It licked its lips,
and stretched its mouth wide open, exposing his white fangs, a display
the watching figure didn't know whether to take as a show of gratitude
or anger.

Then the Jeff became still, before arching its back, the fur sticking up
along the entire length of his backbone, its tail upright, stiff. The claws
shot out of all four paws as a coughing, spluttering erupted from its

ᵧaping mouth. The cat - its back still a rigid semi-circle, leapt onto its side, hissing, screeching, a spray of tuna mixed with spittle and blood shooting sporadically from its mouth, which was now locked open, the lips drawn back far too far, showing not only his teeth but the entire gums. He was still on his side, his back still arched, all four limbs dead straight, digging into the ground, their efforts slowly spinning the cat around. Its head was thrown back, its open mouth spewing a silent scream. One limb - its front right, after three violent swipes in the air started tearing at its chest then its stomach, then throat before returning to the stomach with increased vigour, the vocal chords suddenly bursting into life again, producing an awful, almost human scream, which was temporarily drowned out as another, this time heavily blood-soaked spume of fish was fired onto the fence. As the scream became audible once again the cat's attack on its own stomach became even more violent, skin and fur being ripped away, as first blood and then a thicker less fluid substance drained onto the grass. An extra violent spasm turned the cat around another few degrees so that the watching figure could only see the thrashing animal's back. All the hairs were now stood up, showing the pale flesh beneath. A choking sound was followed by three decreasingly violent twitches, before the cat lay still, but for its tail, which twisted slowly, tensely before coming to rest between its hind legs.

Two, three, four minutes went by before the figure moved, standing up and prodding the stricken creature with a brogued foot. Happy that it was dead, Mr. Clarke strode to the kitchen, flicking the switch on the kettle to the "on" position, before going back out into the garden and disappearing inside the shed, returning to the kitchen carrying a polythene sheet and a blue cat collar. Fussily he arranged the thick plastic sheet on the kitchen table, placed the collar on the side, retrieved a pair of scissors (heavy duty) from a drawer and put them next to the collar just as the kettle clicked off. Back in the garden he put on the pair of gloves he had placed under his chair twenty minutes earlier and, using his right hand, picked the cat up by its collar. With his left Mr Clarke poured the boiling water from the kettle over the specks of bloody matter on the fence and around the area of grass flattened by the cat's struggles. Once empty he returned to the kitchen carrying the kettle and Jeff, whose stiff arched body gave the impression of being in mid-leap.

After carefully laying the cat in the middle of the sheeting, he filled the kettle three quarters full (few things annoyed him more than people not refilling the kettle after emptying it) and taking hold of the scissors cut the collar from around Jeff's neck. Two minutes later the dead cat on Mr Clarke's kitchen table had a new identity - "Spike" (he felt a pang of regret no one was there to see how apt his new name was) courtesy of the nametag and collar he had bought from a pet shop across town ten days before.

Once the body had been properly wrapped up and put in an already half full bin liner and left outside on the path with the others awaiting collection early the next morning, he removed his gloves and after returning them to their correct place in the shed, climbed the stairs to his bedroom.

Mr Clarke was five feet seven inches, with a thick set body and a largish head decorated with a mop of dark straight hair that seemed to sit on his skull as opposed to grow from it. It was constantly being pushed to one side, but not wanting to defy gravity it liked to fall back to cover the creased forehead and rest above the two thick dark eyebrows. His shirt, white cotton, was stretched slightly against his stomach betraying a lack of exercise and an ever-slowing metabolism, while his dark grey trousers with a crease running down the front of both legs to the black brogues that encased his size six feet, suggested a man who took care over his appearance with respect to neatness and economy as opposed to fashion.

The bedroom held four pieces of furniture. A single bed, which had been covered with a quilt and sheet in such a precise manner, it gave not so much a military impression than that of a hospital. Next to the bed, and next to the wall containing the window that looked over the neatly trimmed lawn that Jeff had crossed only minutes earlier, sat a small bedside table, adorned by an old-fashioned brass alarm clock and a small lamp whose deep red tasselled lampshade looked out of place in the otherwise spartan room. On the other side of the bed was an old sturdy wooden wardrobe while against the wall opposite the bed was a chest of drawers, fashioned from the same wood as the wardrobe. An electric razor, bottles of Old Spice pre-shave and aftershave were lined up neatly on the left side, while a pencil, pencil sharpener, an eraser and a twelve-inch Perspex ruler lay on the right side of the chest.

It was to this set of drawers that Mr Clarke now went, gently sliding out the top drawer, which contained his socks (all dark blue or black). Taking its weight, he slid it all the way out, turned adroitly on his heel and put it down on the bed before picking up the neatly folded pairs of socks one by one and placing them in a corresponding position on the bed behind the drawer. Methodically he moved from left to right, taking care to keep them in the correct order so as not to disrupt his strict rotation sock policy that had successfully meant that they all wore out at the same rate, so if one did hole or snag ahead of its peers, it was down to the quality of the sock and Mr Clarke would make a note (written and mental - why try to remember anything when it was just as easy to write it down?) not to buy that brand again.

After the last sock had been transferred he turned the drawer over, revealing a chart Sellotaped onto the underside of its base. The chart fitted exactly and was drawn with black biro onto slightly off white, thick paper. Down the left-hand side, written in black marker were the numbers five down to zero, and then on down to minus twenty, while along the top written in the same pen were a collection of people's names or numbers, each given slightly less than an inch of space. Columns ran down the page below each of the headings, which were written vertically where they didn't fit in horizontally.

At the level indicated by zero there was a double thickness line in black marker running the length of the drawer, from left to right. Along this line were blocks (shaded with forty-five degree pencil lines) mostly hanging down below the zero, though in one case, in the column headed milkman, the block sat lonely on top, its roof resting on the faint biro mark indicating two. There were upwards of thirty columns with space for perhaps three more, mainly with blocks indicating scores of between minus three and minus eight. Third from the left - the column headed 101 BR - the column reached the bottom of the chart, where the number thirty-three had been written.

Taking the rubber firmly in his right hand Mr Clarke located the column labelled 45 BR and after following it down with his left index finger to minus five, proceeded to rub out the 2H pencil lines, down to minus one where he drew a line across with the aid of the ruler to close the box off once more. As the lines disappeared under his white rectangle eraser, the slights and insults, the hurt and sense of injustice caused by them were rubbed from his mind. Recently it hadn't even been his acts of reprisal that had set the record straight, but the alterations they brought about on the chart. As Mr Clarke had watched the cat die he felt no pleasure, no relief, in fact the only emotion he allowed himself during Jeff's death throes was a slight satisfaction that he had got the strength of poison correct. These feelings of wrongs being righted only came as the box was reduced from minus five to minus one. Only then could he forget the abusive taunts in the street; the trespassing in his garden to retrieve their ball; the constant noise and the fireworks that had been fired at his house last autumn. Whereas minus one wasn't an ideal situation he was willing to leave it as it was for the time being. He could have made it into a nice even zero, merely by leaving the cat in their garden so they would see the pain that their beloved pet had experienced in the last moments of its life, but it was a risk he wasn't prepared to take, not for a solitary point anyway. A quick glance across the columns showed how much other work there was to do.

Blowing on the chart and then using his hands to remove the small bits of rubber, his eyes settled on the column that stood out, mocking him and his fists clenched involuntarily, before tearing his gaze away and starting to replace the socks, one by one in reverse order.

Outside he could hear one of the next doors children returning from school and he allowed himself a smile - the corners of his mouth turning up almost imperceptibly.

CHAPTER THREE

During the night Mike's body had arranged itself into the recovery position and it was like this that he woke at eight thirty, fully clothed, the cloying taste of kebab in his mouth suggesting his route home last night.

Five minutes later he had moved position twice, got pins and needles in his left arm and had failed in two attempts to open his eyes, the lids remaining tightly shut, glued by sleep and the light streaming in from the hastily drawn curtains.

Alarm bells rang in his already throbbing head, forcing his eye lids up, his bloodshot eyes painfully slowly focusing on his alarm clock half hiding behind his wallet that he'd managed to rescue from his pocket before collapsing and passing out on the bed.

Cursing himself for forgetting to set the alarm and at the same time dreading the prospect of working eight hours feeling like this, he tried to get both his body and his mind into some semblance of order, swung his socked feet from under the duvet and just about made the sitting position. Pride that he had obviously managed to remove his shoes the night before almost broke through the jumble of other thoughts fighting for his limited attention. Shit, why the hell had he got himself into the state he had obviously got himself into on a Monday or Tuesday or whatever bloody day it had been yesterday? And where was Rachel? These unanswered questions – seemed to be the theme of the week – proved too much and he flopped back onto the bed prostrate.

A voice – quiet, but persistent - somewhere deep in the back of his head, was trying to make itself heard above the curses and drunken mumblings that the remnants of his thoughts consisted of, but its eloquent and logical statements were all but drowned out, only an occasional word getting through, and these found very short shrift when they did gain their freedom.

Tiredness and nausea were also in the mix, and these fought for control as he writhed in slow motion on his bed, groaning into his spittle-darkened pillow. A surge of relief won over its combatant emotions as the voice informed him he didn't have to leave bed this morning. He didn't bother asking why or trying to investigate, just thanked God, Rachel, his mum, whoever had made this possible and closed his eyes again, beckoning sleep and then welcoming it with open, trembling arms as it embraced him once more, allowing himself to be smothered by it, to drown in it.

One hundred and twenty-seven minutes later he awoke choking from it. He couldn't remember waking up earlier in the morning but his mind hadn't been inactive while his body rested, and he was fully up to date with his present employment situation when he woke up for the second time that Tuesday morning.

"FUCK" The word was shouted, waking his vocal chords. "You wanker Mike... you absolute wanker..." Using the heels of his hands he harshly rubbed his eyes and sat up, his head still throbbing slightly but temporarily forgotten. He swung his legs out of the bed, so he was sitting on the edge again, and noticed he'd spilt sesame seed sauce down his trousers last night.

"Fuck. Fuck. Fuck. Do something Mike. Do something you useless tosser."

"Right, come on think, stop panicking and get a plan together." The words, his voice sounded odd, in the quiet room, almost as if they were intruding, but he needed to vocalise his thoughts, give them body and life, before they were sucked back into his still foggy head.

A quick check of his mobile phone told him he'd missed two calls from Rachel last night and one this morning, and that he hadn't called her. Good, he'd be able to deliver the news with a near sober head. See, he was already getting somewhere.

"Good man Mike, Good Man". Despite everything and all evidence to the contrary, he started feeling a bit better. His usually unlimited reserves of optimism – usually blind, but nevertheless optimism – would be tested over this but he was already thinking he maybe had read a bit too much into the meeting. As opposed to well and truly fucked he was slightly shafted. It certainly wasn't irretrievable, and no doubt he would have it all sorted by Saturday when Rachel came back, none the wiser. He'd get himself a coffee, sort his head out and ring Jackson up and have it out with him. There's no way he'd stand for being kept in the dark this time. He'd been caught unawares yesterday, caught off guard, but this time, he'd be ready, prepared. If necessary he'll go to the citizens' advice bureau, get a lawyer, anything. Looking back twenty-four hours on, he couldn't believe he hadn't put up more of a fight, and the fact that he'd gone to the pub and got drunk, almost glad of the opportunity to spend the day drinking in some seedy pub rather try and fight for his job, for his livelihood, fuck knows maybe even for Rachel, was starting to sicken him. More than the dozen or so pints of lager and stout and the glasses of bourbon he'd undoubtedly moved onto, working their way through his body.

As soon as his mind was allowed to wander, to get away from the tight leash he'd tied around it, his optimism faded and fear, gloom and desperation sidled into its place to do their bidding. Still, speaking to himself he quickly, yet clumsily undressed from the clothes he'd worn the day before, down to his boxer shorts.

The kettle sounded its chime to announce to the world, or the kitchen and its clammy occupant at least, that its job was done. Mike left the post he'd brought in from the hall (nothing for him, a catalogue offer and what looked like a credit card bill for Rachel), made his coffee (black 2 sugars) - all the time doing a jig to keep contact between his feet and the cold floor to an absolute minimum - and was almost at the top of the stairs, his right hand holding his "Property of Her Majesty's Prison Broadmoor" mug when out of the blue he remembered the tape.

He stopped, the black coffee spilling over the sides of the mug and looked behind him involuntarily. Quickening his pace, Mike returned to his room, and after clearing a space put his coffee down, spilling more of it. He suddenly felt very aware of and uncomfortable by his nakedness, and quickly pulled on a pair of jeans that lay crumpled on the floor and a sweatshirt that lay next to them.

Conjuring up a picture of the tape in his head he tried to fill in everything else he knew about it. After returning from the toilets via the bar and first seeing it yesterday, he'd sat down and stared at it, scared to touch it, fearing that it was tainted in some way. He also felt that as soon as he did touch it, as soon as he picked it up he was claiming it, taking responsibility for it, and for some reason that suddenly seemed to be the last thing he wanted to do.

He couldn't put his finger on the reason why, but the sight of the tape lying there, waiting for him, had made him feel uneasy. Audio tapes themselves were pretty rare these days, and it recalled past times, days when he wasn't old enough to drink in pubs, times when he'd used just such tapes to record his favourite songs off the radio, or to copy his mate's computer games. In times of satellite television, the internet and mobile phones, it was impossible not to look at it without a certain degree of nostalgia. There was an inherent innocence with tapes, that was lacking in their hi-tech successors. That said, sat there on the dark wooden table, it couldn't have looked more out of place. Less innocent.

The word "Mike" was written in capitals on a white paper strip glued to the top of the cassette. Written in red ink, the capital letters were impressed into the paper suggesting the writer had pressed with some force. The inlay sleeve was also missing.

Scolding himself, for allowing himself to get worked up, he let out a long breath, took a quick glance around the pub and slowly reached his right hand out to claim his gift. There wasn't much else to be discovered. There was no label on the other side of the cassette, and the small plastic tabs that allowed the tape to be re-recorded on had been removed. Despite this, the cassette and its case looked new, its plastic surface still shiny and unmarked.

He'd looked around him, studying the twenty or so other people in the bar, even standing up to give himself a better view, but no one was taking any notice of him, too engrossed in their own conversations, pints, thoughts, their own problems.

And that was it. No mystery man in a trench coat, catching his eye before slipping out of the pub, no beautiful woman, dressed in evening dress whispering a coded phrase into his ear, before placing a kiss on his cheek. Just a tape. Left on a table in the Nag's Head. With his name on it. A few hours after being ejected from his office. Either he'd got over the shock pretty quickly, or maybe because of it Mike didn't know, but he'd pocketed the tape and carried on drinking, for what judging by the way his head and stomach felt now, was probably several more hours.

Fruitlessly, he searched the bedroom, before taking the stairs two at a time into the lounge. He had a course of action now, maybe not a plan as such, but certainly a task to focus on, and he felt better for it. His jacket and coat were lying on the orange settee, the greasy remains of a kebab sat in front of them on the small wooden table. Taking the suit jacket in his left hand, his right quickly frisked first the outside pockets and then the inside, his fingers quickly dismissing the soft packing of twenty Bensons before settling on and retrieving the hard, cool cassette case. Once again Mike became still, forcing himself to breathe as he turned it over in his hands, the suit jacket forgotten and dropped onto the carpet. Quickly he tried to remember if and where he had a cassette player and was sure that they hadn't thrown away his old portable stereo they occasionally used outside in the garden. He was even more sure it was in Rachel's wardrobe.

The tape gripped tightly in his hand Mike climbed the stairs to his room, trying to ignore the fear that was crawling up from his stomach where it had seemed to have made its nest.

CHAPTER FOUR

Making sure he had remembered to lock all three locks on his front door, and then that he had firmly secured the latch on the iron gate that protected the entrance to the small concrete yard in front of his house, Mr Clarke stepped out onto the pavement. Above, the sky was a pale grey colour, and despite being noon, the day hadn't decided what to do with itself yet, though it had kept its options open. A brisk North Easterly wind was blowing, forcing his collar up and both hands into his overcoat pockets. A page of a tabloid newspaper blew like tumbleweed along the path, catching briefly on a lamppost, allowing him to glimpse the headline "Schoolgirl raped by disabled caretaker." Next to it was a black and white photograph of a woman he thought he recognised hugging a giant bottle of wine. Before he could fathom if these two were in any way connected the paper disentangled itself and scraped its way along the pavement before suddenly being tugged upwards by a stronger gust, up and over a wall into someone's front yard further up the street.

Many of the houses stretching out in front of him corresponded to columns on the chart taped to the bottom of his drawer, and before turning left and towards town, he quickly checked to see if anyone he recognised was out or visible lurking at their windows. Seeing no one, he set off, shoulders hunched forward slightly in an attempt to shut out the wind. Mr Clarke's mind, like his body, was rarely at rest and as he strode at an even eighty paces a minute (tested fortnightly on his pedometer) he replayed various incidents in his life, examining cause and effect and planning future acts to redress the balance.

Redressing the balance, that was how he saw it. The world was in constant flux and unless carefully monitored and the results of the monitoring meticulously analysed and acted upon, you would find yourself in a position where you were becoming worn down, bruised, made to suffer continued rejections by the society that you were born into. Born into an equal. You could not expect life, God, fate or whoever you put your faith or trust in, to sort it all out for you, to make everything OK. You certainly couldn't rely on the government or the courts to pay back citizens for wrongdoings, no matter how slight. No, it was down to the individual to take responsibility for not only his or her actions, but also those done by other individuals that directly (and sometimes indirectly) affected them. Of course, not everyone was as conscientious as Mr Clarke, and as careful to ensure that only exactly the right amount of action was taken, so that equilibrium was restored.

Many other people, Mr Clarke would admit, would have taken sterner action against Potter, the ambitious ex colleague at work who had constantly belittled him; lied *to* him and *about* him; destroyed work and eventually, via a malicious rumour campaign, got his employers to force Mr Clarke to take early retirement while Potter got his job, albeit with a different name, and he fancied, a fatter salary. Mr Clarke knew many others in his situation would have considered taking Potter's life, but after very careful consideration - and besides the chart doesn't lie – he knew then as he did now, that he had done the right thing.

The four tabs of LSD he had soaked in Potters coffee on the morning of Mr Clarke's final day at Albright's (he had bought five but he had fed the fifth to the Jack Russell that had bitten him two weeks earlier, with the result that from that day on until its death two years later it had an extreme fear of cats), was done with no sense of malice or revenge - he hated those words - but with one of justice. Two hours later, as Mr Clarke along with the entire workforce, watched Potter, screaming and snarling, trying to first bite off and then eat his left hand - succeeding in only the middle and fourth digits before being overpowered and subdued by three paramedics and two policemen, there was no joy. Nor did he feel pity when he heard he'd since been admitted to a mental institution - up north where his parents lived - indefinitely.

In his mind and in his world that was so simple and black and white it could be completely represented by means of a three foot by two foot chart, him and Potter were now once again on a level footing, and the bar in the column labelled Potter D was now resting - permanently he was sure - on the thick zero line that represented calm, equilibrium, justice. Peace.

He had reached the train station at the top of the high street and had once again noticed how everyone looked dirty, unkempt and completely lacking in self-pride. They skulked about their no doubt dirty business or else they swaggered, swollen with an arrogance stolen or paid for by no doubt equally dirty business. He could taste their bitterness and evil in the cold air he regrettably had to let into his own body.

The tramp was at his normal place by the bus station, an empty can of strong lager lying unconscious on its side, another one clasped in his purple hand. Despite Mr Clarke attempting eye contact, the man dressed in a large black, heavily stained full-length coat and purple woollen hat was too intent on staring at a patch of pavement just to the left of where he was slumped. Mr Clarke quickly pictured the tramp's column and saw that it was lying on minus three. It tended to slowly go down over the months due to occasional violent verbal outbursts that were alarming and embarrassing, and also due to the fact that he forced him to inhale his piss fumes every time he had to use the subway. He would allow it to get a bit lower, before taking action again. The last time had been last winter on the coldest day of the year. After making sure the several cans of super strength lager (including the extra two he had placed there himself) had rendered him unconscious, Mr Clarke had removed the tramp's shoes and socks, and poured some cold water from his flask over them. A year later, not even the sight of seeing him limping on his now toeless feet could clean up the memory of touching his socks or skin.

The newsagents he had chosen had several factors in its favour, namely its general lack of business; its distance from 43 Beechcroft Road; and the large selection of adult magazines. The latter he had noticed with disgust while buying five balls of string several months earlier.

His search of the top shelf was brief but successful and less than three minutes later he was leaving the empty shop clutching a blue bag containing "Bra Busters", "Forty Plus - inches and years", "Big and Black" and "Score". The first three were summed up adequately by their titles, but the fourth he discovered was an American publication specialising in the larger endowed woman and could double for a plastic surgeon's catalogue. Re-joining the pavement before crossing the road

–he'd already decided to go the long way home, not wishing to put himself through witnessing the scum in the high street again - he was torn whether to add the woman who had just served him to his chart. He was sure he had caught the look of disgust on her face, but in the end, he gave her the benefit of the doubt. Even though she peddled the filth, she could not have known the reason he was buying the magazines.

Back at number forty-three, the magazines, unopened, were spread out on the same kitchen table where Jeff had been wrapped up a day earlier, and the same fate, though not so complete was about to befall them. A compliment slip lay on top of them. He had received it with an order of a biology and two chemistry books a while back that he'd ordered from a large bookshop he knew also sold magazines. He had specifically ordered the books in the name of P Foster and had been dismayed the attached slip was not addressed as such, just one of thousands sent out every month from one of their stores, but was confident it wouldn't lessen the impact and in a way added an anonymity to the package in keeping with its contents.

After sealing the magazines and compliments slip in a large brown envelope, already addressed to Mr Peter Foster 68 Beechcroft Road on a printed white label (one of twenty four he had sent off for earlier in the month), the package was weighed using an electric set of scales he kept in a cupboard under the stairs, and measured to an accuracy of four decimal places. The corresponding weight was checked with Mr Clarke's postal services charge book (kept in the bureau in the dining room) and the appropriate number of stamps (kept next to the book) licked and placed in ascending monetary value from left to right on the package.

Carefully he tore off the top left corner of the envelope, revealing enough of the top magazine to leave no doubt as to its contents and after returning the package to the blue plastic bag set off to the post office which contained the only post slot he knew of that was wide enough to take such a package.

CHAPTER FIVE

Several other people shared the top deck with Mike, and the bottom deck was full, save for two seats, one next to a man whose occasional but violent twitches of his head and constant grinding teeth had sent even the weariest passenger upstairs. The other seat was half covered by the buttocks of a fat lady who was still managing to sweat despite the temperature. It always amazed him how many people were out and about on a weekday. He had wrongly assumed that his nine to five, Monday to Friday drudgery was shared by the vast majority of his fellow citizens, but now he realised that more than a few had found another, no less mundane existence.

Such thoughts only paid a fleeting visit to Mike today however. He had far more important, pressing matters to engage, worry and to excite him. He had put the tape into his stereo, trying to convince himself a poor-quality recording of REM was about to fill the room but somehow knowing it was going to be a whole lot more exciting. A whole lot more dangerous. What did fill the room was silence, as the machine slowly transferred tape from one spool to the other. This silence went on for twenty, thirty seconds, one minute - Mike couldn't say. It was only his body crying out for oxygen, making him realise he had been holding his breath since pressing the play button that proved the passage of time.

Eventually there was a sharp click and the sound of background static. Mike was staring at the turning mechanism, stock still, his ears straining to hear some hidden message in the static.

"Michael." The word was spoken, not shouted, but the sound acted like an electric shock to Mike, causing him to jolt back. He spun round to see if anyone behind him had called his name, even though he knew it had been uttered by the speakers either side of his wardrobe. His hands and brow were covered in a sheen of sweat.

"I've organised a little surprise for you. I think you'll like it Michael. There's nothing to be worried about. You'll thank me Michael. Inside a blue Ford Orion registration A987 YJ B parked at the end of Devonshire Street." A pause. "Thank you Michael, see you later."

Mike stood still while the tape hissed static for another ten minutes before emitting another click and a silence replaced the staticky hiss. He paced around the room being careful his footfalls were soundless so as not to drown out any sound that may come from the speakers. Twenty minutes of alternate pacing and standing later and the tape clunked to a stop causing Mike to jolt despite having watched the tape gradually unwind. A shaking hand turned the tape around and he repeated the process but after ten minutes of silence, despite maybe his better judgement he gave in to impatience and curiosity, turned it off, got his coat, swore to himself for losing his scarf and left the house, nearly bumping into a whistling dustman.

And now here he was on the 93-bus trying to get his jumble of thoughts into some semblance of order. Completely new experiences are hard to cope with or plan for as most of our intelligence comes from past events, either experienced or learnt. For the first time in twenty-two years Mike Burley had absolutely no idea what to expect and though he was sure it wasn't going to be anything too disturbing or life threatening, this complete absence of knowledge, his inability to compare it with anything else, he found distressing.

He tried to rationalise what had happened by concentrating on the few facts he actually had. He knew now that the tape had been meant for him. It could easily have found its way onto his chair, but the strange contents and the fact it referred to him in person meant it was almost beyond the realms of possibility that it had all been a coincidence. This meant that it was planned and that this person had either been in the pub or had followed him there. This begged the question - Was it something to do with his dismissal from work? Shit, this was weird. Since he'd seen Rachel disappear on the bus just over twenty-four hours ago, his life had taken progressively more strange turns. The thought occurred to him that he was part of some set up, some TV hidden camera stunt. Everyone on the bus became a hidden stooge, and he found himself trying to look cool, and even toyed with idea of returning home to change into a better pair of jeans and have a shave.

The TV idea didn't sit right though, and though it was the best he had managed to come up with, it only held his favour for half a minute or so, which meant he was back to the beginning again - nowhere.

The voice had been nondescript, occasionally he thought he recognised it but then the next syllable would convince him he didn't. The words were spoken in a slightly hushed way, but also contained a slight smugness that Mike found made him uncomfortable. Sometimes it sounded like the speaker had been trying to disguise his voice, but then he sounded too natural.

Looking back, he couldn't believe he hadn't played it back a couple of times and searched it for clues, background noises etc. Almost without thinking he had left the house, blindly, dumbly obeying the voice on the tape, and sat here his body swaying with the double decker was the first time he'd actually thought about was he was doing, where he was going and what he might find.

He wondered how he would be feeling in an hour's time and started to think that somehow this would turn out to be something mundane and was surprised to find this thought filled him with disappointment.

He wished he had telephoned Rachel, he very much doubted she was behind any of this, but just talking to someone about it may put it into some sort of perspective or at least make it seem a bit more real. He hadn't talked to anyone properly since leaving his bosses office the morning before and that added to the whole strangeness of the situation.

The bus braked sharply, jolting Mike in his seat and bringing his thoughts back to the immediate present, along with the realisation he was hungry - he hadn't eaten yet and it was it was early afternoon. Then, with an emotion akin to terror he saw that he was nearing the stop he had planned to get off at. Another sheen of sweat covered his skin sticking the T-shirt beneath his shirt and coat to his back. He now wanted the bus journey to go on. Forever. He had gradually become convinced that whatever he found at the place mentioned on the tape, or whoever he met there, his life had taken a turn, beyond his controlling, that would mean it would never be the same again. He suddenly didn't want to make that turn, that he was more than happy at the minute plodding along. All of a sudden the 93 bus seemed the safest, the best place he had ever been and outside, especially a place called Devonshire Street and a blue Ford Orion seemed the most terrible things in the world.

But when had his life made that turn? When he had put the tape in the machine and pressed the play button? When he'd found the tape on his chair in the Nag's Head? When he'd been sacked or got the job in the first place? It was impossible to tell. All of a sudden everything seemed connected, even the most irrelevant occurrences seemed to fit into the jigsaw. He realised he had missed his stop - the bus hadn't even slowed down, and he suddenly found himself standing up and then walking down the spiral stairs, the bus's swaying and uneven motion causing him to twice slam into the metal rail.

The cold air seemed even more so on his moist forehead as he stood on the almost empty footpath. He was in the area of town called the Banksmead District, on the opposite side of town from where he lived. In the day it was always fairly quiet, a few remaining factories and businesses providing the occasional delivery vehicle or employee, but most buildings had become deserted in the preceding two decades, either closing down completely or having moved abroad or to a green site. It was at night when it came alive now, with two large night-clubs making use of the large warehouses and of the several pubs that fed off the clubbers most didn't even bother opening in the daytime.

His head down into the wind, Mike set off back in the direction he had just come, before cutting off the main path, up a slight rise between two large buildings. They looked down on Mike through dirty, broken windows, increasing his fears of being watched. The temptation to look behind him was overpowering and he gave into it several times, almost tripping over the frame of a bike that had been chained to a lamppost before being systematically stripped and vandalised. Every time he looked over his shoulder he saw no one, apart from an occasional car on the main road at the foot of the rise. A couple of times he fancied he saw someone jump back behind a convenient wall or retrieve their head from a doorway, but he managed to convince himself it was just his mind playing tricks. He was on his own.

It took Mike fifteen minutes to reach Argyle Road from where he caught his first glimpse of Devonshire Street, a place he had been to perhaps a half dozen times, when he had played pool at a pub called the Cross Keys, half way down on the right. He reached the T-junction made by Argyle Road and Devonshire Street and saw the pub on his right. It looked open but he quickly dismissed any thoughts of having a quick pint or two, though he couldn't think of anything better at that moment, not least because it lay in the opposite direction to the one he had to go.

The road was made up of a large bend that curved gently off to his left, meaning that when the blue Orion came into view - parked neatly next to the left hand kerb - he was probably six hundred yards from it. The slightly tarnished, unspectacular car shouldn't have stuck out too much from its surroundings, but it seemed so alien sat there, so startling to Mike it actually made him stop briefly, his left foot hovering two inches off the ground. He carried on at a quicker than natural pace, trying to force himself to pull himself together. He had known the car would be parked there so why did its appearance scare him so much? He realised it was the first visual confirmation that this was all real. The tape had been real - he had felt it, touched it, but the voice had been too ethereal. He hadn't been able to look upon the voice, to study it, to stare into the whites of its eyes and see if it flinched. As he did now to the car as it gradually came closer, his nervous strides eating up the distance between him and it. He checked the number plate, but he knew what it was before his eyes could discern the black plastic letters. He had only listened to the tape once but its details, sparse though they were, were etched on his mind like graffiti.

As far as he could see there wasn't anyone in the car unless they were purposely making themselves hidden. One hundred yards past the car the road came to an end at a large black meshed gate. Another abandoned factory lay beyond the gate, weeds and grass now making a home of the cracked concrete. On the side of the road the car was parked, a windowless wall stood slightly back from the pavement. A large rectangle was a lighter colour than the surrounding brickwork, evidence of a now departed sign, while on the far side stood what had obviously been a cafe and a rusted sign boasting all day breakfasts still survived.

He reached the vehicle and stopped, then tentatively reached out a hand and touched the boot. He looked around him, subconsciously, for the hundredth time. He was alone. No party was waiting to surprise him, no camera crew were recording the events for a hysterical studio audience. Slowly he walked around the blue car, his eyes studying it but not really taking the details in. His mind was too busy fending off questions that were coming in too thick and fast to make any sense or for any attempts to answer them could be made. After one and a half laps of the car he stopped and looked around again. It seemed colder here and the wind on the sweat on his head was making it ache. The sounds of distant traffic could just be heard but despite that Mike was aware of a silence around him that was almost tangible, and the car seemed to be the focus of it. It was a light blue colour with rust spots and general dirt making it look its age. It was parked neatly, its balding tyres a couple of inches from the moss-covered kerbs, as if its owner had just parked up before heading into town to get some shopping.

Mike's suspicions were confirmed - there wasn't anyone in it. He stood there, hands on hips, at a loss at what to do. He hadn't planned what he was going to do when he arrived at the car. He hadn't thought he would need to, he had played the part of a puppet so far and had been led almost against his will, the puppet master using inquisitiveness and need as his strings.

Mike didn't know what he had expected but this wasn't it, and a sense of disappointment washed over him. His earlier trepidation (and yes fear if he was honest with himself) made him start to feel foolish, but with it came a bravery he had lacked earlier and he found himself trying the driver's side door. With a loud click the latch moved in his hand and the door opened towards him. With it came the stale smell old cars always seem to have, tinged but not overpowered or disguised by a green tree air freshener hanging from the rear-view mirror. The car wasn't as empty as he had at first thought; a woman's shoe lay on the floor, half hidden under the driver's seat. After another quick glance around Mike got in and sat behind the wheel, leaning back, searching with his hand the rear seats and foot well. There was nothing, not in the back, under the sun shields, in the glove compartments or even the ashtrays. His hands on the wheel he rested his head on the headrest and thought about his next move. The keys weren't in the ignition and he was glad he hadn't found them. That would have posed another tough decision. Once again he sensed disappointment, feeling he had been the victim of a shit practical joke. He'd go back home and try to forget about it, maybe returning in a week or two. He also began to wish that Rachel wasn't away this week. He could foresee that every time the telephone rang or there was a knock at the door, he would be convinced it was the owner of the voice on the tape until his mother spoke or the electricity man asked to read the meter.

As if suddenly remembering it, he leant down and picked the shoe up. It was dark red, almost purple, covered in scuffs and ground in dirt that gave away its age even more than the style, which he recognised from his youth. A pixie boot. The thought hit him, and several more fired in with it, hot on its tail. He hadn't checked the boot. Of course - he didn't know how he had overlooked it. If someone had a prize or surprise for him, as the voice on the tape had put it (Mike preferred the former) the boot was the obvious place, and as he stepped out and then around to the back of the Orion he felt sure the journey hadn't been in vain, and the boot would give up a secret - if not the ultimate one at least a clue to its location.

The boot's latch unlocked with a soft clunk and the lid swung upwards revealing its contents.

The body lay in the foetus position, its head towards the passenger side facing out into the grey empty street. The head belonged to a woman, probably in her late thirties, it was hard to tell, the face was splattered with deep red flecks of blood and the skin that had been spared was discoloured by a garish combination of bruises and heavy make-up. The blonde hair, in life, had probably hung down to just below the lady's shoulders, but now in death, it was stuck to her face and the blood on her chest.

So many sights, senses leapt out at Mike as the lid opened - the woman's torn blouse revealing her gaping stomach and a mass of red and white innards; her dead eyes that still seemed to contain a pleading (not fear but pleading); the smell that lay heavy on the released air - a smell that had an earthy warmth about it despite conveying the message of death. So many things vying for his attention, but crazily, the first thing to register on his reeling mind was the one bare foot and the fact that the shoe on the other foot matched the one he had held in his hand not thirty seconds earlier.

The next thing Mike remembered is being bent double trying to be sick, his stomach convulsing again and again, trying to send its non-existent contents spilling from his body as if expulsion of a physical thing would rid it of a memory. Eventually it had its way and a thick, dark orange liquid was spat out onto the road, followed by a little more. The exertion had left Mike feeling dizzy and he stumbled to the pavement and sat on the cold ground, his back resting on the wall, stars swimming in his eyes. Sweat was literally pouring off his face, and he could feel similar amounts on his back, chest and armpits.

He looked across to the car, its boot open to the world, not knowing how or when he had managed to get away from it, only knowing he had because he was sat looking at it now from twenty yards away.

CHAPTER SIX

For the second time in two days Mike Burley was sat on his own in a pub in the early afternoon. On the table in front of him sat a half drunk double whisky, in a dirty glass. The first half of its contents had caused his empty, sensitive stomach to cramp, while the cigarette that was now a stub in the ashtray, hadn't left his tight lips, making his head spin and increasing the nausea that had become as much a part of him as his skin.

The last half an hour - hour, two hours? - had been a blur, his body moving under instinct, not seeming to obey any instructions from his conscious mind. The memory of it was made up of a combination of incredibly vivid scenes, blurred, vague incidences and total blanks, and none of them seemed to bear any relation to their importance. He had returned to the car; shut the boot - trying not to look at the corpse; left the scene only to return at full sprint and use his coat sleeves to wipe his prints from the dashboard, door and boot handles - all the time looking around wildly, convinced the street was about to become crowded with onlookers. Leaving the street in a different direction than he'd come, he had got lost and terrified. Terrified he was going to get lost and arrive back at the car, running, stumbling aimlessly around what he thought were familiar streets, before turning onto a street he did recognise. His fear had become huge and dominating by now, overshadowing all else. It was controlling him, forcing him to run, to constantly swing round to see if he was being followed, watched, spied on, anything. Every now and then he would calm himself down, the rational part of his brain - small, totally surrounded and outnumbered though it was - gaining control and he would slow down to a fast walk. It was impossible for him to maintain it though, and like in the bedroom earlier, and indeed many nights in the past after one too many joints, his mind would free itself of the loose shackles he'd tried to throw around it and had become free, running amok.

By the time he had reached the town centre he had got hold of himself enough to know he had no pursuers and managed to walk at a less noticeable pace. Certain shop fronts and landmarks leapt out with crystal clarity, others couldn't be recalled. A small child carrying a red balloon on a string came swimming back into focus, as did the way the boy had looked at him with fear. He had been scared of Mike - he knew where he had come from, what he had seen.

For the third time in two days Mike tried to get his head together. To formulate a plan. Though a thousand and one things screamed for his attention he did his best to screen them and focus on his most important and immediate problem. What was he going to do with the car? He had started to think and refer to the car and body as one entity. He doubted very much if in his panicky haste he had managed to erase all his fingerprints. He knew for a fact he hadn't wiped down the shoe and couldn't remember doing the steering wheel. How had he shut the door again? Had he pulled it shut when he'd been inside?

In an ideal world (as if this problem would ever arise if he lived in such a place) he could return to the car with a clearer mind and a cloth and remove all evidence of him ever being there, but of course every minute he spent there he risked being seen. Despite that being the most sensible option he knew he would be far too uptight to do a proper job, and he'd simply be in the same situation afterwards picturing the new places he'd left fresh prints.

Two alternatives presented themselves to him. Sitting tight, which because it meant doing nothing, presented itself first and most eloquently. Or going to the police. Doing nothing would be OK if there were no other influences, but there most certainly were in this case. Someone, the sick fucker who's voice he'd been listening to in the serenity of his own bedroom that very morning, had not only killed – butchered – that woman, which in itself was something so far away from Mike's normal sphere of thinking, but he had tried, or quite possibly succeeded in implicating him into it. To have gone to the effort of recording the tape, then planting it, Mike could be sure that he'd covered his own tracks. For all he knew he was at the police station now telling them how he'd seen Mike acting suspiciously with the girl last night, and it was more than his conscience could bear being a good upstanding citizen and all, and it was probably nothing and he didn't want to waste anybody's time, but if anything had happened to her and he'd done and said nothing, well he just wouldn't be able to live with himself.

No, he couldn't sit and do nothing.

This left the police. It was the most drastic and therefore most unappealing option but it was the only one left. If he went, armed with the tape and told the truth he would surely be OK.

Mike wasn't sure his faith in the police force was solid enough to justify his decision to put his life in their hands, but he had made his mind up and if only for the lack of indecision now he had to admit he felt a bit better. Though now there was something else that was bothering him. Something that he couldn't put his finger on but among all the confused messages in his head and all the sights and emotions there was something else, something he had overlooked or up to now ignored. Something big. With all his might he wished it was something good, something positive, but knew with almost as much certainty that it wasn't. That it was something terrible.

He directed his mind and his thoughts towards Rachel. He'd found in the past twenty-four hours he was using her more and more as a crutch – as opposed to simply a crotch as in their first few weeks together – and once again he gorged himself on pictures, remembered scenes, shared jokes from the past three years. He forced his mind back along the crumbling paths of time, to the first days of their relationship, back even before that, to the weeks and months where he hadn't so much stalked his prey as fawned and salivated over it. It was his second year of university, and after a first year that was remarkable academically-wise purely because none of his lecturers could believe he had actually managed to scrape through and pass his end of year exams that would allow his to continue his studies. With their rebukes ringing in his ears, joined by the less well informed but still no less persistent ones of his parents, he had promised himself that he would make an effort, or at least more of an effort this year.

Making more of an effort than last year was hardly going to be a Herculean task, but deep down Mike knew that he probably wouldn't succeed. But at least he would make an *attempt* at making more of an effort than last year, and though he knew this wouldn't be good enough for his lecturers or certainly his parents, it probably would be sufficient for him. And at twenty years of age that was good enough.

Then help arrived from a completely unexpected, but wonderful source. In the first couple of weeks of term, this new work ethic meant he would start attending his morning lectures. This meant that three times a week he needed to leave his house by half past nine to walk the thirty minutes to the university. The walk, mostly downhill, took him out of his terraced street and between both his locals before entering a tree-lined park that, come the summer months was full of reddening bodies, the air thick with warm canned beer and sun cream, vibrating to the sounds of footballs being kicked, girls screaming with mock terror and genuine laughter, and the general hum of happy conversation. The park, the same shape as South America, stretched southwards for more than a mile, and its southern edge – Argentina, nestled comfortably against the city centre with its bustling shopping streets, cafes and pubs. Before it did, a small but fast flowing river snaked across the green fields, in a steep sided gorge it had cut itself in the preceding thousand years, and an ornate iron footbridge crested the gorge and river, its green, peeling railings and faded red tarmac connecting the small southernmost section of the park complete with small cafe and graffitied bandstand, to its larger northern territories. Mike would enter the park around Columbia, taking a path that would have seen him follow the Andes taking in Machu Picchu and La Paz, skirting the arid coastal plains of Chile before heading for the Pampas.

The university, split seventy-thirty over two campuses, sat on either side of the park. The main part where Mike attended his lectures was on the south-east coast, while the smaller campus – that reserved for the more art orientated subjects, was based just off Chile, above the river. Mike would hit this bridge at about ten to ten, the cool breeze that seemed to exist permanently on its crown, and the sound of the rushing water thirty feet below signalling that another couple of hours of academia were about to begin. It was probably into the second week of term, just as his good intentions were turning less so, and his promises becoming hollower when he first remembered seeing her. The Girl On The Bridge.

Mike Burley wasn't shy. He also wasn't the type of person who could go up to a girl he didn't know and ask her out. Not sober. As long as he got to the bridge at ten to ten, he would invariably pass this girl at some stage along the hundred or so metres that made up its span. As the days and weeks went on, the motivation for getting up and making it to the university swung further and further from academic and filial duty to his increasing obsession with the tall slim blonde figure who would be walking from "Argentina" to "Chile", to he guessed the other campus. He would start to make an effort with his hair, with the clothes he wore, choosing his better shirts and t-shirts, the ones he normally reserved for night time. The twenty-minute walk down to the bridge would be a tortuous ordeal, his mind torn between keeping an even pace to ensure his arrival at the bridge would coincide with hers (but what if she was running late?), and the facial expression he should wear. Trying to look casual - normal was, he discovered the hardest thing in the world. Especially when there was turmoil mere millimetres behind the face's muscles and skin. This supreme effort was made even more difficult by the subsequent effort of trying to look either cool, intellectual, good looking or nonchalant. Or ideally all four. There were so many competing messages going out to the facial muscles that in the end the face he showed to the world and more importantly to The Girl On The Bridge, was a frozen mask of fear with the occasional tic or spasm.

After half a dozen of these meetings, he had established eye contact. Fully aware of her presence he would remain looking down at the fading red tarmac, or maybe wistfully over the side at the trees or river below, then at ten metres from his target he would casually look up, and into her gorgeous grey-blue eyes. Their eyes would meet, lock as they passed each other, and he would spend the rest of the journey and at least the first half of the lecture analysing her part in the encounter. Was she just looking at him in response to his manic intense stare? Did she remember him and look forward to their brief but so meaningful encounters, taking more and more time and effort on her outfits each morning, making sure her hair was just right? The rest of the lectures would be spent working on his next move. The smile. It was at this time in his life, more than at any other stage of growing up when he would rue the fact that he wasn't able to go up to someone, a girl, a girl he wanted to sleep with but didn't know, and start chatting with her. He used to hate people who could do it, suddenly he revered them.

Still, one step at a time. The smile. He would stare at himself in his grimy bedroom mirror, going through his small repertoire of smiles, concerned that the image he thought each one portrayed to the outside world was very different to the one he saw leering back at him. This shook his already weakened confidence. The smile he'd hoped to use – a cool nonchalant one that said "hey, I'm at ease with myself and the world, but there's a lot behind this cool exterior you're looking at now, hidden depths of sensitivity, a sharp sense of humour, a sensuality uncommon in modern young men, but don't worry, there's still an element of the rogue in me, and do you know what? You look like my sort of girl, no promises yet but if the time was right I may be willing to take you for a drink," actually came out more as a plea for help, like that of a drunkard who had just soiled himself in a very public place.

He was starting to hate himself for what he was turning into. For what she was turning him into. For god's sake he hadn't even spoken to her and she was changing him. During this period he would scour the pubs and clubs, desperately trying to find her, to encounter her when he would be in a fit state to go up and talk with her. He would take his group of friends to increasingly bizarre and obscure pubs and clubs, surmising that if she lived in a different part of town, the part that she was obviously walking from when they "met" each morning, then she would go to the pubs in that area, a part that was hitherto practically unknown to Mike. During this time, he met several other girls, had a couple of one-night stands, one of which even turned into a two night affair, but they didn't offer him anything approaching what he imagined She would give him.

The searches proved fruitless and besides, a part of him thought that if he did chat to her and nothing happened what would he do then? Would they spend the rest of term saying embarrassed hellos, or more likely would he just revert back to staying in bed of a morning, with simply one more person to masturbate over?

That was another problem with the smile. Once he did it, he couldn't sit back on his laurels grinning inanely at her. The smile was a small, but nonetheless important step onto the ladder, but once he was on it he had to keep climbing or he would fall off never to return. He eventually settled for one that involved the minimum of movement. Standing in front of the mirror he watched as the corners of his mouth moved up almost imperceptibly. He combined this with a small upward movement of his head and a slight widening of his eyebrows. It wasn't a complicated procedure but he practised it endlessly. He tried to let the smile flood into his eyes, to evict the desperate fear that lodged there whenever he thought of performing the smile to Her.

He bottled it the first three days not even being able to look at her, his mind so caught up in producing the perfect smile not only did his facial muscles stop working properly he also forgot how to walk. He would get to the end of the bridge, another opportunity gone swearing at himself, at what he had become. He was regressing back to some horrible awkward fourteen-year-old desperate to get his first shag but not having a clue how to go about it. That weekend he considered two courses of action. Either he would forget it, put her out of his mind, forget the whole morning lecture routine and start enjoying himself again as opposed to letting some unknown girl who would probably turn out to be a self-centred, domineering, sexually repressed bitch (oh no, he knew she wouldn't be, by the way she walked; the way she dressed, how comfortable she looked in her skin, in the world; the way she flicked her hair back from her eyes; the way she swung her blue denim bag back onto her gently sloping shoulders) dominate and ruin his life.

The other option was to drink before leaving the house to give him some courage. To make him grow some bollocks. Even in his desperation, he knew that wasn't a road he wanted to start going down.

The Monday of the next week he had finally done it. His motivational, berating talk for the journey from his front door to the steps leading up to the bridge had instilled him with a brief but unmistakable confidence he was determined would not slither from his grasp. Sensing her in range he looked up and gurned right at her. She returned his look and an easy smile settled on her face. Overjoyed at the fact he had finally done it, elated by the fact she had returned it (with interest he thought), he lost control of the reigns, and seeing the next rung of the ladder in easy reach went for it. He opened his mouth to say…. he didn't know, anything it didn't matter he wanted to stretch out this moment, and found his vocal chords had tightened. A croak crawled out of his slightly open mouth that could, with a certain degree of artistic license have been interpreted as "Alright?" but it didn't matter, she was gone. He turned to see her walking swiftly away, readjusting her bag on her shoulder. He felt fantastic, far too good to go to his lecture so instead went to Fat Sam's greasy spoon for a mug of tea to wait for the union bar to open while he replayed the morning's events over in his cart wheeling mind. It took a couple of hours before the fear started to settle over him, of what he was going to do the next day. Would she be expecting him to repeat the smile that had obviously so impressed her, would she be hoping for conversation, or would that morning's bombshell not even have registered on her emotional Richter scale?

She wasn't there the next day. All kinds of scenarios played through his mind. Was she now on a different course, moved house, had he scared her into taking a different route to class?

That evening he and a group of his mates had hit their usual haunts, fuelled by cheap supermarket wine and subsidised union bar lager. Once again like an adolescent, he found that subconsciously he was comparing all the girls he saw in the pubs and clubs, with the image he had formed of The Girl on the Bridge. In his head he had decided what music she liked – as luck would have it, she had very similar tastes to him, and she had delighted in introducing him to the couple of bands and albums he wasn't as familiar with. She would make tapes for him, giving them names, and he pictured her neat feminine writing on the inlay cards, punctuated occasionally with abstract doodles and other decorations. Likewise their television and film tastes overlapped extensively, though hers still contained some childlike ones that he would chide her about.

The girls he saw in pubs, even those he chatted up and slept with couldn't compete; they weren't even fit to clean the pedestal he'd placed her on, but the advantage of this was he found it incredibly easy to talk to them and chat them up. It was in this mood that he found himself queuing up outside Oasis, the student club to go to on a Tuesday night. People started arriving at nine thirty to try and ensure they would save the £1 by getting in before ten o'clock. It was a dangerous half hour, as thirty to forty-five minutes was really the most you wanted to go without drinking, especially as the clubs notoriously watered down drinks meant that getting back to the required level of intoxication took no little effort.

Midway through an on-going discussion on whether they should get satellite television, Mike turned to get a light from the group behind. Halfway through his sentence he saw her. Her. The question died on his lips, and he found himself staring at her. She hadn't been the one he'd directed his question at but was in the same group, and was in conversation with a mousy girl in a long leather coat. She looked divine, a hint of make-up bringing even more life to her already dazzling features. Feeling the old fears and insecurities shouldering the alcohol out of their way he ignored the questioning look of the smoking girl to his right and lightly put his hand on her elbow, touching her for the first time. Even her denim jacket felt softer than it should have, and his nose sucked in her light, but so sensuous perfume, her pores and personal scent taking the off the shelf product and turning it into something wonderful. She had turned to face him, and after a second of incomprehension her face lifted and she said the two words, that even now, three years later, after all that he had been through in the last week, made his heart lift and thud that little bit harder.

"Hey you."

Three years later, moist eyes closed he could hear those words again. See her red lips form and send them across the electrically charged air. The words that said, yes, she did recognise him, she had noticed his scared, desperate figure stumbling self-consciously towards her three mornings a week for the past month or so. That all his fretting, preening; the sleepless nights and humiliating conversations had been worth it.

Back in the Nag's Head, he finished his pint. It had become dark outside, and the warmth his reminiscing had given his body had begun to cool.

The journey back home reintroduced him to his terror as he began imagining the person responsible for this nightmare to be the man in the dark coat approaching him on the path; the man sat reading a paper in the Audi; the bearded gentleman emerging from Spar. It was dark when he reached his house and was really beginning to wish Rachel would be home tonight. For the first time in his life he really needed someone. Really needed her. And for the first time in his life he was completely alone. He'd ring Rachel, explain everything, then go to the police.

It seemed no warmer in the house than it had been outside and Mike didn't take his coat off when he got in. He had no idea how he was going to tell Rachel. How do you tell your girlfriend you found a tape telling you to go to a car containing the butchered body of a woman? He climbed the stairs and paced around his room trying to summon up some sort of opening line. Imagining her happy answer, then her silence as he recounted his story. Then what? What was he expecting her to say? He realised he was expecting her to come up with a plan that would sort everything out, and that after he had spoken to her it would all be all right. Then he noticed the tape deck on his stereo was open and empty.

He didn't move for five, ten, fifteen seconds, apart from his jaw, which did actually drop, allowing his mouth to open for a scream, a shout of frustration, but nothing came out. He could hear the blood circulating somewhere in his head and feel his eyes starting to fill with tears.

Eventually he made it to the bed where he sat, large sobs escaping from his mouth, not being able to take the impact of this last blow. He would have broken down completely had not a scared voice at the back of his head eventually made itself heard, causing another coppery surge of adrenaline to course through his body. Up to then all he had been thinking about was that the tape had gone. That he had lost his one lifeline, the one piece of evidence that gave his story credibility. The voice reminded him of a far more immediate danger - that someone had got into the house and removed the tape. That person was almost certainly the same person who had killed a woman and left her in the boot of a blue Ford Orion. That same person could be in the house now.

Whirling around he scanned the room. Grabbing a wine bottle candleholder from his bedside table, he stood with his back to the wall, trying to control his breathing. Frozen drips of wax formed a solid fountain around the bottles neck, which he peeled from the glass after snapping the cream candle off at the bottle's opening. Hefting it in his sweating palm, he tried to imagine himself bringing it down onto someone's head. No not someone, the murdering bastard who had butchered that girl. Briefly he considered if the bottle would serve as a better weapon if he broke it, making it into a makeshift dagger, but if it shattered completely he would be left with nothing. No, he determined, gripping the cold glass tighter, small red patches at the tips of his knuckles standing out from its white skin surrounds, it wasn't ideal but it'll do.

The bedroom was small and square; the double bed took up the majority of the space and went all the way to the floor – no room for anyone to hide underneath. The only other furniture was a small wooden chair piled up with his dirty clothes, two bedside tables and a small wardrobe. Its door – ajar – revealed its innards and innocence. He was alone in the bedroom.

Torn between stealth and aggression he considered his next move. First of all he was certain he had left the tape in the stereo. And now it had gone, so he was equally certain that someone had got into the house and removed it. Had he disturbed him (them?), was that why the tape deck was open, or was that done just to mock him, to play with him? Silently, he unbuttoned his coat and never letting go of the bottle with at least one hand, shrugged it off onto the bed. Liberated of its bulky confines he felt more agile, more prepared for the task ahead. Keeping on the balls of his feet, he made his way towards the door, trying to get oxygen into his body and carbon dioxide out without making any sound. His ears reached out through the door, into the bathroom opposite and then down the carpeted stairs, searching out any tell-tale sound, any noise that would betray its creator.

In front of him was the door, half opened revealing the red carpet of the small square landing that stood between him and the bathroom. Slowly, almost silently Mike eased himself out of the bedroom and onto the landing. Below him the stairs led down into the dark hall, the lounge and the kitchen. Even though it went against every instinct in his being he reached out and turned the light out, plunging him and the house into complete darkness. He waited, while he desperately urged his pupils open, the banister and bathroom door gradually appearing out of the gloom.

The bathroom light was operated by a switch on the wall outside the door, and it was to this his free hand slid to, his probing fingers locating then gripping onto the cold plastic switch. A sharp click and the yellow light flooded out from beneath the door and onto his black trainers. He kicked the door, slamming it into the radiator and towel rack, which shook and rang out in dull, tuneless protest. To the right was the bath and shower, the shower curtain pulled out an unusually long way, concealing the bath and shower itself. Its cream, soap-stained surface limply hanging from the stainless-steel rod that stretched the length of the room, held Mikes gaze. It appeared to be moving, rhythmically as in time with someone's breathing, someone hidden behind it, knife poised waiting for the perfect time to plunge it into Mikes throat. Taking two slow steps back towards the door, as if that was his intended route, Mike darted forwards swinging his right arm and bottle in a wide arc that took in the length of the plastic curtain. A cry filled the stark room, the noise as much as the resistance the bottle met forcing the blood even faster through his arteries.

The cry - his cry – echoed around the small bright white room before fading into silence. In front of him, the shower curtain hung limply off its rail, four of the rings had torn through their eyelets, before the remainder had held strong, arresting the careening arm and bottle. Breathing hard he swung round facing the dark landing and stairs, fear and doubt now starting to invade every part of his sweating body.

It took Mike just over fifteen minutes to check every room. It is not until you are in a dark house looking for a psychopath that you can appreciate how many places there are in an empty room that can conceal your adversary; how many places give the perfect cover for someone wishing to spy on you, watch you creep past before leaping out, knife raised over their head. The effort of moving around, every sense straining, trying not to breathe is both mentally and physically exhausting and by the time Mike had thoroughly checked every room, every nook and every cranny, closed every curtain (the black outdoors suddenly seemed terrifying), turned every light on and bolted the front and back doors Mike was completely drained. When he finally returned to his room and sat on his bed he just shook, unable to control his body. Tears slowly ran down his cheeks, but he was too scared to cry, he didn't want to make any noise to alert anyone of his presence and position in the house. Or to mask the movements of anyone else in the house. Even now his mind was questioning whether he really had checked everywhere. Was he sure he'd looked behind the settee in the lounge? Was he one hundred per cent certain that he had looked far enough into the cupboard under the stairs where they hung their coats? Had the intruder managed to double back on himself and make his way upstairs while Mike was making safe the kitchen, and was even now in the bathroom?

When in the hall, he had checked the front door which was, apart from the windows which were all locked from the inside, the only way into and out of the house. It hadn't been forced and the lock wasn't broken. This meant he'd let himself into the house with a key. This in turn meant that as long as he was sure he was alone now – and he wasn't –

70

courtesy of the two bolts and security chain he was ok while he remained in the house. As soon as he left it he'd be leaving it vulnerable again. But that was fine with him. He wasn't in the mood for any trips, unless they took him very very far away, for a long long time, and appealing though that option was - despite the fact he was skint and couldn't leave Rachel - his fleeing would in the eyes of the law seal his guilt as surely as a written confession.

A carving knife he'd retrieved from the kitchen sat next to him on the bed and his hand jumped to it when the telephone rang. The noise filled the house and sounded terrible. If he had wanted to answer it he couldn't have made the journey downstairs. That was if he had wanted to answer it and he certainly didn't. There was always the possibility that it was Rachel. There was also the possibility that when he picked the telephone up he would hear the voice on the tape laughing at him, or telling him where he had hidden other bodies; explaining how he would cut Mike's body up. So he just sat there, shaking and listening to its terrible noise. As he did three more times that night.

His mobile, on the bedside table remained mute. The nature of Rachel's trips often meant she couldn't call, or speak to him, and after the first few times, they'd both got used to the idea that they would have to be content with several days incommunicado. Several times he thought of phoning her, desperate to hear her voice, as if the banalities of her day would wipe away the horrors of his, but the phone remained where it was, the clock patiently ticking off the minutes and hours.

That night, for the first time in eighteen years, Mike Burley slept with the light on.

CHAPTER SEVEN

The newsagent's window took two forms. To the right of the door it was filled with large printed adverts offering the purchaser several different rates depending on which part of the world he or she wanted to call. The window to the left offered a far more varied range of services. These were written in many different types of handwriting, on coloured postcards held in large plastic wallets, and it was the information from one such card - a faded pink one sporting thick black flowing writing - that Mr Clarke was noting down into a small notebook. After a final check he had copied the number down correctly he used his thumb to retract the biro nib and after pocketing both the pen and the notebook set off back to his house.

It had also been a fairly sleepless night for Mr Clarke because he had had to be up early enough to watch the postman come down the street pulling his little red trolley. He had watched with increasing interest as he had delivered to number 62 (a large plastic transparent envelope that was more than likely junk mail), miss out 64, deliver two small white envelopes to 66 and then retrieve the A4 size brown envelope from his bag, turn it over, smile before proceeding up the path to 68's front door, pausing briefly before ringing the doorbell.

His anger that had been fading for several hours was almost completely quashed as the door was opened to reveal a woman in a light blue dressing gown a matching towel wrapped around her head. Automatically she took the offered package. It was obvious, even to Mr

Clarke, watching through a slight gap in his bedroom curtains that the postman was torn between his professional duty and his desire to see the woman's reaction to the package. He dithered briefly, his eyes searching the woman's angular face before his responsible half won the day and he returned to his trolley. The woman was staring at the package, her eyes seeming to grow, as conversely, her mouth and cheeks got smaller and tighter. Quickly, with short, sharp, birdlike movements of her neck, she looked up and down the street before disappearing into the house. Despite scouring the outside of the house no evidence of the inevitable ensuing arguments inside was obvious, and Mr Clarke had to content himself with the sight of Mrs Foster emerging from the front door twenty minutes later, her now naked head looking even more pinched than usual, before slamming the door and striding down the street.

Six hours earlier Mr Clarke had been sat in exactly the same position on the wooden kitchen chair he'd brought up earlier. His head just above the window sill, the net curtain moving with his regular breathing, he had had to wait almost an hour and a half before the black cab had come down the street. Inside the cab, Mr Foster, unknowingly observed, had stopped outside his house, swore, banged both forearms onto the steering wheel before driving off to return four minutes later on foot. He paused next to Mr Clarke's car that was parked - perfectly parallel to the kerb, outside Foster's house, looked around and after retrieving something from his trouser pocket walked purposefully alongside it. He performed one more look around before he walked up his path and into his house.

Mr Clarke hadn't needed to go outside and look at the scratch Foster's keys had made to know what he had done. Foster had told Mr Clarke exactly what he was going to do three weeks earlier - the last time he had parked his Fiesta in front of number 68. He had come home half way through his shift, obviously tipped off by his wife - a tall skinny woman with a shock of bleached blonde hair - and used his fist to bang on Mr Clarke's front door, hardly waiting for him to open it before shouting and swearing, telling him to move his bloody car or he'd pay. Mr Clarke had calmly informed him that there were no allocated parking spaces and that if, like what had happened that evening, someone had parked in the position outside his house and the space opposite was free he would park there again. Mrs Foster had run across the street and had calmed her irate husband down enough to downgrade his proposed action from breaking his legs to scratching his car if he ever parked there again. Mr Clarke had repeated his previous statement before closing the door and going upstairs and altering the appropriate column on his chart. It was a situation that had been simmering for a while and was in danger of getting out of hand if Mr Clarke didn't start correcting things.

The journey back from the newsagents looked like being an uplifting one when the position usually occupied by the tramp with the frost ruined feet was empty and there seemed to be no evidence of him, but this feeling quickly evaporated when a commotion on the other side of the road caught his attention. A woman in a dirty skirt and thin blouse that paid no respect to the cold weather, was making her way down the pavement in bare feet, hitting herself with open palms on her thighs and arms in a pastiche of trying to keep warm. Her dirty, lank hair was tossed one way then the other as she stared wildly and accusingly at each passer-by, who to a man tried to avoid any form of contact with the woman, not least with the eyes. Her slow procession down the high street was accompanied by her shrill shouts of "Don't make me go back... don't make me go back there." Her actions should have invoked pity or at least curiosity in her fellow pedestrians but instead she was met with embarrassment, fear and Mr Clarke wasn't the only one who was feeling hatred towards her.

It was still in this state of mind that he passed number 101, the place that was subject to the most activity in The Chart, practically all of it in the same direction - the wrong one - he hated to admit. He couldn't go passed the building normally without it causing his hackles to rise and today he found it almost impossible to breathe he was so angry. He had automatically decided that this was where the bare footed woman had just come from. For three years now the occupants had made his life close to unbearable. There was a constant stream of them in and out of the place at all hours of the day and night, their cars always speeding up and down his road. They had targeted him personally in the past as well. They had been in his house, his garden, had verbally abused him and threatened him with violence.

He had been formulating a plan for a year now, but still he wasn't completely happy with it, and something this big had to be prepared to perfection. He planned to even everything out with 101 in one go, but he was prepared to wait. He wasn't going to rush in and endanger himself or his plan. His mind going over the intricacies of his plot, he continued on home towards number 43, once again finding solace and calm in his meticulous planning.

Mike woke with a start, a cacophony of emotions, feelings and fears vying for his attention. His stomach whined and grumbled at him to feed it; paranoia whispered that there was someone in the house; his memory flickered and stuttered stills from dreams about Ford Orions, psychopaths and dead women; his rational, normal mind, or what remained after the previous day wept and asked what he was going to do. But loudest of all and in a voice he did not recognise, one word was shrieking at him in the sound equivalent of red neon:

"SCARF".

He listened to the word, and recognised who it belonged to. It was the nagging voice that had been telling him quietly but insistently that there was something he was overlooking. It had discovered what that something was and now it had summoned all its strength and was shrieking its findings out with all its might, loud enough to wake him.

Once again he saw the dead girl lying in the boot, a cheap gold earring just visible in her ear; tight, dark blue jeans stretched over thin bent legs; the mouth-like gash in her stomach with an intestinal tongue; and his scarf that lay under her body and ended on her left upper arm.

It wasn't a particularly rare scarf and he was sure they were available from many high street shops, but he knew beyond a shadow of doubt that the one in the boot with the woman was his. The one that he had mislaid about two weeks ago.

Complete helplessness and despair forced more tears from his red-rimmed eyes, but these emotions were soon replaced by injustice and anger and as he strode downstairs to use the telephone he almost wished the person responsible for this was in the house now. He wanted to see who he was dealing with, to know who to focus his anger on; to beat his fists into; to scream and scream at, until their ears bled.

CHAPTER EIGHT

Mike Burley was sat in the same chair he had six days earlier. Had that really only been six days? When he entered the pub shortly after two o'clock on a wet miserable Sunday afternoon, he'd collected a pint of Guinness from the bar and was relieved to see that the chair he had come to think of as his own was unoccupied, despite the pub being fairly busy. He had spent a lot of time at this table over the last six days. And put a lot of money over the bar. Despite this he realised, pocketing his change, he still wasn't even on nodding terms with any of the bar staff.

"Shit pub," he thought and asked himself why he kept coming here. But he knew why. It was the cheapest, least pretentious pub in walking distance from his house. Also it provided a bit of stability in his life and god knew he needed that right now, whatever form it came in.

It would be different today though, he had arranged to meet Rachel at 4ish, as long as her train came in on time. She had stayed an extra couple of nights, using the opportunity to visit an old university friend. Originally they had sort of planned for Mike to go up on the Friday night but he had declined the invitation.

He hadn't really come to terms with what had happened, and he certainly was not coping, but he *had* become slightly numb to it and that wasn't all down to the alcohol. He had changed the locks on the door, enabling him to venture out without needing to check every nook and cranny of the house on his return. Of course, he still did a thorough search, but as the days passed, these searches took less and less time, as he got more adept at doing it, and also as his confidence in his home's security grew.

Rachel had taken his sacking (he had told the truth to her, well almost, the term "forced redundancy" had been used) better than he had imagined. Everything else that had happened since then had leant his voice a frightened, desperate edge and Rachel had mistakenly put this down to his dismissal. She knew he would be hurting, and her having a go at him wasn't going to help the situation. The lies he had told her about the efforts he had been making to find himself another job also eased her attitude towards him, and her frustrations were limited to a couple of sharp comments about him to her work colleagues.

Mike and Rachel had been going out three years now. The night they had met properly in the queue for the club, they had gone inside, found a table in the quietest part and talked. It wasn't like he was chatting her up; they just talked, exploring each other's lives, hopes, fears. After all the time he had spent imagining, inventing, fantasising about her, it was so good to hear her voice, her thoughts, so she could start to become a real, solid, breathing human being. An absolutely incredible one. At two the lights came on, and before any doubt or panic could creep back into his mind, she had stood up, taken his hand, kissed him quickly on his lips and whispered "come on let's go home."

Twenty minutes later they were in bed, and he was exploring every inch of her body, spending as long on her hair, neck, fingers and back as the more intimate parts he had pictured, touched and kissed in his mind night after night. He relished in exploring her warm, soft, fragrant skin, delighting in discovering its hidden, moist secrets, his mind racing along with his heart.

He had woken the next day, with her arm draped over his shoulder. He had watched her sleep for almost quarter of an hour, her body perfectly still, apart from a slight parting of her lips as she drew breath and exhaled, and the occasional movement of her eyes beneath her closed lids. Despite, or maybe because of having woken in somewhere akin to heaven, he didn't want to wake her. If he could have stayed there, in her double bed under that light blue duvet watching her sleep, reliving the previous night, again and again, replaying whole conversations in his head, he would have done. For ever. If she woke, the dream may shatter. Now that he had come so close to having her for his own, now that he had tasted her and felt her body on his he couldn't possibly cope with letting her go.

As it happened she woke, and after a second to allow her to focus on the face inches from hers, a smile washed over her face and flooded her eyes.

"Hey you again", she said, then leant over and kissed him and he was back in heaven. Properly this time, with the gate firmly shut behind him. They spent the day making love and getting to know each other. Hours turned into days and as they are inclined to do, days into weeks, and they became a regular site around the campus, in the bars and park.

Over the next three years the sex had become less frequent and not as experimental, but their friendship had become stronger, lust being replaced by healthy, contented love. They had practically been living with each other for the last few months at university so when they started to officially, it was a seamless transition and the fact that it now needed no effort to see the other one, only made things easier. They shared enough common interests and ambitions that they always had things to talk about or occupy their shared time. They also each had enough friends and other interests to ensure that they never had to rely completely on the other person or were forced to spend twenty-four hours together.

Now the only thing that occasionally bothered or worried him about his relationship was how much he loved her. How much she was part of him. How perfect she was for him. How gutted, heart wrenchingly devastated he would be if she was ever to leave him or even did anything to hurt him. He loved her, loved everything about her. He loved the way her left eye closed slightly when she was concentrating or was about to say something she considered off the wall; loved her laugh that started silently, just an open mouth, before the laughter flowed from her eyes and came out of her mouth in great gulps; loved the way she tasted in the morning; loved the way she lit and took the first drag from her cigarette, staring at the orange tip, rapt with concentration, left eye almost completely shut; loved the way she hugged him and stroked his shoulders in bed, and promised she would never leave him.

The decision not to tell Rachel about the tape or the car and body hadn't been a hard one for Mike to make. He just assumed it was something that he had to carry around on his own. There was nothing she could do, nothing to really help his situation. She couldn't make the body disappear or make time reverse and if he told her it would be for purely selfish reasons. She would make it easier for him to cope with whatever was going to happen and she would give him someone to talk to about his fears and surely that would alleviate some of them? But what right had he to burden her with all this shit? Surely that would be just passing on the disease that the owner of the voice on the tape had infected Mike with the moment he had left the tape on his chair. No, he loved her too much to tell her the whole truth.

There was also the nagging doubt that maybe she wouldn't believe that he was innocent.

He was contemplating trying to win back some of the money he had lost in the fruit machine over the last few days when Rachel came in carrying an umbrella and her holdall. She was holding the door open with her back while shaking the wet umbrella outside. The first thing that hit Mike as he watched her was how beautiful she was. Maybe not in a model type of way, in a textbook way - though certainly she was very pretty, but in a way only a boyfriend or husband, a girlfriend or wife can detect. In a way that went below the way the skin covered the bones and flesh. Tiny habits and foibles that were only familiar to those who had studied them for hours, and that gave away exactly what they were thinking at any precise moment. All those made someone truly beautiful and Mike was astounded not only how good she looked but also that it had taken a week apart and for his world to fall apart for him to realise it.

They hugged for several seconds, both squeezing the other as tight as they dare, then kissed before Mike went to the bar to get a drink each. Rachel eased herself out of her coat and pulled a chair from the opposite side of the small table to the side perpendicular to where Mike's chair sat.

They talked at ease for twenty or so minutes without mentioning his sacking, Mike avoiding it more deliberately than her more subtle methods, but when it eventually did come up Mike struggled to remember exactly what he had told Rachel, and what he said he had done about looking for a new one. It was so far down his list of priorities at the minute he only gave it any attention when he was forced to lie about it to Rachel.

"As I said I've got my c.v. in practically every agency in town, but you know what it's like, you either never hear from them again or they just offer you anything, some of the jobs they've asked if I'd be interested going to an interview for.......... I mean I may be wrong, but I can't remember telling them I wanted to be a fucking zoo keeper."

She laughed and took a long thoughtful sip of her wine. "I know you don't want to take the first thing they throw at you but... you know, you never know what something's like until you try it. I didn't dream of finding already overpaid accountants even better paid jobs when I was doing my O levels."

"What you're trying to say nicely, is buggers can't be choosers."

"No I'm not, honestly. More along the lines of any port in a storm."

"Come on Rach, this is hardly a storm." He was getting annoyed but was desperately trying not to show it.

"I know, I know. OK, any nice port, with a pub."

"There's absolutely no point in me rushing into anything and ending up with another job I'm not happy in. I've got an opportunity, maybe for the last time in my life, to wait for something to come along that I really want to do." Too late he realised he had left himself open to the obvious question.

Rachel didn't disappoint, "What is it you want to do Mike?" The question was said pleasantly enough, but he knew there was an underlying impatience and slight annoyance, underlined by the use of his name at the end of the question.

"I don't know... lots of things, that's the thing, I can wait to see what comes..." He was having to think on his feet for the first time in a week, a task not made easier by the battering his mind had taken recently; by the alcohol; by how bad lying to Rachel suddenly made him feel.

"I was thinking I may write a book..." This wasn't a complete falsehood, it was something he had been toying with off and on for a couple of years - had mentioned it in passing on several occasions to Rachel, but he was just as surprised as her when he heard himself saying it. But maybe not as disappointed.

"Write a book." It wasn't a question.

"Yeah... you know I've always wanted to. I'm not going to have this much time on my hands again until I retire." Or in prison he thought.

"You've mentioned it before but I thought you meant it as a hobby not a bloody career choice."

"I never thought I'd be out of a job so quickly. Anyway, it's just something I can do while I'm looking for a job."

There was a silence, Mike couldn't think of how to fill it, so took a slow draft of his pint.

"What sort of book?" She seemed generally interested, the slight hostility was fading.

"Err... well there's nothing concrete yet, but I've got a few ideas." He tapped his temple with a forefinger and lit a cigarette, forcing his memory back to a drunken conversation he'd had with his mate several months earlier. "There's one idea I've got... it's a beauty actually... ground breaking you might say." Encouraged by the returning memories and by Rachel's interest he gained in confidence and eloquence. "Remember at school, in the infants, you always got read those stories about kids who went on adventures in strange, magical lands after climbing a special tree or sitting on a certain chair or whatever?"

She nodded, though she knew there was no need.

"Well, mine is like that with one big difference, something that will make me rich and you a very happy, proud girlfriend." He finished his pint. "Get the drinks in my love and I'll tell you what it is."

"Look at the master story teller cranking up the tension!" she laughed. Rachel got up and walked to the bar, Mike following her with his eyes, having his first sexual thought for six days.

Rachel's return had already made him feel better, if only temporarily and though he didn't know how he was going to conceal the state he was in from her, he was so, so glad he wasn't going to be alone again in bed.

"Go on then Enid, spill the beans?" She'd returned with the two drinks and carefully placed them on the table before sitting down.

"Well, as everyone knows, the chair or the tree or whatever it was - the thing that was the path between the children's normal life, reality, to the places where they had adventures," Mike lit another cigarette, surprised how well he was doing, even beginning to convince himself, "... the wardrobe in The Lion the Witch and the Wardrobe is another example... well as everyone knows, those things are simply an analogy for drugs, but partly because of the times they were written in and partly the way they were written, the writers got away with it."

"I didn't know they were relating to drugs," She paused, taking a sip from her wine, a frown creasing her forehead, "or maybe I never thought about it."

Mike opened his mouth to continue but Rachel cut across him."So when they were running around in Narnia fighting against the ice queen and saving whoever that lion was called, they were actually just off their tits on smack. Bloody hell, that's horrible."

"Not literally, as I said it's just an analogy." Rachel still looked disturbed. "Well anyway, that's where my idea comes into its own. All the previous ones have been so far removed from actual drugs or the process of taking drugs that they were too obscure to be obvious. In my stories the kids will go to one of their Grandma's houses and eat the special soup she makes them. The actual imbibing of the thing that lets them transcend into magical lands is too close to drug taking to go unnoticed."

"Why do you think, no, why do you want it to get noticed? You think the children buying it will think they're hard or cool at school, reading the kiddies equivalent of Trainspotting?"

"No, it will just create controversy, which is what any new writer needs. You know, all publicity is good publicity and all that shit. I can already hear the disgust from the Daily Mail readers, up in arms, starting campaigns to put an end to this corruption of their precious little children's minds."

"Grandma's magic soup." She said it in a mock dramatic way "It's certainly got a ring to it, but do you really want to be responsible for creating a generation of pre-teen smack heads? Think on my love, while I go to the loo." She rose, pecked him on the cheek and strode towards the ladies.

Outside it was dark, and rain periodically spattered on the window to Mike's left, sounding for all the world like bony fingers trying to get his attention. His mood was easing slightly, the human contact bringing a much-needed injection of reality back into his life. He had been living inside a bubble for six days. A bubble that only included him, a cut up woman's body, a Ford Orion and a TDK tape. The only people he knew or even recognised had always been at the end of a telephone line or speaking from a television on the outside of the bubble. They, along with the pedestrians on the streets, people in the pub, even the various bar staff hadn't managed to penetrate it. Rachel was in danger of entering it, and maybe she was the only person capable of bursting it, but he was too scared to allow her in.

"How are Dave and Sal?" He hated the fact that nowadays Dave or Sally were never referred to in the singular. They were now simply half of an entity.

"Usual. His insane jealousy and her perpetual flirting and taking the piss. They'll live together forever and happy ever after." Rachel reached over and retrieved a cigarette, pausing slightly and looking at the white cylinder poised an inch from her faintly lipsticked lips, her smile fading gradually.

Watching her, Mike realised she was drunker than he had thought; she rarely smoked unless she was at least merry. Her smile suddenly grew again as she remembered something from the weekend and she leant forward conspiratorially.

"Sal was telling me last night that Dave is convinced now that she's having an affair with this bloke from work…"

"He's always convinced she's having an affair, with the barman, the bloke who came round to read the electricity meter, the guy waiting for the bloody 57 bus"

"I know, I know, but this is different, at least from what Sal was saying. He really does think she is. I think the other times he was just, I don't know, looking for a denial, or attention or something, god knows, but for some reason this is the real thing. So to speak." With a red painted fingernail, she fished out a small piece of cork from her wine before continuing. "Every time she goes out or is slightly late home from work he thinks she's been off having sex with him. He doesn't let on to her this is what he thinks. Or not obviously anyway, not in his mind."

She lit the cigarette, took a gulp of her drink and leaned further in. "I shouldn't be telling you this, but he's started, every time she comes back, well he comes on all loving and what have you, takes her to the bedroom, and you know, well, goes down on her. Every time, and he thinks she doesn't know why he's doing it." She broke down into peals of laughter, only cut short by Mike's puzzled face.

"What's up with..."

"Oh come on Mike, surely I don't have to...."

"Ohhh, I get you, to see if she's been...."

"Yes, and she's loving it, pretending she thinks he is just horny all the time. She's even taken to going out more, and becoming secretive."

"Poor bloke."

"Get off, he deserves it, there's no way in the world she'd ever go with anyone else, he must know that, deep down."

"Jesus, he's going to have a jaw like Arnold Schwarzenegger soon."

There was a pause while they both imagined the scenario, Mike in perhaps more detail and length than Rachel would have liked.

"They passed on their love, and were sorry you couldn't come up."

"Did you tell them why?"

"Yeah, you don't mind do you, I thought it..."

"No of course I don't. They'd only have assumed we had had some massive argument if you'd made some crap up. I was going to say I'll email him, but I can't anymore can I? I'll give them a bell when I get my head sorted."

They stayed for a couple more hours, got a cheap Chinese takeaway which they almost finished before going to bed and making love. It would be the last time they would have sex, and neither enjoyed it. Mike was overcome with guilt suddenly - quite what for he didn't know, but it killed any spontaneity from his part and his actions became awkward and clumsy. They were both relieved when his jerky motions culminated with two bigger jerks and he became still before rolling off. They both lay in silence, Rachel knowing it should have been better than that after a week apart, blaming it on his sacking and alcohol, Mike thinking of a dead woman in the boot of a Ford Orion.

CHAPTER NINE

The room is almost dark despite the air around the bell tower in the church half a mile away still vibrating from the proclamation of midday. There isn't a television which is the most striking thing about the lounge and the strange collection of settees and armchairs arranged in a near circle around the wall give it a symmetrical feel uncommon in the later part of the twentieth century, where most rooms are arranged with a definite focal point - usually a television set, but occasionally and refreshingly, a window with a view. On closer inspection the chairs have all seen better days and are sporting well-worn injuries, and the carpet - once grass green, now earth brown - offers views of the floorboards beneath. Apart from the three men there are only a few scattered newspapers on the floor and settees, and a bucket against a wall that contains the dried remains, and distinctive smell of vomit.

Spoon gradually allowed his eyes to focus, not wanting to force them, playing them the way an experienced angler does a large fish hooked on the end of his line, occasionally letting it out, gradually pulling back, reeling it in until voila, clarity. He waited ten, twenty seconds and scanned the room, his eyes doing the work of his neck and head. There were two other men in the room - Al who looked either dead or heavily asleep but was neither, and Danny. Danny hadn't been there when he'd come in and was probably waiting for Shafeeq to drop by.

Danny, the only person Spoon knew who had a proper beard, who until then had been boredly flicking through a ten-day old copy of The

Mirror, seemed to notice Spoon's eyelids had opened and glanced up giving a friendly nod of acknowledgement. Spoon returned the nod and attempted an "all right?" but his dry throat wouldn't allow it and didn't even allow a croak to escape.

Spoon was twenty-five and probably looked early thirties. He was good looking, maybe not to everyone's taste, but he had never found it too hard to get casual sex - sometimes so casual he fell asleep during it. He wore his hair in a grade four all over, not so much as a fashion statement, more for ease of maintenance. Three days stubble sat comfortably on his face, trying to compete for attention with a small scar just to the side of his left eyebrow and the two blue tears under his left eye. He had never been to prison, and had certainly never killed anyone, but had got the tattoo in a particularly heavy month a couple of years earlier. He couldn't remember if he had got them as a joke, as a dare or in an attempt to look hard or gain respect. Each possibility seemed as alien to his nature as the next, so each was as likely.

He had been staying in the house, the squat, the crack house, the drugs den depending on what paper you read, for a year and a half now. It wasn't perfect he knew that, but it was free, it kept the rain and the worst of the cold out and people knew where to find him. He looked upon it as more of a home than he had anywhere since his early teens. He tried not to do business there, preferring to go around to his customers' flats or to use the bars or parks. Of course, he wasn't one to ignore an opportunity if it presented itself on a plate, but the ambitious, daring young man of a few years ago had gone, or at least grown up or evolved into a careful but content and, yes happy, individual. He could probably make three or four times more money than he did at the moment, with very little more effort, but it would mean dealing with people he didn't really know and hence completely trust, and that was only a small step away from triple locking your door again and constantly looking over your shoulder. This was not the industry to tread on people's toes. You didn't grow market share by a clever marketing strategy and shiny sales literature. You did it by removing people's teeth and fingers and carving your initials on their foreheads.

Also, if he was one hundred per cent honest with himself, he didn't entirely trust himself not to look at the money and the opportunities and think - what if? To consider, even for a split second, trying to see how big he could be. No. He had tried that once and failed, but most importantly he had been handed another chance and he didn't think it fair to whoever had seen him worthy enough a candidate for that second chance to let him down. He had his small circle of customers who he knew totally. He also knew that they needed him and couldn't live without him.

Occasionally someone new would enter the circle, occasionally someone would give up. Occasionally someone would die. As long as you didn't get greedy and start to make it go a bit further, or by selling more than you needed to just get you by, you were sorted. He allowed himself a little each day and no more. He vowed he would always stick to smack as well. It was safe and you knew where you were with it. He had been down too many new-fangled routes, jumped on too many all singing, all dancing bandwagons before, and had always returned to what he knew best, and had vowed never to be unfaithful again.

He had sold his first pill at sixteen and had not had a choice since. He had started by being the one who always had some on a Friday or Saturday night, and just by selling to his mates meant he got his free, and that he was always able to be where it was going on. He was the first to be invited to a party or to be told of a forthcoming new club night. He enjoyed the attention and the respect that came with it, something his less than mediocre schoolwork and poor footballing ability had failed to provide for him.

Gradually he was selling to a wider and wider circle of friends until he would sell to anyone who put a ten-pound note in his hands. He was taking more and more himself but soon discovered that trying to conduct business with half a dozen ecstasy tablets in your system wasn't to be advised. He would find any transaction involving change or too many notes almost impossible, and coupled to acts of over generosity where he would heavily discount prices – especially if they were particularly chatty, fit or claimed to know such and such a friend – meant that he rarely took home as much as he should and even made a loss on some of his "better" nights.

It was around this time that he had started to get delusions of grandeur, and decided to cut out the middleman, and get his pills straight from the top, allowing him to shift more at a healthier margin. It also brought him into contact with the most violent, paranoid people he would ever meet. He started getting his pills supplied directly from Steve, a ridiculously hard Brummie, with a lisp and MUM tattooed on both forearms. He took Spoon under his wing and encouraged him to push more and more pills for him, inviting him out to his local pub where he would talk about some of the deals he had done, some of the people he knew and what Spoon could expect if he played his cards right. Every few stories would be punctuated with one telling of a particularly violent beating he had handed out; or how he had punished someone who had crossed him; or how someone had started to cry when he cornered them in the car park of a club with a machete; or how they had literally shat themselves when they got home with the pills they had stolen off him to find him sat in their lounge.

On several occasions Steve would take out one of two firearms that he owned, a small black revolver and a shotgun. He would either move them from one secure hiding place to another, or would simply move it to a position where Spoon couldn't help but notice it. He never referred to them, Spoon guessed it was Steve's idea of being subtle, but it was plain that it was all done for Spoon's benefit, to ensure he was under no illusions who and what he was dealing with.

Spoon wasn't too stupid to realise he was in very real danger of getting in far too deep, but he was ambitious enough to ignore that fact. He said to himself that this was something he had to do in order to make it big and that a little more risk now would enable him to move up the ladder and experience riches and a lifestyle that was only possible outside the law.

Also, he was strict with himself what he'd get involved with and what he'd stay clear of. Basically, he restricted himself to pills and speed. He sold the occasional nine bar, but apart from that he left everything else alone. Unless you had the infrastructure to store, and move large quantities, there was no real money in hash, and the stuff stank. Before long you were a walking advert for any half-trained sniffer dog. Coke dealers were a law unto themselves, and in terms of violence and downright ball breaking nastiness were on a different level entirely. Though Steve would never admit it, from several comments Spoon had heard, even he didn't get involved, and let them get on with their business while he concentrated on his.

As for Smack, that was left for the junkies and grebos. The young ambitious Spoon, didn't want to dirty his hands with the likes of them.

At first everything was fine. Steve gave him his own club to operate in, where the bouncers turned a blind eye to anyone Steve told them to turn it to. He was moving upwards of two thousand pills a week, half of those good ones, half shit ones he paid a quarter of the price for. He should have been taking home two or three grand a week but for the reasons explained earlier this was rarely, if ever the case.

If everything had carried on as it seemed it was going to, Spoon would now be either one of the richest men in town, in prison or with one of the biggest habits in the world. Or dead. But he had forgotten one major ingredient in all business, no matter how unorthodox. And it was the ingredient of competition that was going to rock Spoon's boat. There were two other main dealers, along with Steve in the area Spoon worked and though there was no love lost between them they all knew where they could and couldn't sell and toe stepping was kept to a minimum.

Then things changed. Spoon had noticed for a while that a couple of other lads working for Steve were working his clubs but suddenly there were several others. Rumour had it that Max - Steve's main competition who normally went by the name of the film hero made famous by Mel

Gibson - had had a big deal go badly wrong, leaving him tens of thousands out of pocket, and in a desperate measure he had started to spread his wings. It got to the point where on a quiet night there would be almost as many selling as those buying.

Steve saw his profits starting to shrink, and responded in a predictable manner. He firebombed the club that Max part owned. Max responded in an equally predictable manner by going after everyone and anyone who worked for Steve. A couple of the lads Spoon knew well - the whole business was far too shallow and self-centred to meet anyone you could call a mate - were stabbed and he knew it was only a matter of time before he would be followed and knifed. Spoon had to think fast. He couldn't really stop because he knew nothing else and though, if he really looked at himself he wasn't really enjoying it, it was so much his way of life, and he had got into such a routine, he wasn't even able to think about doing anything else.

A club called Clockwork Orange had opened up twenty miles or so away, and a couple of weeks earlier Spoon had gone purely for social reasons. It had been an old school mate's birthday, and Spoon had been invited mainly because everyone knew he would come carrying. The club had been shit but had been full of young naïve clubbers and as far as he could tell only two dealers, who didn't seem to know what they were doing.

Spoon decided to abandon his current clubs and make a fresh start. He didn't tell Steve and though he hadn't been able to give him what he owed him for the last couple of weeks he felt confident enough to ask for three times his usual weekly amount.

At the time, Steve was operating out of a greasy spoon owned by Little Nick, an annoying Irishman who owed Steve for putting the bloke having an affair with his missus into hospital. That was six months ago, and it was obvious that in Little Nicks eyes he had repaid the debt, but had no idea how to tell Steve this.

Steve had only hesitated for a second before going into the back room. Conversation was almost non-existent between them nowadays and it was almost a year since Steve had invited him out drinking with him. As he handed over the three bags he stared into Spoon's fidgety eyes slightly longer than normal. Spoon couldn't tell if he had failed to pick up a signal Steve had flashed at him, or if he had been trying to read his thoughts. Either way he left with his heart pounding and a lone bead of sweat making its way slowly but deliberately down his spine. He was only to see Steve once more in his life.

Two nights later he went to Clockwork Orange confident his luck was going to change, and his career was going to start heading upwards again thanks to his piece of forward thinking. He took most of what remained of the three bags, looking forward to a profitable night, and was going to try to get invited back somewhere for a smoke, where he could off-load a shed load of pills get some contacts and maybe get a shag. He didn't even let the prospect of crap music and an inexperienced D.J. dampen his spirits. He got in past the bouncers without any problems and found a good place on the first floor.

It had been a slow start, but he was refusing to let his spirits drop - with the aid of four pills, one more than he'd promised himself, and the music wasn't half as bad as he had feared. He had just sold a few for half price to a gorgeous Spanish looking girl in a fur bikini, and two duds to a spotty kid who couldn't have been more than sixteen, when he felt a hand on his shoulder. He turned around to face the barrel chest of a bouncer dressed in a bomber jacket complete with breast and back motifs. The bouncer was saying something but Spoon couldn't make out what, and only realised he had been speaking into a small microphone attached to a headset a split second before two more hands grabbed both his arms from behind and he was half carried half pushed twenty yards to a door, through it and into a corridor that was no lighter than the club but where the music was reduced to more of a vibration than actual sound.

For the first time in his life he could actually feel his testicles tighten and try to retreat into his body, as hands were frisking him. The bouncer who had first apprehended him was speaking but he couldn't hear the words, all he could make out was the deep bass reverberating in the door and in the walls around him, and the noise of the hands as they roughly searched his pockets. All three bags ended up on the floor in front of him, their contents spilling out onto the dark carpet. His balls were just about realising that there was no way they were going to fit from where they had dropped years earlier, when the small bundle of money followed the pills.

Spoon registered he had just been asked a question and opened his mouth to answer, but realised he had no idea what the question had been. The combination of MDMA and adrenaline had formed a heady cocktail that was sending his mind cart wheeling, allowing it to focus with incredible clarity on certain details, but unfortunately extremely irrelevant ones - one of the bouncer's shoes; the headset around the first bouncers large round head; the way the leather tag on the end of the same bouncer's jacket zip vibrated with the bass. Almost everything else was too ethereal for him to get a handle on.

"Pick this shit up and fuck off." It was the first bouncer. "If I see your face in here ever again I'll fucking kill you." It was shouted, only partly to overcome the background noise.

A massive rush of relief flooded through Spoon's body, weakening his knees making his descent to a kneeling position quicker than would normally be possible as he mumbled apologies and thank yous. He started fumbling for the nearest bag when the first foot caught him on the cheekbone, sending him sprawling onto his side. Several more crunching blows followed, first to his head again, then his body, then his groin before returning to his body. Then he felt himself begin to fly as he was hauled off the floor, carried the hundred metres or so to another door and then he was outside on the metal grill of a fire escape stairs. The door was slammed behind him. Silence. The cold air stung his senses, the warm blood quickly cooling on his face and neck.

Two days later, returning from casualty - the pain had got too much and he had been forced to go to hospital where he had been diagnosed with two broken ribs and severe bruising to go with his two missing teeth and broken nose - he had turned into his street to see Steve walking out of his front door, followed by two other men he recognised, one carrying his widescreen television, to their waiting BMW. He quickly jumped back behind the corner house, breathing heavily, his heart threatening to do more damage to his ribs, and his purple balls once again attempting to return to their birthplace.

It took Spoon an hour and a half and four Bacardi and cokes to pluck up enough courage to return to his house. Once there he picked up what clothes and bits and pieces he could fit into his holdall, his passport and his remaining stash of eleven pills. This took a little over five minutes, a time lengthened by his continual wincing and frantic looks over his shoulder. He also took his two largest kitchen knives and left his flat for good. That night he met up with an old friend who he knew Steve didn't know existed, sold his pills a few c.d.'s and two tops, and said goodbye to his friend and hometown forever. By lunchtime the next day he was on a plane headed for Ibiza.

***

Back at the squat Al hadn't moved and Shafeeq had just come in, sporting a floor length, cream leather coat.

"My man," he said to no one in particular, his face split by a broad smile. He proceeded to shake Danny's and Spoon's hands, saying their names before offering his heavily ringed hand. He hadn't seemed to have noticed Al's inactivity until just after offering his hand. Seeing his gesture wasn't going to be returned his smile somehow widened and he used his hand to ruffle Al's hair instead. This only succeeded in moving his head an inch to one side.

"How's it going Shafeeq?" - Danny.

"It's going well my man, it's going good."

"Do you know the Stranraer Alloa result?" Spoon asked.

"Two one, home win."

"Carlisle Torquay?"

"Carlisle Torquay, let me see, let me see. One one." He beamed at Spoon and then passed a look to Danny.

Spoon picked up a piece of paper that was sat on the chair next to him, crumpled it and flung it to the corner nearest the door. "Shit."

CHAPTER TEN

Mike Burley was sat on the 93 bus, on the top deck again but slightly nearer the front than he had been two weeks earlier, when he had looked out the window and thought about hidden cameras and TV shows. He had thought about retracing his steps many times and had made it to the bus stop on two previous occasions, only to walk away before the bus had even come into view. This time he had stayed and waited the eleven minutes it had taken for the big blue frame to loom around the post office. His heart had jumped at the sight, but he had forced his trembling hand into his pocket to get the fare and less than a minute later he had found himself in a seat on the top deck, its upholstery slashed allowing its innards to protrude.

Outside it was grey, the sun failing to make an appearance for another day, while the sky seemed pregnant and its waters looked if as if they could break at any time. A woman who had just got on, climbed the stairs and for a moment looked like she may sit next to Mike before a look of distaste appeared unchecked on her face and she made her way to the back of the bus. Mike just managed to keep the reins on his paranoia as he realised he had been scratching his groin with a vigour that was almost painful. He remembered Rachel had picked him up on it the night before, or the night before that and he realised he was developing it as a nervous twitch, that though unfortunate, seemed pretty tame compared to the maelstrom that had caused it and was raging in his head.

That had been one of many things that had made it obvious to Rachel that something was wrong. She hadn't a clue what it was, but she was positive that there was something Mike was keeping from her that was putting a massive strain on him and their relationship. She had confided in Sarah, a friend from work, her worries and that he seemed deeply troubled but was adamant that nothing was wrong. The thing was, she had told Sarah, was that he genuinely didn't seem worried about being sacked, or the prospect of finding a new job, and he swung from talking about it in a carefree, almost apathetical manner to being aggressive towards her, snapping at her for worrying about it, as if it really, really did not matter. Rachel stopped short of suggesting Mike was nearing a nervous breakdown but only for fear of looking either melodramatic or stupid. Sarah had thought about it long enough to take two sips from her sauvignon before suggesting that maybe Mike was having an affair. Rachel had denied it vehemently and truly believed Mike wasn't capable of doing that to her, but, unbeknown to her, the seed had been planted.

Mike had desperately wanted Rachel to return and though he was thankful for someone to hug at night, she had brought with her more problems for him. While she was around, he had to play a part, to act and he was finding it increasingly difficult. He was convinced she had begun to suspect the truth. During the day, while he was alone, he watched the news obsessively, tuning into the radio or TV every half hour expecting and dreading the newscaster to bring him news of a grisly find in the Banksmead District. He tried to temper this behaviour in the evenings and at weekends, but found himself sneaking off so that he would be alone when the news reached him, knowing he couldn't cover up if Rachel was in the room with him when the story broke, or worse still, if it was her who told him.

They had started to argue at ridiculously small things and he found that he was looking for something to get angry about, something far removed from his problems that he could use as a vent for his tension, and Rachel was taking the brunt. The day after she had arrived back she had got home after work and found out she'd been locked out, her keys no longer able to unlock the front door. Mike arrived forty-five minutes later, smelling of alcohol and had got angry and then stupidly apologetic when questioned. Her wait outside had done nothing for her mood and she had gone too far when he admitted losing the original keys. They had made up later but the easy, good-humoured conversations of only two weeks earlier had eloped with their sex life.

Two days after the key episode, Mike had attempted to sort things out and had prepared a meal, setting the table with an extra effort that included two candles and the better cutlery. The night was ruined however when he lost track of time and burnt the meat, and it soon developed into the regular pattern of silences, forced small talk in an attempt to lighten the mood, and Mike disappearing at almost half hour intervals into the bathroom or bedroom where he tuned on the small pocket radio he had bought several days earlier for just this use.

Back on the bus, he was three stops away from where he would have to alight if he was to return to the Orion, to the scene of the crime. One more guilty step he thought miserably.

Most of Mike's waking thoughts were occupied by the events, real and imagined leading up to the time he had opened the boot, and what he and the owner of the voice on the tape had done since. He hadn't assigned a face or features to the owner of the face. He assumed the identity of twenty or more people a day - the man on the back seat of the bus who had caught his eye for a split second too long; the gentleman who opened the door for him at the newsagents; the skinhead on the fruit machine in the Nag's Head; the driver of the black BMW who was pretending he was looking for a house number.

Over the days his mind had created a shortcut that meant that when he had somehow managed to think about something else, it wasn't necessary for him to then go along the laborious path of him finding the body; realising whoever had done it had been in his house; that that somebody was obviously capable of murder and had a reason to dislike Mike; knowing that he was in very real danger of spending the next ten years in jail and finally to complete and utter despair, fear and paranoia. No, now it had managed to burn a path from anywhere to the despair. This innovation saved approximately six minutes a day.

The rain had just started to fall in big heavy drops, as the bus stop that would take Mike to the rusty, now slightly strange smelling Ford Orion, disappeared out of sight behind the bus. On the top deck, Mike sat, hunched slightly, stroking the goatee beard he had started to grow. He was telling himself that next time he would definitely get off.

CHAPTER ELEVEN

Six thirty a.m. and all was quiet on Beechcroft Road. At the end of the street a milk float mounted a speed ramp, causing its bottles to rattle before turning right into Fir Avenue. It was dark, the streetlights dripping orange pools of light onto the white, crispy pavements. A couple of lights were starting to be switched on in the houses but generally it was a scene of cold, tranquillity and sleep. The progress of the milk float had been keenly observed by the occupant of number 43, and after seeing the white and blue vehicle disappear out of sight, he rose from his chair, his legs grateful for the increased circulation. After putting on his thickest coat and gloves, he collected a bottle of milk from the fridge, checked the foil top one final time and happy the hole left by the syringe was practically invisible, left the house. A quick glance left, right and to his left again satisfied him he was alone. He walked purposefully across the road to number 68 - which was showing no signs of life, was relieved to find the gate was already ajar and gently pushed it wide enough to allow his frame to pass through. Careful not to make a noise on the frosty path he made his way up to the front step, took the bottle of skimmed milk from beside its full fat brother and replaced it with the one from his pocket. Another glance behind him and six strides later he was back on the pavement and walking briskly in the direction he had watched the milkman come from fifteen minutes earlier.

Mr Clarke had been born almost forty-two years ago, about fifty miles from where he now lived. The younger of two sons he had been brought up in a loving but strict house, his father always wearing the trousers while his mother existed in a drab shapeless dress, a light blue apron and a mental straight jacket. Looking back with the benefit of the sexual revolution and the introduction of near equality it is hard to believe that his parents enjoyed a happy relationship - he certainly couldn't recall them ever laughing or showing the outward signs of enjoyment - but they provided each other with exactly what the other needed and in return received what *they* yearned for.

His mother found satisfaction in keeping the house in a state she always believed a house should be kept in, in order to bring up a healthy family, and took pride in following her husband's instructions to the letter. If she failed to carry them out as instructed then she knew she had done wrong, so felt she fully deserved the rebukes and criticism. It just made her try harder next time. While she busied herself with the physical parts of family life it left time for her husband to concentrate on the educational aspects, both moral and scholarly. And of course the not insignificant job of earning the money that ensured they could keep the house she meticulously cleaned, and could eat the food she put on the table at five forty five every night (one o'clock and five thirty at weekends). On the few occasions he would come across his mother in tears, he always put it down to some weakness in her, and would always quickly leave, not willing to hide his shame and embarrassment.

His unremarkable home life spurned a similarly unremarkable record at school, never standing out either socially, academically or sportingly. The few people his own age who onlookers would have assumed were his friends were merely people who found themselves in the same position - not different enough from the assumed norm to be bullied, but not individual enough to be popular or to actually enjoy their time at school.

From as early as he could remember Mr Clarke had always kept a diary. Not one in the way that the majority of people do at some stage of their adolescent lives, full of unanswered questions of why no one understands them, or about some member of the opposite sex, and how their plan to eventually woo them into some sexual liaison was progressing. It didn't even contain a glorified list of that particular day's events. The diary he kept hidden under his mattress contained only numbers. One, written in black ink, carefully in the middle of each page representing a day. These numbers ranged from minus five to five and represented how his day had gone. If it had been a good day, as in it had been chicken for tea, or he had seen the Braithwaite kid from up the road fall off his bike or get in trouble from his father for throwing stones at old Mr Partridge's house, he would put a one or two in the diary. If he had been told off at school however or his father had come down on him after discovering him without a handkerchief in his right hand trouser pocket, then a minus one or two would take its place, depending on the severity of the telling off.

The majority of the days were therefore represented by a number between minus two and two. Occasionally a minus three would appear (like when he repeated that word he had heard the Braithwaite kid using, while at the dinner table) and he remembered the odd three, usually around Christmas and birthdays.

He would spend hours at a time in his room putting the figures together, grouping the days together into weeks and months to see if any stood out as particularly good or bad ones, but they rarely did. The mediocrity of his life was being proved by mathematics, but this made him happy. When at the end of a year he put all the numbers together (always done on the afternoon of New Year's Day - one of the few things he really, really looked forward to) they nearly always ended up just one or two away from the magical zero figure. Nothing would make him happier than when after all his calculations the small black calculator his father would let him borrow, produced a small solitary circle. He was a firm believer in complete equality, in that if something bad happened then it stood to reason that something good was going to come around the corner to balance it up. Conversely anything good that happened always left him feeling worried and looking over his shoulder, waiting for the forces of nature to punish him. As his mathematical ability progressed, so did the graphs and tables he would produce on January the first, but they generally showed the same results.

Mr Clarke's contact with the outside world, apart from the one that actually touched him on his journeys to and from school, was very limited. He was allowed to watch an hour of television a day and the news never entered his viewing agenda. This meant the only current affairs he knew about were those opined by his father over their evening meal, complete with his very individual and black and white outlook on life. The teachers at school offered no further insight into what was actually happening in the world around him - they were content to see out their remaining years in the profession trudging through the same syllabus they had done when they were keener, less bitter individuals. Happy to not so much nurture or even prune the pupils but to create bonsai reproductions of themselves.

Mr Clarke would make sure that he saved up enough television time to enable him to watch an entire episode of Star Trek. For years he would watch episode after episode, repeat after repeat and came to almost idolise Mr Spock. He loved his approach to life and to the variety of obstacles that were placed in his way by a combination of the Styrofoam aliens and the shortcomings of the rest of his crew. To Mr Clarke, Spock was the real hero of the show and in his opinion should really have been the captain, positive that he would have made a far better job of it than the far too emotionally driven and at times foolhardy Kirk. As much as he loved Spock, he hated Bones, the doctor who always poked fun of the science officer. Bones was supposed to be a man of science, but to Mr Clarke this was the most unrealistic part of the show - Bones just didn't have what it takes to be a doctor, certainly not one with the responsibility of looking after an entire starship.

At the end of each episode, when order had once again been restored (more proof if more was needed that his theories on equality were correct) there was always a scene on the bridge involving Spock, Bones and Captain Kirk, and it was always the latter two having a joke at the formers expense. As a result of Mr Clarke's tender age and naiveté this was always lost on him and as the programme ended on Spock's face, an eyebrow raised in incomprehension of his fellow crew members jibes, before returning to his instruments, he would swell with pride believing that once again his hero had not only got the better of the evil extra-terrestrials but also of the Captain and the doctor.

One of the first signs of his advancing years and slightly less advancing maturity showed itself at the end of one episode. One Tuesday night he had enjoyed an episode - the first of the brand new series - particularly impressed with the way Spock had out thought a race of green skinned mutes with his peculiar brand of logic and science. Then, still glowing with the feeling of a job well done he watched with mouth actually agape as Bones and the Captain took the mick out of him. What made it worse was that Spock didn't even seem to realise what was happening. Suddenly it was as if everything he had believed and held to be an undeniable truth had been wrong, had been a cruel joke. His mind sped back to all the previous episodes and he realised that his hero was the laughing stock of the rest of the crew and that whenever they had praised him, their mocking tongues had always been placed firmly in their cheeks. That was the last time Mr Clarke had ever watched Star Trek.

***

The ringing tone clicked off and a woman's voice answered.

"Hello."

"Yes good morning... I'm ringing regarding your advertisement in the newsagent's window."

"Which one would that be honey?" Her voice sounded thick with either sleep or lack of intelligence.

Mr Clarke had hoped it would be an easy process, and felt his cheeks redden.

"...The one advertising... a massage."

Silence. He felt obliged to fill it but wasn't sure how to go about it when the voice on the other end did it for him.

"Well, what about it?" she didn't seem annoyed or even impatient, just going through a tired old ritual.

"I'd like to order one." He said lamely, feeling his earlier confidence seeping away.

"Right. When would you like it honey."

Mr Clarke objected to the use of the word honey, its implied affection seeming hideously out of place in the current circumstances, but he swallowed his growing resentment to the voice and its owner.

"Straight away, it's very important that you can come straight away." Oblivious of the pun he had just unwittingly delivered, he carried on, his hatred giving him renewed confidence. "It's no good if you can't get around here in the next hour."

"Jesus, you are eager aren't you?"

He could hear her beginning to slip into her act and he found himself gripping the green handset harder and harder.

"OK honey I'll see what I can do. What's your address?"

A minute later and the initial transaction was complete. He had got her to promise she would make it at the agreed time, and though he was sure he couldn't trust her completely it was the best he was going to get, so had to just sit and hope. It occurred to him that he hadn't verified that she was as she described herself on the blue card in the newsagent's window, but as it had hardly been a flattering description in the first place he didn't really see any scope for artistic licence. The words "Big Jamaican Mama" didn't leave much to the imagination so he sat back down at the window feeling confident it had gone as well as could be expected, especially as it involved relying on what he considered scum.

Five minutes earlier, when he had seen the bleached haired figure walking quicker than what you would normally consider as a natural pace, coming up the street, both arms folded across her stomach, leaning forward, making her progress almost look like a controlled stumble, he knew he could put into action the final part of his plan. Reaching across to his note pad he looked down at the names, numbers and brief descriptions by each one. He had taken down three numbers hoping that two back up ones would be enough in case the first one was unable to make it in time, but he had hoped that one would be enough as he didn't want to talk to any more prostitutes than was absolutely necessary.

Now he just had to sit back and wait, slight excitement tinged with the worry that always comes when a plan had to rely on external forces that one had no ability to control. He went through in his mind every step of his plot, and tried to think of anything he could have done differently, any small thing he had overlooked that would jeopardise the end result. Unable to come up with anything he settled down, almost content, his eyes glued on the traffic.

Just over fifty minutes had passed and he was feeling the beginnings of anger and frustration well up in his stomach when a figure coming from the opposite direction the bleached hair woman had arrived from, caught his eye. It was of a large black woman, with an equally big black mass of curly hair, dressed in a large but dated fur coat. He had expected her to arrive in a car but was sure that this was the woman he had spoken to on the telephone. She appeared to be looking at the house numbers, and a combination of her size and unsuitable footwear meant her pace was less than half that of the bleached haired woman but no less awkward looking. His heart almost sank when she appeared to go past no. 68 but at the last second, she stopped and went up to the front door with a confidence that suggested this was one of many such visits this week alone.

From Mr Clarke's vantage point, he could clearly see her raise her hand to the doorbell and give it a long press. He had to remind himself to breathe as he watched to see who would answer the call. It wouldn't be a disaster if Mr Foster himself opened the door, but it would be so much better if it was his wife, and he was fairly sure that she would be experiencing stomach cramps serious enough to stop her being able to lie in bed. The door began to open inwards, just as it appeared the woman in the fur coat was going to knock on it. Mr Clarke leaned even closer to the window and then a smile cracked his face as the door opened fully to reveal Mrs Foster's dressing gown covered body, behind the bulk of the woman on the doorstep. An exchange took place that was hard to gauge but for ten or so seconds could have been that of any taking place between a householder and a door to door salesperson. Then suddenly, and violently it took a turn for the worse as the smaller of the two women burst into life and pushed at the larger one, shouting at her while clutching at her stomach with one arm. The fur woman refused to budge and now appeared to be shouting back, while Mrs Foster now with most of her attention aimed at someone behind and above her. Several seconds of this passed, with two passers-by temporarily stopping on the opposite pavement and enjoying the show, before Mr Foster appeared behind his wife dressed only in a pair of black Y fronts.

A shouting match ensued with each giving as good as the other two, no one seeming to be on the same side as anyone else. After two minutes or so of this with the fur coat woman stretching her hand out obviously wanting financial reward for her efforts, she gave one final shouted insult before turning and stomping off through the gate and back in the direction she had come, turning and yelling something first at the Fosters and then at a woman pushing her bike laden with shopping who was taking too much interest at the goings on for her liking. Her inability to walk with any dignity or speed lending her exit even more theatre. The married couple carried on their argument seemingly oblivious of the third party's departure, and after a minute of each one screaming at the other the confrontation was ended by the woman, when in an impressive show of strength, physically pushed her husband down the path and after briefly doubling up and vomiting painfully on the step, straightened up, strode into the house slamming the door behind her.

In the safety of number 43, Mr Clarke sat very happily, the smile still visible on his face, only slightly dampened by his regret of not having opened his window to allow him to catch at least some of the words being shouted. As he watched his near naked neighbour banging on his front door in an attempt to carry on the argument inside with a bit more dignity and warmth, Mr Clarke was torn between watching him and going and updating his chart.

CHAPTER TWELVE

Mike could hear the bird that spent every morning on the branch of the tree outside his bedroom window going through its small and annoying repertoire of chirps and whistles. On about its thirtieth rendition he couldn't help himself and he leapt out of bed, threw the curtains open and tried in vain to pull the sash window up. Failing that task, he took to banging on the condensation covered glass not caring if his fists went through the glass or not. Whether the bird had actually been scared off or simply become bored he didn't know, but he was greeted with silence. He returned to his bed and sank below the duvet allowing it to devour him and protect him from the daylight that had been allowed to rush in from the outside world signalling the start of yet another day. Once again he considered putting on some music but quickly rejected it. All his c.d.'s seemed hollow and shallow and somehow pointless now, reminding him of the time just a few weeks, days ago even, when they would listen to them together, singing along. Now they seemed as if they were simply trying to cover up something rotten in the background but failing dismally, like washing with cheap soap to get rid of an unpleasant smell on your hands.

Just as quickly he dismissed the idea of putting the radio on, knowing the banalities spewed by the overly happy d.j.'s would be even worse. Besides the radio, along with the television had ceased to be objects of entertainment, but had merely become a means of discovering how long he had left before the authorities caught up with him.

He had slept alone last night, after a massive row with Rachel. It was the worst they had ever had and was possibly the last one. She hadn't even shouted bye when she left for work, but had just shut the door with exaggerated force. Already he was dreading her coming back from work, not knowing how he would handle it or what she would do. He knew he should do something positive to try and sort it out like tidy the house or go and meet her for lunch, but knew he wouldn't for a variety of reasons.

Firstly it would take far too much effort. Not that he wasn't desperate to do something to show how much he loved Rachel, and to prove to her he would never do anything intentionally to hurt her, but he was finding it increasingly hard to motivate himself to actually get up and do anything. He was even getting to the point that he actually didn't know if he could be bothered to run if the house caught fire. He wondered if this was what depression was, but in asking himself the question he thought that he was probably answering it in the negative, in a Catch 22 kind of way.

Secondly, and for the thousandth time in recent times, he knew he hadn't done anything wrong and certainly nothing to deserve this. Rachel had arrived home late from work the day before, and hadn't even bothered to put on the mask that said that everything was all right. She had stomped into the lounge where he was sitting staring at the blank television set; met his gaze, seem to go to say something but then stopped herself and left the room. Mike had almost got up to follow her but knew he wouldn't be able to say anything and would probably make matters worse if he just followed her around, mute, getting in her way. He had planned to get a meal ready for when she got home but hadn't realised it was an hour and a half past when she usually got home until he had looked at the clock when he'd heard her key in the door.

She returned to the lounge ten minutes later, still in her coat and scarf, but she had obviously been crying.

"Mike... do you know where I've just been?"

It must have been the most rhetorical question ever asked - he had no way in the world of knowing where she'd been. He didn't help by answering in a strangely optimistic, questioning voice "Work?"

"No, Mike I haven't been to work, well I have but I'm not on about that." Here she started to cry again, or rather tears started to come from her eyes but her voice didn't break. Instead it got stronger and louder, though still under control. "I've been to the fucking clinic Mike, and do you know why I've been there? Do you know what they said when I was there?"

Mike didn't know he was still capable of it, but he was genuinely shocked. He sat up, opened his mouth to form the word "no" but nothing came out.

"I'll tell you what they said Mike, I'll tell you what they fucking said," she took in a deep breath like a swimmer coming up for air, "They said I had fucking lice, Mike. Crabs." This last word was shouted. In any other situation the word would have sounded absurd, even comical, but now it sounded horrible.

"Crabs........?"

This was so much of an unexpected almost surreal turn of events, that Mike, particularly in the state he was in, found it hard to grasp what was going on. He just found himself repeating the word like an imbecile.

"Yes crabs. And I wonder how on earth I got them Mike?"

It suddenly dawned on him that she was implying that not only was he somehow involved in this but that she appeared to think that he was the cause. "Rachel, I don't understand what you are saying. How have you got that, them... surely you know it's nothing to do..." somewhere in his head it was like a clock mechanism that has suddenly got to the part where it is ready to chime the hour. Up until then he had hardly noticed, despite Rachel's digs that he had been itching for days maybe even weeks. "Ahhh..."

"You dirty, dirty disgusting bastard, who have you been fucking? Mike how can you?" Now she seemed to lose all her strength and she practically collapsed into an armchair and started to sob, "...Mike how could you?"

This spurred Mike into action or at least into movement and he leapt up and went to go over and comfort her, to hug her, to tell her that he loved her, and that he really really honestly hadn't slept with anyone else because he would never ever do anything like that because he loved her so so much.

She looked up maniacally at his approach. "Get away from me you bastard," she shouted, "don't ever touch me again...how could you...you complete shit...I loved you...bastard.........." Her voice finally broke, and she suddenly seemed to shrink, as if something inside her, something that gave her her poise, her strength, her energy had left.

Mike stopped in the middle of the room, mouth open, starring at her, unable to move.

The third and probably the most important reason why he wasn't going to go and meet her from work or take her for a lunchtime pint to get to the bottom of this and try and save his relationship, was because it would involve going outside, out of the house. And that thought terrified him. He hadn't left the house for several days now and lying there in bed he would have been very happy if he knew he would never have to leave the house again. In an attempt to raise his spirits, he reflected that this was probably as low as he personally could go, so there was only one way to go from here. There was another way out of course but he didn't even want to think about that.

CHAPTER THIRTEEN

Shafeeq had done his usual entrance and had taken a seat, opposite Spoon and Danny and next to Al who was - as usual - asleep or unconscious or a combination of both.

"I'm telling you man there's some shit going on out there, there was this guy in a Mondeo at the bottom of the road all yesterday, and there's been a window cleaner van opposite on and off for weeks, and no fucker ever leaves or enters it and there ain't no one having their windows cleaned around here. I'm telling you man it ain't right, and it ain't me bein' paranoid or nothin'. I didn't even turn up this street yesterday man, you know what I'm sayin', I just carried on walkin' straight past." He took a long drag on his Marlboro cigarette, "I just carried on walkin' straight on past." He used the middle two fingers on his left hand to demonstrate how he had just carried on walkin' straight on past.

"I know what you mean Shaft, you aint the first to notice something. If it is anything, they'll get bored soon enough or their budget will run out. They'll soon fuck off."

"Yeah well, I'm still not happy, I don't need to be coming here you know, I've plenty of other places to go man, without me comin' here and putting my black ass on the line for you guys." He glanced towards the curtained window, "I don't need to be comin' here man."

"We know mate, we know, don't worry." Spoon said it and Danny nodded his agreement.

"yeah well, it's easy for you sayin' not to worry, you're sat in here, I'm the motherfucker walkin' up and down past 'em." His fingers showed them the walkin'. "I don't need this shit man. Don't need this shit."

A silence settled over the room, and Shafeeq contented himself with rubbing at a dark spot on his jacket, which seemed to divert his ire away from the local constabulary.

"Anyway, how's it going?" Danny settled down with the cigarette he had been rolling, offered it to Spoon who declined, and lit it.

"Yeah not bad Dan, not bad Dan my man." He smiled, either at his little rhyme, or at something he'd just remembered. "Did I tell you about that Maria girl that was gettin' it from the old Shaft? Well you won't believe this man, I tell you, you won't fuckin' believe this man....."

Spoon half listened to his latest tale of extraordinary sexual conquest. He did enjoy them, especially as he was probably the only one in the house who knew there was probably only some truth in them. The rest of his thoughts were taken up by what Shafeeq had said earlier. Whatever faults Shafeeq had, he wasn't stupid and he wasn't prone to imagining or making this kind of shit up. He wasn't the only one to mention it either, Danny had been the first to think that maybe he had been followed a couple of weeks earlier, and Spoon himself had noticed a certain Cavalier and Mondeo once or twice too often for his liking.

Shafeeq had come to the end of his tale and was laughing loudly, as was Danny. Spoon hadn't heard the ending but felt obliged to join in.

"You kidding me man." Danny managed, in-between laughs. Spoon had noticed before that Danny changed the way he spoke when

Shafeeq came around and he wondered if it was pissing him of as much as it was himself. Come to think of it there were several things that Danny did that pissed him off. He always told crap, obvious jokes as if he spent his life digesting the back catalogue of every crass comedian so as to regurgitate the material at inopportune times. Spoon delved back into the recesses of his often fallacious memory looking for the first time Danny had come into the house, or who'd introduced him but returned empty handed. If he had to put money on it, he'd have gone for Al, who did seem quite pally with him. He made a mental note to ask him next time he woke up.

Back in the room Shafeeq was off on another episode, this one involved even more hand movements and gestures than usual. Danny, who was hanging on his every word, was making encouraging noises while rolling a cigarette.

Shafeeq returned to his chair, and lowered himself down, looking at his audience as he did. "All the Chinese are the same, they all do it every last fuckin', one of 'em." He stopped, shaking his head in bewilderment. He tapped out a Marlboro from its packet and gestured to Danny for his lighter.

"I shagged a chink once" Danny began, reaching over with the lighter to Shafeeq, not noticing Spoon rolling his eyes. "Not bad at the time, but you want to shag another one half an hour…"

" Shaft, what was the Wigan score last night, please tell me it was a home win?" Spoon cut across him, retrieving a pink betting coupon from his jeans pocket.

"I'd love to bro, I'd love to. Unfortunately due to some shocking defending and a last minute equaliser, it was only a score draw my friend. A score draw."

"For fucks sake" A crumpled coupon joined its brothers and sisters in the corner of the room, "One fucking game every…fucking…time."

Shafeeq, quickly caught Danny's eye who was trying not to grin. He didn't feel guilty about making the scores up. In his opinion, if people were foolish enough to give their money to corrupt thieving bookmakers on the results of a game that was run and played by even more corrupt and thieving players, officials and businessmen, one more piece of dishonesty was neither here or there.

Silence once again settled on the house, broken only by Shafeeq and in particular Danny exhaling smoke. That was another thing that fucking annoyed him about Danny, the way he exhaled his cigarette smoke with an exaggerated blowing noise. Even the fact that Danny had a beard was starting to annoy him. "Jesus" he thought "I think I just need to get out of this house for a bit."

The dark of the room was replaced by that of the approaching night, only this didn't come hand in hand with the cloying smell of cigarettes, sweat and vomit. He found himself thinking, not for the first time recently, if it was time for a change, if not of lifestyle, certainly of scenery. "How?" He spoke the word, asking the cold steel lampposts; the black and white cat perched on a cooling car bonnet; his mother, one hundred and eighty centimetres under the ground; his father, fuck knows where, but probably pissed out of his face in a gutter; a god, who he doubted existed but dared never quite completely dismiss. And finally himself. "How the fuck are you going to escape?" He knew he wouldn't even try. He was tied to his small band of customers, and until they all either died, quit or fucked off he was going nowhere. At the grand old age of twenty-four he hadn't the strength to fight anymore, to stand in the way of whatever fate, god or whoever had in store for him.

CHAPTER FOURTEEN

November the thirteenth. It would probably go down as the worst day of Mike's life so far, but that may have something to do with the state he was already in when it found him. Ask an AIDS victim what his worst day was and they would very rarely tell you the day the infected needle punctured their skin, or the night they had quick, rough, though otherwise unspectacular sex up against the wall beside Boots, where the quick, disappointing climax led in turn to a much slower, more final one. They would be almost as unlikely to say the day that they were diagnosed. It's the day, not far from the end that they fall victim to that fatal cold virus or the lethal chest infection that will finally overcome their already battered and bleeding immune system. The day when the false hope, fed and nurtured over the preceding weeks, months and years is finally all but extinguished.

November the thirteenth found Mike Burley asleep on his bedroom floor, an assorted pile of Rachel's clothes in an untidy heap underneath and around him, and two puddles of sick, one the size of a dinner plate the other that of a saucer. Several feet away lay an empty bottle of vodka that had been kicked by a thrashing leg in the night and had rolled towards the door. Even in his emotional and confused state last night, after he had drained the last of the imperial spirit from its container the thought had occurred to him that he had just finished the last drop of alcohol in the house and that if he was going to continue living his life in the way he had become accustomed he would have to leave the house to get some more alcohol.

November the thirteenth may about to be bad, but November the twelfth had been no picnic. It had been four days since Rachel had been to the clinic and since then she had stayed around Sarah's house, coming in briefly one night – with Sarah – to collect some more clothes. Her friend's presence and particularly the way they had seemed so together; the way Sarah had looked at him so disdainfully, (in his own fucking house); and the way Rachel had refused to look at him, had made the ten minutes or so when she was in the house a hundred times worse than the thousands of minutes he had waited for her to return. All his plans of sitting down and talking and of convincing her that he wasn't the guilty party here, had disintegrated and after a couple of aborted attempts he just sat there and scowled at Sarah wishing he had at least been watching the television as opposed to sat staring at its black, inactive screen, and that he wasn't cradling an almost empty bottle of Canadian rye whisky.

Afterwards he had wished that he had made a meal beforehand to show that he wanted to make a go of it and at least try to sit down like reasonable adults and talk things through. Maybe that way Sarah would have been made to feel uncomfortable and that it was her who was intruding. Maybe that way he'd have at least been able to talk to Rachel, get across his side; maybe that way they'd have made up, promised to live happily ever after and he'd be lying next to her now instead of her cold empty clothes.

The next he saw or heard of her (she was not taking his calls at work, or answering his texts) was straight from work on the twelfth. The first thing she said was that she wasn't staying long because Sarah (precious fucking Sarah) was sat outside in the car waiting. Mike was more than tempted to say that heaven forbid Sarah was put out at all and made to wait in the car for more than a couple of minutes, after all, all we are talking about is our whole fucking relationship here, but he didn't want to start out on the wrong footing. By the time his lethargic body had risen from the settee to follow Rachel she had already been up in the bedroom a minute and when he came up behind her, his mind desperately searching for an opening line that would not sound too dramatic, too corny or too lame, she had already half-filled the suitcase that lived on top of the main wardrobe.

"Rachel…" She didn't look round, didn't even flinch "I love you Rachel…"

He noticed that she was making far too much hard work of transferring the contents of her two drawers into the suitcase and was relieved to see at least she was affected by the situation. It had been her coldness, her hardness that had hurt him most two days before. Slightly encouraged he made another step towards her and placed his hands on either side of her waist.

"Don't touch me Michael." It was stated, no emotion, no cracking of the voice. This was even worse than the use of his full name. Unperturbed, or rather knowing that maybe this was his last chance he squeezed harder and tried to pull her slightly towards him while he moved his head into the back of her neck, smelling her hair for the first time in days. He had just registered how wonderful it smelt when she spoke again, shattering any feelings of pleasure that were in danger of being rediscovered.

"I said don't touch me Michael." A pause while no one moved. "Michael get your hands off me, I'm trying to pack."

Inside Mike was wishing he could break down and cry, to beg for forgiveness, to throw himself completely at her mercy, but he wasn't capable of such emotion anymore. He just stood there finding himself remove his grip on her and take a step back. Two minutes later she had closed the suitcase and had put her hairdryer and several other "essentials" in another bag. She turned around and looked at him.

"I'm leaving Mike. I just can't live with you anymore. I find it hard to even look at you anymore. What you've done to me…" she looked around the room as if literally searching for the right words, "I wouldn't do that to anyone Michael. Anyone, and certainly not the person I was supposedly in love with and wanted to spend the rest of my life with. Still, more fool me for not seeing it earlier and being stupid enough to actually believe that we had something special. I thought we had something that no one else had. I used to look at other couples and even feel sorry for them because I thought that what they had together wouldn't come close to what I thought we had. How wrong could I have been?" She stopped, knowing that she had said more than she had planned and was in danger of breaking down. She could do that in the car with Sarah, she just had to get out the house.

This was Mike's last chance. The words had stung him but at least they had stung his mind into some sort of action and his head started to clear slightly and began to form something approaching an eloquent argument. He realised he was almost blocking the door which was good, it would mean that she would actually have to wait for him to move or at least have to ask him to move. He had one last chance, and the ball was in his court.

He watched her pick up the two bags, and then found himself looking at his feet as he stepped back and allowed her to pass through the bedroom door. He heard her rush down the stairs, the case banging into the banister, then she was opening the door, a large sob escaping from her before the door slammed shut with a horrible finality. Then silence.

It had taken five hours, the rest of the whisky, the remainder of the vodka, a few tears, a lot of soul searching and self-hatred to get Mike from standing in the bedroom looking at his stockinged feet listening to the girl he loved leave their home and leave him, to lying in the same room, surrounded in some of the few clothes Rachel had left. At some stage in the night, he wasn't sure when, but logic suggested it was near the end, he had sought them out and buried his face in them, smothered himself in them. Trying to get a trace, a sniff of Rachel but all he could detect was Surf.

***

In an impressive show of strength of character and motivation he hauled himself to his feet and after a very rudimentary tidy up - which consisted of pouring warm water onto the two puddles of sick; standing the empty vodka bottle up and returning Rachel's vest and jeans to the drawer (neglecting to check for signs of their nights adventures) - stood under the shower for twenty minutes allowing its hot cleansing water to saturate his body. He stood almost motionless, occasionally shifting his position slightly, directing the water onto previously neglected areas hoping the water would cleanse more than the surface grime and sweat. He hoped it would wash away the inner filth, the guilt, the fear, the knowledge that he had been shat on from everything and everyone around him. But as he stood naked in the bathroom, shivering, he knew his skin - previously too thin, had acted as a barrier, not only keeping the water from entering but also not allowing anything to escape its confines.

After eventually drying himself off he found some clean clothes - another good sign - and poured some cereal into a bowl before realising he had no milk. He managed to eat almost half of it before his already dry mouth refused to allow any more in and retired to the lounge sitting down in a different chair than usual, trying anything to break the habit and schedule he had fallen into over the last few days. He was thankful for his thumping headache and slight nausea, for it gave him something to concentrate on.

November the thirteenth. It was now ten twenty-five, forty-five minutes since Mike had risen and he had made steady progress in attempting to rid himself of the heavy cloak that had weighed down on him over the last few days. If he carried on like this, he thought, in a few days he'd maybe go outside (he ignored the tightening of his stomach at this thought), and then he'd concentrate on winning Rachel back, and convincing her how it had all been a terrible misunderstanding. He had flung open the curtains and had allowed the dismal drizzle soaked light to drift in, and now he was sat looking in the direction of the television that he had actually turned on, sipping a mug of coffee (his plain green one - the prison one no longer seemed a harmless joke). He had even discovered that he preferred black coffee. A ruddy faced fat chef was throwing a selection of ingredients into a pan, smiling and telling the watching public that they should be there, so they could smell the aromas bursting out. Mike very much doubted if it was anywhere near as exciting as the chef was claiming and almost allowed himself a smile as he thought that the last thing this man wanted was another meal, especially in the middle of the morning.

Despite himself he found his thoughts drifting back to Rachel. He hoped she was thinking of him now. He also hoped she was feeling shitty. Normally he would never wish any harm or ill thoughts on her, but right now - and he didn't think it was through malice or bitterness - he really hoped she was going through hell. But the only way he could picture her was her laughing, sharing a joke with Sarah. He contemplated ringing her up, if only to cut her joke short, but just as quickly rejected it. He had nothing to say to her. That was the awful thing. He had nothing to say to her. That was why he had allowed her to leave the previous night. Not through cowardice or because he had given up or because he wouldn't give the world for her to stay. He had absolutely nothing to say to her.

The chef was now smiling smugly as a tall woman with a severely cropped bob poured compliments onto him out of a food crammed mouth. Mike wasn't sure if she was a member of the public or a minor celebrity, but she was playing up her part, glad of the attention - making the most of her Warhol allotted slice of fame or desperately trying to inject her career with some much needed airtime. Either way it seemed to Mike a crappy forum on which to do it. Their self-satisfied faces were replaced by a clapping crowd which in turn were ousted by a list of people wanting credit for putting on the show. Not for the first time he wondered how many times it would take for Malcolm Bailey (for example), the chief grip to get bored of watching out for his name scroll up the screen. How long it would be before he would not tune in with a couple of minutes to go. Slightly less time, he concluded, than before he failed to point it out to anyone else in the room after happening to stumble across some closing credits.

Dismayed he realised he had been waiting for the programme to finish before getting up and fixing himself another black coffee and forcing a bit more cereal into his mouth. He returned, placed the brimming mug on the coffee table, noticed it had actually begun to rain and returned his gaze to the television, gearing himself up for the next bland offering - probably an opportunity to see how his licence fee was being spent on doing up somebody's front room and garden.

Instead the screen was filled with the image of a car. A blue Ford Orion, with rust patches. It was a car he had seen only once in person but one that had been emblazoned on his brain for 10 days. Though this time there was something different, which meant it took fully two seconds for him to register what he was looking at. When he had seen it before, it had been on its own, deserted, abandoned, waiting for its private liaison with him. Now it was surrounded by yellow and black tape and several men, some in uniform some not, one in a white plastic overall. The camera shot swung back to a stern looking reporter wearing a light brown Mac, its collar up against the rain. His mouth seemed to move in slow motion and as a result the words coming out became slurred and impossible to understand.

The reporter finished and the screen was filled with the face of the news reader in the studio, but Mike wasn't there to see it. He had run upstairs and was desperately putting his trainers on, grabbing his wallet and keys. Both feet successfully in, he fled downstairs, picked up his coat and frantically tried to put his keys in the door. Now he could hear the newscaster saying how a lottery grant was helping local school children, but he was giving his full attention to the key in his sweating hand. For days the house had seemed a sanctuary, a haven that had protected him from the awful things that happened outside its wooden door, brick walls and glass windows. But now the insides had been poisoned. The outside had cunningly used the television as means of entry and it had infected the whole house. At that minute Mike couldn't think of a place in the world he would less like to be. Eventually the key turned, and he flung the door open and ran out into the rain and the cold and the outside world.

CHAPTER FIFTEEN

There was no sound, but the imaginations of the three men watching meant they could almost hear the man screaming and choking to death. The man, of average appearance in every way apart from the way he was dressed and the fact he had a noose around his head and was hanging from a wooden beam, was clawing at the inch thick rope that was eating into his neck and up under his chin. His struggles and flailing legs had started a slow spinning motion that offered a three hundred and sixty degree view of the spectacle. The chair that the three voyeurs had seen his desperate legs searching for minutes earlier was now upturned on the floor behind him, no use at all. When his left thrashing leg had knocked the chair over, the man's body language had seemed to change (as much as it can when you're strung up by the neck from a beam), his faced had gone rigid for a couple of seconds, before he had spat out an orange ball from his mouth and started his silent screaming.

Doug sat in the middle. He was the only one of the three not sporting a moustache, and not resting his feet on the table in front. He was also the only one not making jokes about the video being played on the colour television in the corner of the small square white walled room. The only other furniture was a metal filing cabinet against the wall on the left and a chipboard noticeboard above it. Faded yellow sheets of paper were haphazardly pinned to it, along with some yellowing white ones. The door, in the wall behind the three D.C.'s had its glass window papered over, while above them a bare light bulb struggled to cut through the smoke curling up from the three cigarettes.

Back on the screen, the man's brain had failed to tell his erect penis that it was no longer a game, as it pointed alternatively to ten and two o'clock as its owner continued to rotate, albeit increasingly jerkily. His neck was an array of red gouges and gashes, as his finger nails tore into the straining flesh, trying to get underneath the murderous cord. His lips, starting to turn colour, formed unheard syllables and words, and it was these that Doug was focussing on, trying to put out of his mind the larger picture, the fact that he was watching the last minutes of someone's life. It was impossible to make out what the man – in his mid-forties Doug would guess – was screaming. Whether it was the names of his wife or children, prayers shouted at a deaf god, or just a long wordless scream full of despair, rapidly fading hope, fear, and regret that his life was to end like this.

Doug realised D.C. Laithwaite – "Call me Lathers, everyone else does" followed by a steely grip and some vigorous hand pumping was his invariable greeting – had asked him a question, and this time was waiting for a response, something that didn't usually stop him. Lathers was his partner on the latest OP, and beforehand the thought of spending up to eight hours a day alone with his acerbic wit and endless storytelling, "Dougys", cajoling and insults had hardly filled him with excitement, but he soon discovered that conversations with Lathers rarely involved two people, and you could tune out without him caring or seeming to notice. And if he was honest with himself he did find him fairly entertaining at times, and Doug found himself almost looking forward to the days sat observing the squat.

"Say that again, I was trying to see what matey-boy was saying."

"Course you were Dougy, course you were." Lathers' strong Yorkshire accent didn't appear to come with a volume control, or if it did it was set permanently midway between normal conversation and a shout. "Hey Sniffer, reckon this is right up Dougy's street this." His thick set head with matching thick black eyebrows and moustache nodded in the direction of the television. "Best keep this under lock and key or he'll be taking it home for some overtime, 'ey, what do you reckon?" He leant across Doug, making a gesture like he was shaking a can of coke.

"Reckon you're right, too worried to put his legs on the table an' all look Lathers, scared nature will take its course…"

"You needn't worry there Dougy, not as if we'll be able to see oat from up 'ere. Anyway, if you can drag yourself away from gimp boy here," another nod towards the television, "I was asking a question. Why do these S and M characters stuff an orange or satsuma into their gobs before stringing themselves up?"

"Is it a joke?"

"No straight up Doug, serious question."

There was silence for ten, twenty seconds as Sniffer – a thin-faced D.C. whose Black Country twang seemed to have been lifted straight from a sitcom – and Doug chewed over the question. Raised voices moved along the corridor outside in the direction of the D.I.'s office, discussing the body of a suspected prostitute that had been found that morning.

"I imagine it would be to keep their airwaves open…?"

"Do you imagine that my dirty Brummy friend, do you indeed? And when do imagine this, when you're at home and the lovely Lisa is knelt in front of you keeping her airwaves open with your very own little jaffa?" Swinging his legs down from the table, he placed his hands onto his black denim clad knees, and faced his two pupils. "Dougy boy, any idea? "

"No, go on then, enlighten us." Doug turned to face the big head full on, fully expecting a weak punch line to follow.

"Well, let uncle Lathers fill you in about the facts of life. Jesus Christ, you'll be asking me about the birds and the bleeding bees next. Anyway, the reason they do it is, so that if they get a bit carried away, go too far like, and start to pass out, the body's reflexes automatically bite down on whatever is in their gobs – in this case, the aforementioned citrus fruit - and the sour juice revives them. Brings them round like. The mistake they make though, is that you may as well use a pigging tennis ball as an orange, it aint gonna save you. Not sour enough you see. Oranges may taste alright and be good for your skin, but when it comes to their reviving qualities they're worse than useless. What you need is a lemon. Bite down on one of those fuckers and it'll bring you out of a fucking coma."

Lathers leant back, retrieved a match and cigarette from their respective packets, struck the match, lit the cigarette, inhaled noisily and shook the match out before flicking it in the direction of the ashtray sat in front of Doug on the Formica table. Doug watched it fall short, and returned his gaze to the television screen. The man, who along with his life, appeared to be coming to a climax, had stopped spinning and was facing the camera he'd set up ten minutes before. His hands still grasped the rope but now his legs were performing a kicking motion that reminded Doug of a scuba diver making for the surface.

"They could use limes as well."

"Hark at fucking Einstein 'ere. Yes Sniffer they could use limes as well. With your gob, you could use a fucking grapefruit."

He laughed and contemplated the image for a while, his smile straightening his moustache. "Mind you, wouldn't have helped this bugger," Another nod of his big head towards the television. "A lorry load of lemons wouldn't have saved him, 'less of course he could stand on 'em."

"Shit, I'm getting pins and bloody needles." Sniffer stubbed his cigarette out and stiffly lifted his legs down, rubbing his thighs with the palms of his hands.

The man on the screen had stopped moving, swinging slightly from side to side like a pendulum in some grotesque grandfather clock. His penis – spent, hung limply, as did his arms, the talon-like hands and gashes on his neck the only evidence of the violent struggle for life only moments earlier. Doug tried not to look at his face, at the lolling tongue, and bulging eyes, but couldn't help himself.

"Who found him?"

Sniffer, still rubbing his legs, watched Lathers reach across to the video, turn it off and eject the tape before answering Doug. "His missus, came home from work with their four year old kid, went upstairs and found him like that in the games room."

"Games room, Jesus Christ, I bet these weren't the type of games they had in mind when they set up their family home." Lathers carefully returned the tape to the brown evidence jiffy bag and stood up.

"Right doesn't seem to be anything else for us here. Obviously old gimp boy here had taken to sneaking home from work to film himself and this time he got more than he bargained for."

Doug, elbows on the table, rubbed his eyes with the palms of his hands, trying to erase the image of the man. "I'm as open minded as the next man, but shit, what's wrong with a copy of Escort or something, beats me why people start having to do shit like that."

In his job, he was always determined to see the individual; the father struggling to cope with the mortgage; the teenager bullied and beaten at school with nowhere else to turn; the single mother desperate to feed her bawling kid; as opposed to just the name on the charge sheet. He got some stick for it, mainly light hearted, some not, from the others in the nick, especially his D.I. but it was the only way he could work. Or rather the only way he could live with himself after work. But in this case he was desperately trying to separate the family man with the wife and two kids he'd read about in the folder sat at his desk twenty minutes earlier, from the limp hanging figure that was still burned into his retinas.

"I'm with you on that there Doug." Sniffer – unfortunately not named due to his exceptional detective work, but rather because of his habitual winter cold and summer hay fever - watched Lathers leave the room with the brown jiffy bag in one hand, his cigarettes in the other. "Still, as they say, it takes all types."

They both listened to the loud tuneless whistling as Lathers made his way down the corridor to his desk, at the other end of the building.

CHAPTER SIXTEEN

The drizzle had come down and washed the earth for several hours, before the sky had exhausted itself, and had lent the grass and trees a sweaty appearance. It hadn't been a cleansing wash, the like of which Mike Burley had attempted earlier in the day, but a wash from a dirty, festering flannel that had sat in the sink too long. The grey sky looked flat and almost within reach, punctuated by the occasional patch of darker cloud, making its slow progress from one horizon to the other. A crow, suddenly bored of its surroundings took off with a jerky hop, skip and jump, stretching its heavy black wings and slowly rising, before disappearing behind the row of council houses that skirted the park. The distant sound of the bypass could be heard, but after a while you could ignore and eventually forget its constant drone, the newfound calm broken occasionally by a crying child or shrieking toddler.

This was as peaceful as the city got, and it was to this quasi oasis that Mike had found he had run to. The playground had been deserted and in the last hour and a half only one mother and child had disturbed his peace, and that had been short lived. Something about him had quietened the child dressed in a red coat she hadn't yet grown into, and disturbed his mother enough that after one go on the slide they had returned to the rusting gate in the corner from where they'd arrived five minutes earlier. The child, from under a protective arm had looked back twice to the figure on the middle of the three swings, only to be admonished by her mother, before being hurried through the gate and out of sight. Mike watched them go, his body and swing performing a slow but steady pendulous motion. At the top of each arc, the thick metal chains connecting the yellow plastic seat to the flaking supporting bar let out a metallic groan. After a while he returned his focus back in front of him, looking out to the duck pond in the distance and the outline of the mosque just peeking out above the trees. Using his arms and body, he kept up a steady rhythm allowing himself to become lost in it.

If this was the city's lungs, then the city had smoked far too many cigarettes, and done precious little exercise. The grass and scattered trees were gradually losing their fight against the encroaching bricks and concrete. What had once been a wild and natural terrain, had become over the course of a couple of generations, and many more flawed council initiatives, a poor imitation of what it had once been. Again and again, they had changed it, built on it, cut it up, remodelled and re-landscaped it, in an attempt to make it more natural looking, more like it was before they started planning on how to improve it, until now, it resembled nothing more than a neglected window box, stuck on the front of a tower block. Though the city's regulations stopped any more encroachment, the city had found other ways to eat into it and claim it as its own, Exhaust fumes perfumed the air, while glass bottles and garish tin cans and plastic wrappers added splashes of colour.

Mike and Rachel used to come here occasionally. It was a short cut to one of their friends' houses, and sometimes they'd stop and have a race on the swings, to see who would be the first to get their heads level with the bar, or they'd take it in turns to push the other on the roundabout, spinning it faster and faster until they lost strength from laughing. Rachel had found the park particularly incredible. She came from a village in the middle of the Dorset countryside. After a childhood spent amongst rolling fields and scattered copses, where there would be more shades of green in her view from her bedroom window, than there were houses in the village, she couldn't believe that this would be the only grass that the children growing up would see. On one evening the previous summer they'd come here, on the way back to their home. Stoned, they'd arrived at the playground just as the orange July sun was bidding farewell to the sweating city. Mike had got stuck on the slide, his denim shorts becoming wedged half way down. Giggling they'd freed him and had sat on the scorched earth, becoming lost in their thoughts, a mixture of happiness, warmth and hashish taking them off to their individual worlds, each preceding step and leap of logic instantly disappearing without a trace. Rachel had returned first, and had said how the park was like one of those paintings you saw of lions and tigers and elephants from the seventeenth century. The ones drawn by people who had never actually seen the real thing, and had only second, third and often fourth-hand   descriptions of what their subjects looked like. Still, confident that their audience had even less idea, they created more and more of them, each one getting further away from the actual, and closer to the imagined.

Mike had loved the idea, and had once again marvelled how Rachel was capable of looking at the same things as him, but seeing them in a completely different way than the black and white - conventional he guessed - way that he did. Sometimes he'd try to see things with a different slant, to imagine how you could describe the scene in front of him in a less literal manner, but always gave up. He supposed it was like humour - if it didn't come naturally to you, then it wasn't something you could force. Morally, Rachel was a lot more black and white than him, and he would occasionally mock her for her almost puritan views on some issues, especially compared to his more ambivalent ones. But when it came to seeing the beauty in things that he was blind to, or of seeing hidden depth or meaning in the simplest of ideas or objects, it was a talent he was very envious of.

He remembered how, that evening, they had started having sex, just next to the slide, under the soft blanket of the night sky, only stopping, in more fits of giggles, when the near silence was broken by a group of teenagers throwing their empty lager cans into the stagnant waters of the laughingly named duck pond.

On the swing, Mike came back to reality with a start, angry at himself for letting other thoughts and memories penetrate the wall he'd tried to build out of his efforts to keep him swinging. He didn't know if the saltwater flowing down his face was tears or sweat.

***

Spoon hesitated and changed direction - away from the small fenced off playground and the junkie on the swing, where he was originally headed - and towards the wooden bench overlooking the small pond. He'd left the house for some fresh air and to get away from the junkies and the filth they lived in. He had started to feel more and more that he was better than the others in the squat. That the squalor, the cyclical conversations, the hand to mouth, needle to vein, score to fix to hit to comedown life was somehow below him, and that he was only there temporarily. Passing through. That thought scared him. He'd rather be happy with the scum, the detritus, with no delusions of grandeur, illusions on ganja, or other sparks of ambition. Hadn't he learnt his lesson? He was in his rightful place, and as soon as he realised that, and extinguished the false hope that had begun to burn deep within him, the better it would be. Using the sleeve of his coat, he dried off the surface water from the scarred and graffitied bench, took out a cigarette packet from his jacket pocket and a sheet of folded paper from rear jeans pocket and sat down. A shiver went through him, almost causing him to drop the joint he'd just removed from the packet, and he tried to remember the saying – "someone just stepped on my grave"? Something like that, though he was sure there was a goose involved somewhere down the line.

There had been a park - not as nice as this, where he'd grown up. It was on the other side of the town from where he lived and where his friends and the other people who went to his school had lived, so he used to go there when he wanted to be away from everyone and everything he knew, or when he was just feeling down. Like when his father was drunk, or had locked his mum in the bedroom. He used to go there and pretend he was in some strange and foreign land on a mission to observe and report back on enemy activity. The people in the park became underworld characters, the old man walking a dog would be there to meet and exchange messages and the names of spies operating in the area – maybe even his own, with the couple strolling arm in arm; the mother with the pram – an agent carrying ammunition or radio equipment; the gardener - one of the local militia, who would arrest and torture Spoon (or plain old Rudy, as he was back then) if he managed to spot and capture him. After spending hours on his belly, hidden behind a slight rise in the ground carrying out his mission, he would return to his native land (the border marked by a corner shop half way home) where he would be awarded with a dozen or so penny chews and a can of pop. Ten minutes later, he'd be back home among the tears and whisky, waiting for the day he could escape for good.

The joint was half way down before he allowed himself to unfold the piece of paper. It was crumpled, and he used the palm of his hand to flatten it out on his thighs, careful not to make the tear he hadn't manage to avoid while removing it from the magazine back at the squat three days earlier, any bigger.

One year, he couldn't remember if he was thirteen or fourteen he'd had a particularly bad time at school. By then he had managed to create a wall against his torrid home life, his father rarely scarred him anymore and he was too angry with his mother for putting up with it all to allow too much pity or sympathy in, but a new threat had come in the shape of Gary Maxwell and his small gang of hangers on and sycophants. For some reason, probably because he didn't suck up or hang on, he'd taken a particular dislike to Rudy, and his strange name was an easy in. The friends he had had, drifted away, not wanting to come under fire themselves, so for six months Rudy was very much on his own, doing his time at school trying to avoid getting hit or having his books or football stickers stolen, before running home, dumping his bag, changing quickly before escaping into the make believe world of violence in the park. It didn't bother him too much, the attacks and abuse at school. From what he'd seen this was the norm. It was what happened, it was what you did when you were growing up, before being shat out into society for real.

That year, he'd been horrified when he found out that the school was having a special re-enactment in the park - his park. Apparently, it was the centenary, or bi or even tri centenary of some battle that had taken place where the park now stood. At first he'd not wanted to get involved with the town wide event, hoping that if he ignored it, somehow so would everyone else and the park and Rudy and the foreign agents, spies and messengers would be allowed to carry on out of the sight and minds of the rest of the town. It was impossible however not to be picked up and carried along in the momentum that had gripped the town. There was talk of television cameras and even someone who used to be in Emmerdale Farm was rumoured to be making an appearance. Rudy's class had a key role in the proceedings, and were to re-enact the siege. Naturally everyone wanted to be on the victorious side, and Rudy's originally ambivalent stance meant he was pushed towards the losing side. When he finally realised that there was nothing to do but take part and try and enjoy it, he took the proverbial bull by its seemingly tailor-made horns and found himself with the starring role. Even his parents had promised to attend and his mum had helped him with his costume.

The big day arrived, and was welcomed by a bright blue sky and slight breeze. Dressed in his jerkin, and tights he'd waited dry mouthed for the bugle call which was his cue. Eventually it had come, ringing out over the hushed spectators, announcing the surrender. His skinny legs - made to look even more so by the green tights - strode out from between the mock city gates the infant school had helped construct, to his mark, his eyes desperately searching for his parents faces in the crowd, while going over one last time his well-rehearsed speech. By the time he'd reached his position and was face to face with Gary Maxwell, naturally enough the leader of the victorious side, it was obvious his parents weren't there. Despite the growing lump in his throat, he delivered his lines, maybe not with the pomp he'd practised, before turning on his heels and retracing his steps, the cheer of the victorious army ringing in his ears, and tears stinging his eyes.

He had returned home an hour later to find his mother with a black eye, and no sign of his father. He didn't read the write up in the local paper, so was unaware of the praise for his part, particular mention going to the emotional delivery of his speech announcing the town's surrender. He rarely went to the park after that. Looking back, he guessed he had grown up, and no longer found solace or escape in childish games, but from then on he always felt that the park – his park - had been sullied. Not only by his parents' snub, but also because it was no longer his secret. As soon as the outside had been allowed into the world that had existed solely for him for a few brief months, it could no longer exist. One of the next times he'd had gone there he had lost his virginity, and the experience and memories of that night was enough to make him blanch now, nine years later.

A breeze suddenly sprung up, disturbing the black stagnant water of the duck pond, sending thick, lazy ripples across its surface away from Spoon's bench. Holding onto the sheet with his hands, his eyes hungrily explored the page, as if it was a treasure map. He'd never even heard of Granada three days ago, but now it represented all his hopes, his dreams. His escape. He studied the three colour photographs, desperate to find a clue, a key, anything that would tell him how he could join the people milling around, starring at the architecture or enjoying a coffee in the pavement café. He had never seen anywhere like it, and barely knew places like this existed outside of children's imaginations.

The first and largest photograph showed the Alhambra, a huge thirteenth century palace. A small inset showed tranquil water gardens and fountains, bordered by dozens and dozens of exquisite pillars, which looked barely strong enough to have held the ornate roofs up for hundreds of years. Snow-capped mountains framed the reddish bricks from behind, while lush green forest in the foreground added to the whole aura of something stolen from a fairytale. Another photograph showed a cluster of small quaint white houses clustered around narrow winding lanes, with a larger more modern city in the valley below. The final photograph showed a large church or cathedral towering over more of the picturesque houses and a small square with tables. Ten, perhaps a dozen people were sat at these tables talking and laughing amongst themselves, drinking coffee from small blue and white cups, or simply taking in the breathtaking view across the valley and towards the Alhambra itself. Despite the damp air and chill breeze, a warmth infused through Spoon's body, absorbing it from the sun reflecting from the tables and chairs in the photo on his lap, lapping up the smiles and calm on the people's faces. He made a promise to himself, there and then - just like he had the four other times he had spent time alone with the ripped-out magazine page – that whatever happened, whatever it took, he would go there, to Granada. That was where he had been running to all his life, that was the place he had always belonged, it's just that he never before had a name for it, or an image with which to hold in his mind and focus on. It had been in Danny's News of the World magazine, and he'd been flicking through it absentmindedly, half listening to Shafeeq and Danny and incredibly Al discussing for the fourteenth time that bloody week, about moving to somewhere else, as they were now all convinced they were being watched. They all knew they wouldn't go anywhere. This was perfect, it had running water, all but one window was intact and for most of them it actually felt like something approaching, if not home, then security.

He'd almost got to the end of the magazine, where there was no more chance of any more pictures of celebrities topless on the beach, and normally at the stage when he would have returned it to the pile on the floor, when, in the holiday section he'd seen the page that was now sat on his lap. He'd read the article twice, and studied the photographs, with amazement, excitement and then that dangerous emotion, the one he had desperately tried to eradicate from his life, so once more it didn't grow and eat into him like a cancer – hope. Carefully, with trembling hands he had torn out the page, unaware that the rest of the room was silent, its occupants staring at him, and had left the room ignoring Danny's comment about him going for a wank.

He had walked and walked that evening, the picture in his back pocket, his hand occasionally flitting there to check that it was still there, that he hadn't lost it or even worse, it hadn't been some dream or hallucination brought on by the smack.

He didn't know how he was going to do it, but he was going to save up, even if it was a fiver a week, until he had enough – however much that was – to leave this shithole, and start a new life, this time a real life in

Granada. He knew it would take years, but he didn't care. Five years waiting was better than the next 30 years slowly rotting.

He stood up from the bench, carefully folded the page and returned it to his pocket. The junkie, he noticed was still on the swing, though he had stopped swinging and was now just sat looking towards the pond, to where Spoon turned and left the park, towards the trees and mosque.

CHAPTER SEVENTEEN

How are great plans born? Are they worked on over months and years, chiselled and shaped, altered, adapted like a stone sculpture, gradually taking shape? Or are they the result of a lightning bolt of inspiration? History tends to favour the latter, with the likes of Archimedes and Robert the Bruce coming to the fore. Meticulous planners, though equally successful maybe, never make for as good copy. It was this thought that occupied Mr Clarke that morning over his eleven o'clock cup of tea, but not the reason for the slight frown that played over his face, causing an extra line to traverse his forehead and a normally well-behaved lock of hair to hang mischievously an inch below its allotted position.

No, what was causing this particular melancholy mood to ruin an otherwise perfectly made cup of tea, was the fact that he should have been happy. Very happy. After three years he had finally decided on a plan to eradicate number 101, or rather the bar on the chart that represented number 101. The bar that had been growing steadily like a tumour for almost half a decade. The bar that had mocked him every time he had consulted, updated or studied it. The bar that had ruined every single little victory. That bar represented every slight, every insult he had had to endure, every break in; every theft; each and every piece of abuse – both verbal and physical; character slur upon character slur; every malicious stare and malignant rumour. It represented every day of misery, pain, loneliness, fear, inadequacy of downright fucking shit that it had put him through.

Hot tea spilled onto his shaking hand, and the lock of hair had briefly made it to his V shaped eyebrows before being roughly flicked back to place. Gradually, purposefully, he controlled his breathing, his grip easing on the white cup. He silently reprimanded himself for using foul language, albeit only thought and not actually spoken. He never swore. That was something that the scum did. The dirty, filthy, thieving classes that he was trying to eradicate, and who had their tendrils into every part of society and were obviously even getting into his own head, forcing him to use to speak like them. This on, what should be a marvellous day, the first step on the final march to victory, and he was sat here, his tea ruined by their poison even in his own kitchen.

That wasn't the only reason his tea didn't taste quite so sweet that morning. He was worried that though he had finally settled on a plan, it wasn't the right one. That it wasn't perfect. He was only too aware that something on this scale could only be done once. He would only have one shot at it, so if it wasn't perfect, if it wasn't the right one, well, that just didn't bear thinking about. If this didn't work, his dream of equality, of perfect equilibrium and order, of balancing the chart would never be fulfilled. Hence, Mr Clarke's musings about Scottish Kings to be and Greek philosophers. He had been hoping for a eureka moment, while behind the scenes his mind had been patiently quarrying, chiselling and honing. When the lightning bolt had come – while ironing the sleeves of the third of the following weeks seven shirts – it was merely to inform him that there would be no others. There wasn't going to be another instance like when his brother went into the hospital to have his appendix removed and came out a week later blind. That was a one off, a fantastic, remarkable one off, but just that, and if he sat around waiting, hoping for another opportunity to come knocking on his door, all that would happen, was the bar on the chart would continue to grow, to eat into him, until it would eventually consume and destroy him. He would have to settle for Plan A, not plan b, because there was only one and there only ever would be just one.

By the time he had hung the seventh shirt up onto the wooden hanger in his wardrobe the night before, he was a happy man. Something akin to contentment had settled on him. For the first time in years he went to bed thinking the tide was beginning to change. He may still be swimming against it, but now he was making headway, and the current was no longer as strong.

That was last night. He had awoken this morning, fully expecting to start the wonderful process of putting the plan together, of formulating and arranging the minutiae, the intricacies, the layer upon layer of details that would result in the final creation. But instead, that was when the doubt had set in. They hadn't come alone either. Knowing they wouldn't be welcomed with open arms, they'd brought back-up. Familiar fears, insecurities and doubts, dressed up in various guises and fashions. Some dated back to the fifties, sporting the coarse, school uniform he'd spent nearly a dozen years in, others had come to the party in denims, some in cheap Marks and Spencer suits, still others in the dark blue of the constabulary. One, he saw with horror, but no real surprise was dressed in a skirt that just touched the top of two white fleshy knees and a diaphanous white blouse that wasn't even bothering to hide the pert pink breasts beneath with their even pinker perter nipples. With dismay he found his eyes drawn to her, they lingered on her legs, crawled up to her breasts then her long, thick dark hair, before settling on the round, open face with the heavily mascaraed eyes and bright red lips, that opened ever so slightly, the colour designed to evoke thoughts of her other, more intimate opening.

Long interred feelings tried to dust themselves down and make themselves heard, but as the look on the woman's face changed in turn from affected lust to surprise, to terror, pain then pleading, these once again died, and were replaced by the more familiar revulsion and guilt. Wildly he swung his mind's eye trying to refocus on anything, groping for the mocking schoolboy or skinhead, but before he managed it, he could not help but notice the ripped bloodied blouse and the thick dark stain spreading through the denim and down the once white flesh of her legs. In times like this he would normally run to the chart, finding solace, strength and hope in its logic and mathematics, but this time he just sat there, his straight back against the simple wooden chair, both fists clenched, his arms out straight resting on the kitchen table.

"Why? Why? Why now? Why can't you leave me alone?" The questions started out in his brain as an angry, defiant challenge to the hordes that were threatening to overwhelm him, but by the time it was ejected through stiff closed lips it had turned into a desperate plea. Gradually the stiffness left his body, his back became slumped, his arms reached for his face, the fingers searching and kneading the bones, flesh and skin of his cheeks and forehead.

Debra Murphy loved life. That was not only how she had described herself, but also as others had described her after she had had it ripped from her. She had grown up as a bright-eyed girl through the sixties, marvelling at all the sights, sounds and promised experiences that as an eleven, twelve and thirteen year old were just out of reach. Her mother, whenever she described her childhood and teenage years, would always refer to them as grey. That colour seemed to have permeated every aspect of her mother's countenance and history. Everything from her job in the laundrette – six days a week for thirty-five years – to her dull, unspectacular marriage – seven days a week for thirty-nine years - was tainted with grey. Her skin, the colour sucked out by the forty cigarettes she smoked a day, had even taken on the hue of her life. In the evenings, Debra would sit on the lounge floor while her mother would comb and plait her long dark hair. She would listen to the stories of her mother's childhood; of the people who came into the laundrette; of the history of when her parents had come across from Ireland, all the time breathing in the smell of her mother – soap and cigarettes, which was wonderfully comforting, and promise herself that she would be different. She would live. She would not settle for second best. She loved her mother with every fibre of her body, but she couldn't understand how she could have just accepted the first card that she was dealt. Debra had promised herself, again and again, that she would go through every card in the pack until she found the right one for her. If she didn't then she would order a re-deal and would keep doing so until she was happy. And everything she saw outside on the streets, on the small black and white television they had just got, gave her hope. Colours were everywhere – Jackie Mason at school even had a colour television set. A new freedom had seemed to sweep the past away, and with it the drab colours that it had wrapped itself in. Even though her mother pretended to look down her nose at what was going on, Debra knew deep down that she was happy that her daughter would have at least a chance at something approaching happiness. She had got a job at a firm in the centre of town. Her time was split between covering reception, doing some typing and filing and running errands to and from other companies in town. The pay wasn't amazing, especially after she'd given a sizable cut to her mother, but it was enough to enable her to get the latest T Rex and David Bowie records, to gradually increase her wardrobe and to keep her in make-up.

Her job brought her, for the first time, in contact with men, real men, and with it the revelation of how much power she could wield over them courtesy of wearing a short skirt, or not wearing a bra. She was the youngest woman in the company, and the majority of the fifty or so men who worked there would go out of their way to spend time with her. They would give her errands that would invariably involve both of them, or she would arrange and rearrange their filing systems. She would enjoy the feeling of their eyes boring into her as she leant down with their coffee, or stretched up to put a file onto the top shelf. Most nights she would be taken out for a drink where they would talk about their wives and girlfriends, and how they didn't understand them. Debra, was a good listener, after hours of practice with her mother, and though rough calloused hands on her thighs, neck and breasts weren't as comforting as the feel of her mother's hands through her hair, it still felt good and made her feel something approaching special. Her job also brought her into contact with the men at the other firms she visited on her errands, and she preferred these as she didn't have to put up with the women from those offices looking and talking down to her.

It was at one of these that she met George. He worked at the accounting firm that she delivered the papers to twice a week, and there was something about him that she found intriguing. He wasn't like the other men, who pawed her and pored over her. He was a strange mixture of childlike innocence and old-world chivalry, yet she sensed that he was desperate to open up, to throw off his ponderous, conventional self and to start living. It was this that had so endeared him to her. She saw him trapped behind the defences that he had built around himself to protect him from the outside world, but which had gradually become a prison from which he was unable to escape. She saw that like her, he wanted to live, but unlike her, he hadn't been able to do this on his own. That was where she longed to help him. She started to see it as her mission to help him, to free him from his mental chains, to open the door to his prison. To let him feel, like she herself had, the beautiful wind of freedom on his face.

It wasn't easy. It wasn't that he wasn't very good with women. He wasn't very good with people. Six months after being thrust into society, having men thrust themselves onto and into her, this was a new challenge for Debra. She thought he was quite cute as well, in a slightly weird, sergeant major type way, though she knew that if he had been like all the other men she certainly wouldn't have made any extra effort with him. She was the one who had to manufacture situations where they would be together. She would take bags of shopping along with her, when she went to the accountants where George worked, or reams of writing paper, and then ask him he if wouldn't be a darling and help her carry her bags, as she wasn't very strong, and the bags were so heavy, and her arms were aching so. Then she would come over faint, or go over on her high heels just as they were passing a particularly quiet pub, with an especially small and dark snug, and while she let him go to the bar she'd find the smallest, cosiest seats, undo another button on her blouse and watch her flustered, awkward man bringing their drinks over – her Martini and lemonade or Babycham, his pint of bitter or lemonade.

Talking to him, leaning over in front of him, or resting the swell of her breasts against his arm, was like watching a man fighting. Fighting the fears, restraints, taboos that he had put in place to protect himself from the outside world. It wasn't until later the thought occurred to her it may be the other way around.

The thing she liked most about these evenings though was the fact that she did the talking. Yes, she was a good listener, but she also had things to say herself. As well as her shirt and bra, there were a lot of things she wanted to get off her chest, and despite all the other blokes' fawning interest, it soon evaporated into lust, introspection and self-gratification once they realised that she was theirs for the night. Though he may not have listened, she found it therapeutic to talk to him about her loving but unadventurous mother, her distant, bland father; to tell him about her hopes and dreams for the future, how she was going to visit all the countries in the whole world. There was a world atlas in the reception at work and she spent hours flicking through its pages, marvelling at all the strange sounding places. She was fascinated by the different colours of the countries as well, and was only half sure that they weren't actually that colour in real life. England – the only country she had ever been in, was represented as green, and although looking out the window it certainly didn't look green, she had seen colour photographs taken from an aeroplane and she was amazed how green the country looked. So now she wasn't sure, that if, when she went to Holland she wouldn't be surrounded by orange trees, or Egypt wouldn't be a blaze of red, and

Chile covered in dark blue rock. She had asked Derek, a cocky salesman at her work, if the colours in the atlas were real. He had just smiled at her, and gone back to kissing her neck, and moving his hand up her thigh. The next day, she had entered a room where he was laughing with two other men, and she was sure she had heard him telling them what she'd asked. After this she had resolved to keep quiet, and find out for herself.

Several months, and a dozen or so of these meetings passed, and gradually she was having to try less hard to get him to come for a drink. He was even opening up to her, and as long as she didn't ask direct questions, or push too hard she was starting to find out a bit more about him. Rarely did he mention his family, and it didn't sound like he had many other friends. Occasionally he would make a comment – usually stern, about his brother, or he'd mention his father who he seemed to have a fearful respect for - then he would stop himself, and she could almost see the shutters and barriers being resurrected. After two pints of frothy bitter, he would move onto lemonade, and would look coolly at her as she downed her drinks, her eyes becoming more and more closed as her mouth, blouse and legs did the opposite. Several times she would try and embrace him, or kiss him, and he would always stiffen, and then would finish his drink and leave, ignoring her apologies and pleas for him to sit down for just one more drink.

Despite this slight opening up, she was starting to lose patience, and had started to ask herself what she actually wanted from him. If it was something as crass as the thrill of the chase, then there were better targets that would be a lot less hard work. She wasn't sure, why she was trying to help him. Did she feel sorry for him? Maybe. She had also started to think that maybe he was gay. She had read in the Daily Mail only that weekend, that there were more and more of them around, and that you couldn't always spot them straight away. Added to this, she had started seeing Dean from her own work a bit more frequently. Although Dean was married, he assured her that it was on the rocks, and they were practically living separate lives (though she wasn't under any circumstances allowed to ring him at home or see him at weekends). Sometimes she thought that it would be nice to have a man, her own man who she could show off and have him walk her around town, proud to be seen with her. One who would buy her clothes and jewellery and not make her feel like a prostitute. Sometimes she thought this, but other times she would scold herself, for trying to go down that route. The easy route her mother had taken, the one that led – maybe not directly, but inevitably to a terraced house, an ironing board, a stack of bills and thirty years of frustration, boredom, unrealised dreams, and unfulfilled desires.

She had started to catch George looking at her breasts, and now he didn't always recoil instantly away any more when she leant on or over him, though the strain and sweat on his face these incidents caused proved it was going to be a long process, and not one she was sure she could be bothered to go through any more. She was no longer sure she was doing any of this to help him, and that maybe it was purely for her own satisfaction and self-confidence, and this thought that stung her.

She had almost made up her mind to give up with George by Valentine's day. The cloudiness of her motives, the time and effort with very little result were part of the reason. But there were also a couple of signs – disturbing signs – she had started to notice in George. Flashes of darkness that would occasionally flicker, if not on his face but in his eyes. As if after weeks and months of scratching away the surface, of gradually eroding the barriers, she had opened up little peepholes with which to let light flood in and see what was beneath. Or to allow what had been so purposefully caged and hidden, to escape.

Valentine's day was going to be perfect. Dean had booked a room for the night at the Delta. She knew it wasn't The Ritz, but it was going to be only the second time she'd ever stayed in a hotel (the other time being a guest house in Scarborough) and it was a further sign that Dean was starting to deliver on his promises. Whether this was a good thing or not, was not something she wanted to think about too deeply at the moment. She was just happy that for one night she'd be treated special, no quickie in the pub car park or in the back of his Ford Granada. But the one thing she was looking forward to more than anything else was waking up next to her man. Even if it was only her man for that night. She was starting to tire of a couple of hours of heavy flirting, followed by an hour of necking, ten minutes of frantic sex and breathless whispers of endearment followed by two minutes of mumbled farewells, as they guiltily returned to their other lives. Their real lives, leaving her alone with hers, holding onto the taxi or bus fare that had been hastily thrust into her hand or skirt pocket. She could cope with all the rest of it, even enjoy it again, if they didn't inevitably lead to that final stage, the hurried goodbyes, apologies and pecks on the cheek under the car interior, street or moon light.

To wake up in the arms of a man, under his firm protective embrace was her new dream. She didn't care that she was starting to yearn for the things she had originally been so desperate to avoid, and didn't see them as mutually exclusive. She was young, and learning her way in the world, who was to tell her she couldn't move the goalposts of her ambitions slightly?

Deans face told her all she needed to know, and a lot more than his stuttering, explanation. She didn't want to listen to his probably made up excuse. She also didn't want him to see her cry, so she spun on her new for the occasion red stilettos and walked with an even more exaggerated swagger than normal, her face gradually caving into despair and loss, the tears mercifully hidden from his gaze.

She decided to get drunk, find the first man who looked her way and take him to the hotel room Dean had paid for with cash the night before. Then if she still felt like it, she would tell Dean all about it the next day. Unfortunately, the spectacle of a young provocatively dressed woman on her own, knocking back Martinis didn't produce the kind of attention even her fairly indiscriminating revenge plan had in mind. Tom - part time glass collector, occasional bouncer and full time drunkard was the first to make his move, and he decided to dispense with any preamble. His thick, phlegm, salt and pork-scratching speckled lips greedily attached themselves to her white exposed neck, while his big hairy hands easily fended off her attempts to do the same, and made for her barely concealed breast. Those in the bar that could be bothered to watch, cheered him on, the cries turning to laughter, disapproving jeers and finally to shouts of abuse, as Debra threw the remnants of her drink at him which missed; the contents of his pint which scored a hit; and was then marched out by the bearded landlord for upsetting his regulars. She was ejected into the dark, damp street into the dark, damp figure walking quickly along the pavement. For the second time that Valentine's day Debra descended into a flood of tears, as George was forced by the site of her buckling legs and pleading helpless eyes into making physical contact. He caught her, steadied her, holding her like someone minding a stranger's child, and walked her to the pub they had spent several evenings in two hundred yards down the road.

The next two hours was spent with him nursing two pints of warm bitter, and her downing Martini after Martini telling him how all men were bastards and how all she wanted was for someone to put their arm around her and tell her truthfully that they cared for her. George, not sure that he did care for her - though some of the unfamiliar sensations he had started to feel when he was with her, or even when he simply thought of her, suggested that maybe he did - was even less sure of whether she was expecting him to put his arm round her and *tell* her that he did. The whole minefield of social and particularly sexual relationships was one that he had successfully, and up to now fairly easily avoided, and in a life that was so regimentally and rigidly ordered, represented a loose cannon he had no desire of standing in the way of.

So why did he spend so much of his time thinking about Debra? Why, after the initial shock of her being thrust onto him outside the Bluebell pub that evening, had his heart and other unfamiliar organs lower down stirred? Why had he started to not only enjoy but to recall the sight of her fleshy white thighs, her equally white but firmer breasts? To crave the feel of them on his arm, left there to receive such attention? Why had she been sent to ruin the ordered life he so wanted? Why was he encouraging her? Why so many hated questions when all he wanted was answers?

Two hours later and the tears were a thing of the past. She no longer hated all men, only Dean and the men from the Bluebell. George was nice. She liked George, and hoped that he liked her. She wanted to help him, she said, and wanted him to help her. She also wanted him to buy her a bottle of wine from the off-license next door, and to take her to her hotel room. Her hotel room, where she was going to spend the night, maybe run a bath, drink her wine and show that bastard Dean she didn't need him.

Fear settled once more onto George's face, he would get her the wine, but he wasn't sure about taking her to the hotel room.

"Are you going to make me walk up there on my own?" She leaned closer to him. He watched her red smudged lips as she talked and smelt the vermouth on her breath. "What if that man from the Bluebell sees me...or if he's waiting outside now?"

"OK, Debra, come on. I'll get you your wine. If you insist. But I really don't think you need any more. And I'll get you to your hotel safely. But please don't ask me to go in the room with you." The desperation in his eyes matched hers.

The Hotel Delta occupied three floors on a back street opposite a multi storey car park. A square red neon sign told any passers-by that there were vacancies and that some rooms were en suite. Debra had handed the keys to George outside the off-license. In her excitement at lunchtime, she had insisted that she checked in to the hotel, had stored her small overnight bag in the wardrobe, placed her sexiest nightie on one of the pillows, and arranged her small but carefully selected number of toiletries in the small bathroom. All an attempt to give the room a feeling of permanence, the impression that this was their home, even if only for one night.

The reception was empty as they entered it through a white painted door that had stood ajar, spilling wan light onto the damp cigarette littered pavement outside. During the ten minute walk from the off-license to the hotel, Debra had got less and less capable, and hung heavier and heavier on his supporting arm, and as he practically carried her over to the lift he was relieved that she would be in no position to pressurise him into staying for a drink, for a chat, for a…

The dark wooden lift doors opened with a metallic moan revealing a dull corridor, any light produced by the haphazardly spaced light bulbs quickly absorbed by the dark red wallpaper. Cheap prints of pastoral scenes hung at eye level along the corridor, the one opposite the lift depicting an Edwardian couple enjoying a picnic by a stream was cracked, and its plastic frame badly chipped.

A brown plastic sign to the left of the picture told George that room 306 was to his left. Wine bottle and key in his left hand, Debra Murphy in his right arm, he slowly made his way in that direction, her dead weight starting to take its effect on his tiring limbs. Supporting her, he inserted the key, trying to be as quiet as possible so as not to wake her. Pushing unwanted thoughts away, he planned to put her on the bed, and then quietly leave her be to sleep it off. The door opened onto a square room lit by two bedside lamps that stood on dark brown Formica topped tables either side of a small double bed. Something small, green and lacy decorated one side of the bed, while a door to his right, opposite the bed led into what he guessed was the bathroom. He closed the door with his foot, and was carrying her to the bed when she started to stir, opened her eyes, and took in the semi familiar surroundings.

"You are such a darling Georgey, what would I have done without you."

"His arms sprung open letting her go, and she fell onto the bed looking up at him, smiling. No one spoke for several seconds, Debra looking at her hero trying to work out what it was that was so different about him, letting her eyes take in his concerned features, his lean but masculine physique. He stood there, mute, his plans disrupted by her miraculous recovery. The pressure of the situation, of being in such an intimate location with a woman sending his head spinning.

Nimbly, she sprung up from the bed, put her hands on his shoulders and gently kissed his forehead. "I'm going to the bathroom for a second, you wouldn't be a love and open the wine, there are two glasses and an opener over there. She nodded to one of the bedside tables, the only furniture in the room save the wardrobe and bed.

"I'm not sure you need any more Debra" He repeated. "I don't want any. I don't like wine, and anyway I need to get home..." His hesitant voice tailed off as she gave him another peck turned smartly and walked to the bathroom, her eyes never leaving his, and her smile becoming larger, more suggestive before being obscured by the door closing behind her. His heart was racing, unsure whether it was rising panic, due to the new situation he found himself in, the exertion of carrying her the quarter mile or so to the room, or the thought of her behind the thin door three feet away.

He sat on the bed, the unopened bottle resting between his legs, the cheap plastic corkscrew in his upturned palm. He could hear her moving about in the bathroom, and unbidden images forced their way into his head. Three minutes later the door opened slowly, and she walked out. Her hair looked neater, her lipstick brighter and no longer smeared, and a strong, almost cloying perfume accompanied her into the bedroom. Not knowing where to look, his eyes briefly registered that her blouse was undone almost to her navel before settling on the less distressing site of the corkscrew that was twisting in his sweating, taught hands.

He sensed, more than saw her approach him, his heart thudding so much it was actually causing his white sweat sodden cotton shirt to beat in time with it. His mind was whirling, and pictures and images started to kaleidoscope, images from the room, memories from the past hour, fantasies from the last few months crashing into and merging into each other. Gradually he became aware that Debra was holding something in front of him, and that another sense was trying to gatecrash his addled brain. Slowly his eyes focused on the filmy red material held an inch from his hose, knowing what they were, but at the same time not understanding how he knew and not entirely sure which category they fitted into. The smell that filled his nose, which coursed into the membranes and synapses in his head, told him that this was real. But at the same time, this was the smell of his fantasies. The thoughts that had been desperate to let themselves be known over the previous days, months, years, this was their scent. He backed away from her, from her smile, from the thick odour that he couldn't stop breathing in, in big greedy mouthfuls. Using first his hands, then his legs and feet he backed away onto the bed, until he was laying down, his body at a slight angle off the thin brown blankets supported by his elbows.

Taking this as a sign of supplication Debra mounted the bed, pulling her skirt up over her thighs to allow her legs to straddle his and his eyes to see her dark, matted hair between them. He stared at it with horror, terrified, but unable to take his eyes from it, like watching an approaching train hurtle towards the stalled car on its tracks, its engine desperately but uselessly turning over.

He was begging her to leave him alone, shouting it, but wasn't sure she could hear him. He couldn't hear himself, the words blocked out by the roaring in his head. Frantically he lashed out at the opening that was coming closer and closer, that was opening to embrace him. The corkscrew in his hand he struck out again and again, penetrating a woman for the first and only time. His vision was blurred with red, the pumping blood in his own head combining with that coming from Debra. Again and again he thrust at her, shouted at her, to stop it, to stop him.

He came to, looking up at the multi storey car park. The rain was heavier now, and soaked his hair face and suit. A terrible, all-consuming cold was devouring him, causing his limbs to shake and his teeth to chatter. A cold that was coming from inside, from within his stomach as opposed to from the sky and the rain. With one last look at the Hotel Delta behind him, the red neon blurring in the rain, he set off down the road.

Twenty-two years later the same cold crept back up his spine, along his nerves and into his muscles, tendons and ligaments. Stiffly he rose from the kitchen table, the remaining tea in the cup cold and forgotten. Slowly, but resolutely he climbed the stairs to his bedroom. To his chart.

CHAPTER EIGHTEEN

"I tell you who I saw yesterday. Gecko…"

"Jesus wept, that's a name I ain't heard for a while." Spoon shook his head and whistled as if he'd just been told that Lord Lucan had been spotted in the neighbourhood.

"Yeah man, he was walking out of Woolworth's, large as life." Continued Shafeeq.

Danny looked up from the cigarette he'd been meticulously rolling using the tobacco he'd just borrowed off Spoon. "Who's Gecko?"

"One of Spoonys old mates…" Shafeeq laughed, leaning forward towards Spoon, "used to be best buddies didn't you?"

"Yeah course we were, course we were. You used to sell to the mad fucker didn't you?"

"Shafeeq doesn't turn no man down. As long as his moneys got the queens head on it man, its ok with me. Tell the man the story about Gecko, Spoon. Danny won't have heard it."

"I can't be arsed, you tell him."

"Don't give me that can't be arsed shit man, it's your one funny story you got man, come on tell the man."

Spoon sat up straight, stretching his back and rubbed his palm across the stubble on his chin.

"OK, give me that fag then Danny." He reached over, took it, studied it before putting it between his lips and lighting it. "Gecko is about forty say forty five years old…"

"Why's he called Gecko?" Danny asked, cutting Spoon off.

"That's not important... come to think of it why is he called Gecko?"

"The fucker can probably climb walls." Shafeeq laughed, Al unconscious on the settee, stirred slightly, grabbing everyone's attention, before Spoon continued.

"Anyway he is that's all you need to know." He took a drag of the cigarette, his eyes watching the tip flare orange and crawl towards his cracked lips. "So he used to hang around with a few boys we know and was living with this massive girl, I'm telling you she was huge, twenty stone if she was five. Anyway this Gecko absolutely doted on her, I mean absolutely loved her, like you can't love anyone any more than what Gecko loved this girl."

Shafeeq leaned back on the wall, a smile creeping across his face, his head nodding slightly.

"But by all accounts she didn't really give it back, I mean she liked him and everything but she would shout at him in the middle of the street, in the boozer, just constantly giving him shit an' all, in front of his mates, always trying to make him look small…"

"That fat fucker would make anyone look small..."

"... but Gecko would put up with it without batting an eyelid, I mean he's a funny looking bloke ain't he Shaft?"

175

Shafeeq nodded more vigorously, his smile turning into a grin.

"It was probably the first woman who'd shown him any affection." Spoon took another drag on the cigarette, a frown creasing his forehead. "It's bugging me now why he's called Gecko... anyway, where was I... right yes, they were generally happy together, and at this time Gecko wouldn't touch anything, I mean he'd drink and have the occasional reefer but that's where he drew the line. His woman on the other hand, she would take anything she could get her fat greedy hands on, I mean every time you saw her she was fucked up on something, and always pissed. But she knew that whatever state..."

The door opened and a large man dressed in a bomber jacket and faded blue jeans walked in, an anxious look on his large round face.

"Alright Terry?" the room's occupants said in unison before returning their attention to Spoon.

"Not really lads, I've…"

"Sit down Tel, Spoon's telling Danny the Gecko story..."

"There's…"

"Terry, sit down and stop moaning." Shafeeq adopted the patronising teacher - naughty pupil tone that everyone tended to with Terry.

Terry obeyed, and somewhat timidly sat down on an empty chair, his actions completely alien to his appearance and size.

"I've lost my drift now Tel..."

"Sorry Spoon, I didn't mean to...it's just..."

Danny leant over, took Spoon's packet of tobacco and started rolling another cigarette. "You were saying his fat bird was always pissed up or strung out."

"Right yes, so anyway whenever you saw her she was always off her head and be taking the piss out of Gecko, who just seemed to smile and take it. She knew that however bad she got, and however much she shouted at him, however much shit she gave him during a night, Gecko would always make sure she got home safely. Even if it meant carrying the fat fucker, and as I've said that's no easy task, and Gecko ain't a big man. No one could understand why he took so much shit from her, I mean she was horrible looking, massive and treated him like something she couldn't even be arsed to wipe off the sole of her shoe. But you know, he loved her and it makes you do strange things at times I suppose." Spoon said this as if an old man looking back with a sad fondness over his own experiences.

"Sounds like a fucking muppett to me boys."

"Well, apparently, they had this agreement that when they got home no matter what sort of a state she was in and I mean nine times out of ten she would be unconscious, dead to the world at this point, no matter what state she would be in he could put her to bed and then climb on top of her and shag her."

Danny stopped rolling and looked up. Shafeeq, grinning like an idiot was nodding his head, willing Spoon on."

"Come to think of it, that was probably the main reason she got into these states - the thought of a horny Gecko sweating and puffing on top of her, taking a fistful of downers was the only way to get through the experience. Anyway he would watch her get gradually out of her face all evening, taking all this shit and abuse on the chin, just smiling and supping his pint, and then when she passed out he would bid farewell to his mates and drag her back to their flat, and make sweet loving."

Spoon took a final drag on the cigarette, and readjusted his position in the worn chair, letting silence fill the room for two, three, four seconds. "Then one night, it hadn't been any different from any other, they had spent their usual evening down the Nag's Head, then come eleven, eleven thirty he took her home, got her to bed and had his wicked way with her, and fell asleep. The next morning he woke up, and still feeling horny he climbed back on and rode her again. After several minutes of huffing and puffing, he realises something is different, that she feels different...colder... the fat fucker had died in the night – heart attack the coroner reckoned - and here he was giving one to her..."

The room erupted into howls of laughter and thigh slapping.

"I fucking love that story man, love it."

"Anyway, as you can imagine this would do strange things to a man and Gecko, who adored the fat son of a bitch lost it. He's never been the same again, blames himself for killing her, and apparently can't rid himself of the feeling of her cold fat body in his hands and on his skin." He paused reflectively, "It's a shame because he's a nice bloke and he's best shot of her, but he's just a fucking nutter now."

An easy silence settled in the room, before Spoon broke it, remembering Terry's desperate entrance, who despite his earlier edginess now seemed to be at peace with the world, his large frame dwarfing the chair he was sat on, a content if slightly imbecilic grin on his face.

"What can we do for you then Terry?"

Slowly he swung his massive head to look in Spoon's direction, a puzzled expression there now instead of the smile. He held Spoon's gaze for a couple of seconds before this too was replaced by a look of anxiety.

"Oh yeah, this morning on my way over to see a couple of guys, I reckon I was followed, there was a funny looking bloke in tracky bottoms and he was behind me all the way up the high street and then left to Hannover Street and along past the rec. Then after meeting a couple of lads there I came back the way I'd come and he was behind me again. I even went into Woollies for a bit to see what he did. He didn't come in and when I left I couldn't see him but five minutes later there he was, behind me again. After what you were saying last week, " he motioned towards Shafeeq, " I thought I better come and warn you."

Everyone opened their mouths to talk but it was Shafeeq who won, as usual, "Please tell me Terry you didn't come straight here, with this fucker following you, please tell me you ain't that stupid, man."

"No I came straight round, I thought you'd want to know, you said everyone should keep their eyes open." It was obvious Terry still thought he had done well, and was half expecting praise.

"You stupid bastard Terry." Shouted Shafeeq.

"Terry." Spoon said it more full of despair and disbelief than anger.

"Spoon, the dumb fucker... I'm going hit the cunt, I swear to God I'm going to hit him."

"What... I'd thought you'd want to know. Spoon what have I done wrong?"

"Terry if you were being followed, and by the way, if you managed to spot the bloke following you it begs the question what sort of fuckers are they employing in the police force nowadays, but if you knew you were being followed didn't it occur to you that maybe you shouldn't lead them to here?"

Slowly, it showed on his face that he was beginning to realise the stupidity of his actions. Spoon made a mental note that he must play poker with Terry one day, and went to say more, but just shook his head. Even Shafeeq bit his lip - it was almost impossible to stay angry at Terry for too long, though he had seemed to make it his life's work to test this.

"Should I leave then?" He half stood up, looking questioningly at Spoon.

"No, the damage has been done now Tel, sit back down."

Terry was the biggest and strongest person Spoon had ever met, by quite some distance. He was also the thickest person he had met by an even greater distance. He was a few years older than Spoon and still lived with his mother. Because of his limited intelligence he was constantly being taken advantage of. His size made him an important asset and he earned money being the runner for Italian Tony a medium sized dealer no one else in the house had any time for, but to be fair to the Mediterranean he did treat Terry well enough and though he had many opportunities to cheat him, he very rarely did. Terry's loyalty was never questioned but Spoon wouldn't fancy Terry's chances under stiff questioning, so tried not to use him, and only did when he needed the threat of his muscle. Terry was so big he was hardly ever called upon to test his strength, kind of the human equivalent of a nuclear deterrent. Terry was actually called Mick but he had been saddled with his nickname after Terry Fuckwit in Viz magazine. It had taken off so well, that even his mum referred to her only son as Terry, and Shafeeq told the story of how when an old acquaintance rang his house and asked if Mike was there she told him that he must have the wrong number as no one of that name lived there. Spoon was inclined to believe this story, after several experiences involving Terry's mother.

CHAPTER NINETEEN

Mike Burley had managed to cut down the time he spent in the shower to about ninety seconds. Admittedly it didn't result in the thorough clean that a longer wash and soak would have given him, but one and a half minutes every other day was better than nothing and said to the world, to himself, that he hadn't let himself go. The shower was the place he felt most vulnerable. It was the one place in the house where he was surrounded by noise. Noise that would mask an intruder. He toyed with whether to shut the bathroom door or leave it open. Shutting it would make it even harder to hear the muffled smash of a downstairs window, but would offer about ten seconds more protection. Originally he had opted on leaving it open, but forty seconds in he had panicked, shut it, and had showered with the door bolted shut since.

Back in his room, he quickly dried off, taking extra care with the area around his penis and between the top of his thighs. The rash (he refused to believe the accusations from Rachel, despite growing evidence) had become almost intolerable over the past few days, not so much the itching, but the wounds his nails had inflicted to alleviate the itching. He had broken through the skin in several areas, the flesh not having time to heal before his next onslaught and now looking down, his whole pubic region was a mass of raw flesh and moist yellow scabs. He patted it dry, wincing as a scab stuck to the damp cotton and came away from the skin.

He caught sight of himself in the full-length mirror next to the wardrobe. His red eyes, staring back at him from underneath a mop of damp dark hair. A week's stubble covered his features - not quite long enough to be termed a beard - the discomfort and itching unnoticed due to its harsher twin a couple of feet below. Slowly his eyes tracked down his reflection. A dozen or so hairs were clustered around each nipple and a thin trail led between them meeting in another small patch in the slight hollow between his pecks. His chest was definitely getting harrier. That would have pleased Rachel. She maintained she loved hairy men, and would tease him about his hitherto naked torso, rubbing it vigorously with the flat palms of her hands, claiming it aided growth by stimulating the circulation. He would counter that that may well be the case, but he certainly didn't want to go out with a girl with hairy palms. She would smile, give him one last extra firm rub and kiss his grinning lips…

He forced his eyes down, pushing the painful memory away. Down over his still flat stomach and into the untidy patch of matted hair. It looked like the fur of a diseased animal from this distance, and he was half glad there wasn't anyone to see it. Any woman. Rachel. Looking at his penis, hanging limp and dejected, he wondered about the next time he would have sex. Who would it be with? An image of his faced pushed up against the cold brick wall of his cell flashed before his eyes, and he mentally groped for an antidote, settling on the equally painful but at least real memory of the last time he'd slept with Rachel.

It was cold in the bedroom, and his still damp body had started to shiver, dislodging a couple of drops of water from his shoulders so they started their own descent of his body, one down the centre of his back along his slightly ridged spine, the other to the right, heading for his liver and kidneys. The tickling of the water, the spasmodic movement of his body went unnoticed as his thousand yard stare sought out images and sensations beyond his trembling figure, through the glass and brickwork, back into a different time, a safer more innocent one, where you didn't get fired from work for no conceivable reason; you didn't receive tapes directing you to cars where butchered women slowly rotted; where the woman you loved didn't suddenly accuse you of infidelity and leave; where you didn't spend your entire day looking over your shoulder waiting for the next onslaught.

To a bedroom three years ago, where a smoking Audrey Hepburn looked across from her cream wall at the flickering, dancing, figures on the one opposite. The cavorting shadows – magnified, animated versions of the soapstone sculptures on the overflowing bookcase against the wall, life breathed into them by the thick foot high candle sat in the black fire grate in the wall opposite the double bed. The room with its unique smell - a delicious blend of Rachel, her perfume and the candle. The smell that would linger on his own clothes and skin for hours afterwards.

To the drunk, laughing couple on the bed, exploring each other's bodies, minds, desires and secrets with their tongues, lips, fingers and questions. Sex with Rachel had been different from any other he had had. It was the first time he had actually cared if the person he was with was fulfilled, and not just for his own self-esteem. After weeks and months of idolatry there was always going to be the risk that real life didn't live up to the reels and reels of fantasies and idealised scenarios that had played through his mind. The truth was though that it far surpassed anything he had imagined. Anything he could have imagined, as his narrow perspective had only been able to draw upon his own numerous but monotonous experiences coupled with an equally steady but two-dimensional stream of pornography.

It may be trite to say that it was the addition of love that made the difference. It may not be true in any case, but they clicked, dovetailed. In the pub, in the club, on the street, on the phone, and in the bedroom. It was a time of discovery, not just of the other persons inner self, but of their own. Completely at ease, they could express feelings and desires that they had hidden away, scared of letting them out not only to the public but to themselves. Suddenly, they were free to talk about and experience everything, to release all the pent-up energy, realise their specific needs without fear of recriminations, loss of face or embarrassment. And the joy of releasing their own inner cravings and appetites, was matched by the thrill of seeing those being liberated by their partner, and absorbing and experiencing them.

Rachel possessed a self-confidence that set her apart from any other woman he had ever met. It wasn't one that could be mistaken for arrogance, but was one as a result of a having a firm set of standards and morals – albeit ones slightly at odds with society's standards and morals – and having complete and utter faith in them. The combination of these meant she would progress both academically and in her career far quicker and further than Mike could ever hope. It also meant that the comfort she felt in her own skin, in herself, resulted in the absolute comfort of allowing others – Mike - inside her.

They would talk, laugh, tease while making love in a way Mike never thought you could. Sometimes, they would give themselves completely up to it, totally absorbed by the physical contact and sensations, but at other times, it would just be an extension – a wonderful, luxurious one, of their evening, their discussion, their interaction.

Like an elixir he feasted on these memories, of how she would love to taste herself on him, uncoupling herself so she could go down and…

The noise downstairs brought him back to reality, to 1996 and the cold bedroom. The final bits of water on his body had either evaporated or been absorbed and he stood cold, dry and naked in front of the mirror, his eyes desperately refocusing back on the present, his penis now awake and pointing to the ceiling. His hearing, the only one of his senses that hadn't been able to enjoy the reverie strained for any more clues of what had disturbed him.

Silence. Then a whistling. Relieved, he peered down the stairs, saw the post on the mat, quickly dressed and went downstairs to retrieve it. Three for Rachel, one for him. He took a little encouragement from the fact that Rachel hadn't given him a forwarding address. This meant she would have to either come and pick up her post herself, or at least contact him to tell her where to send it. This meant he had at least one more chance.

The letter addressed for him was in a brown A4 envelope, the thinness of which suggested it only contained one, or at the most two sheets of paper. His name and address printed on a small white label, had been stuck onto the envelope at a slight angle. He studied the frank, but it was ineligible apart from the date that informed him it had taken no longer than twenty-four hours to reach its destination. The familiar clamminess returned to his skin, the exaggerated thudding of his heart as it endeavoured to pump the adrenalin rich blood faster and faster around his tense body.

Had the killer – he hadn't managed to think of another title for the owner of the voice on the tape, apart from several four-letter ones – chosen a new method of communication? What was this going to tell him? Where would he be sent today? Whose body would he be forced to gaze down on that morning?

Just as the thought that maybe he should take this to the police right away, before he opened it and keep intact the only solid piece of evidence he had, just as this idea was making itself known, it was rudely shouldered aside by the image of Rachel, half naked in thorny undergrowth, her pale white skin made to look more so by the deep red gashes along her once so flat, smooth stomach.

Feverishly he tore at the envelope, almost expecting to see photographic evidence of the imagined scene. What he did see was a letter from the personnel manager of his company. Relief flooded his system, and he took the letter - shaking in his talon like grasp to the lounge where he sat down, took one, two, three deep breaths to bring order once more to his battered system and read the letter.

Maybe he had been half expecting an apology. Maybe, the tiny part of his brain that had been given the task of concerning itself with his job situation was thinking that the letter would be simply saying that yes, he had had his punishment - a week's suspension, and that he was to report back at work on the Monday, and a line would be drawn under the whole matter. The myriad of dilemmas that would have faced him then were of no consequence however. The letter didn't say that. Instead it was informing him that he was to attend a meeting at 10:30 the following Monday. Also present would be Jackson and Nigel Greenspan the acting MD while the official one was convalescing after undergoing another cycle of chemotherapy. It went on to say that he was entitled to have someone there to represent him, but that he should be aware that despite the very serious nature of the offence they had decided to keep the matter internal, so it would be in his own interests to choose someone from within the company. It said that any questions would be dealt with in the meeting and that apart from contacting the person to represent him, he should under no circumstances make any other contact either by telephone or in person.

He sat on the settee in silence, the black words swimming slightly on the white paper under the intensity of his stare. His right hand – empty, slowly clenched and unclenched itself into a fist, and after a minute or so his left joined in, taking the letter with it, until it was a tight ball, the shape of a comet, with a white tail left by the gap between his thumb and index finger. Just as it seemed that this movement was going to gradually consume his whole body he sprung up, and hurled it at the wall opposite.

"Fuck you." It was roared, spittle following the comet. "Fuck you. Fuck you, fuck you, fuck you." Like a boxer, Mike prowled the ring. In a strange way he felt free. It had taken a lot. Far too much, and he had taken more than anyone should have to, but he had finally decided to take things into his own hands.

For twenty-six years Mike had been pushed around, forced, coerced, bullied, manipulated. Controlled. He, like millions of others around him, was one of life's flotsam and jetsam. It was easier to follow, to be led. That way you didn't have to take the responsibility or make any decisions. If you were sent down a dead end, or made a wrong turn, you simply shrugged, turned around and waited for the next instruction be it implicit or a barked order. He had never thought of it in such black and white terms before, but it had been something that he had accepted, if not wholeheartedly embraced. There was always some personal stigma involved, some guilt that man, having come out of the oceans; down from the trees; from Eve's loins or the hold of a spaceship – whichever theory you subscribed to – that having been given his freedom, it was some kind of betrayal to give up that freedom so willingly. Up until recently, this certainly had not concerned Mike. His natural instincts were to trust whoever or whatever was pushing the buttons, pulling the strings, and to be fair it had given him no cause for complaints.

In the last three years he and Rachel had often questioned what would have happened if they hadn't found themselves next to each other in the club queue that night. Would he have ever been brave enough to make a move on the bridge? If he had, would he have come across so awkward, so uncomfortable, that he would have blown his one chance? The thought genuinely scared Mike, whereas Rachel, more adept at making things happen, paid it no mind, reassuring him that one way or another they would have found each other.

Recently things had changed. The puppet master had either grown bored or been usurped. As opposed to a gentle push in this direction or an implied nod in another they had started taking direct action, leaving explicit instructions on tapes, on letter headed correspondence. The direction he had been sent had also changed. Gone were the dead end jobs - literally, in their place butchered women. He was being pushed, nudged and cajoled into areas he was no longer willing to go. It was time to fight back, to make a stand, to spit in the face of whoever was wearing fate's cloak.

Glancing around the untidy lounge, he quickly took stock. He had been running. No, retreating. It was time to regroup, gain strength and start to plan his fight back. It was no good simply waging war on the world, dealing out indiscriminate blows no matter how much he felt like it. He had to find his aggressor, track him down, find the clues he must have left, follow them and then destroy him. In order to do that he needed to get focused, to get strong, throw off the depression, the doubts, the self-pity, the fear that had been gradually crushing him. That was something that would have seemed impossible only twenty minutes before but now, he was confident he could achieve it. One step at a time.

First he would deal with this bloody rash. It had been more than embarrassment and stubbornness that had kept him from going to the chemist to get what he imagined to be fairly routine treatment. He had come to think of the rash as his own hair shirt, and used the discomfort, the pain to remind himself that this wasn't a dream, but a reality that needed to be dealt with. It was also easier to focus and deal with an actual pain, one he could if not actually see, could certainly visualise. He did not need it any more. It was no longer a substitute, but a hindrance and he would get it sorted.

The other thing he had to do was to start sleeping. He was exhausted. For four days he had refused to sleep in the house. He would spend the nights in the lounge he now looked down on, curtains drawn tight, television down low. Fear of the consequences of the alternative, kept him awake, and more than outweighed the soporific qualities of the cheap whisky he would sip with moderation throughout the long hours. In the days, he would go to public places, libraries, museums, galleries and try and sleep, the security that the crowds gave him allowing him to snatch half an hour here, twenty minutes there, before being awoken by uneasy dreams, pins and needles or security guards.

He looked at himself once more in the mirror, this time head on with a steely glaze. He had no desire to push through into the past. He had to take hold of his present, to stop running, to face his pursuer head on, in an attempt to salvage his future.

CHAPTER TWENTY

Grey. That was the word, the colour, which had not so much sprung as crept upon Doug's mind as he peered through the net curtains. Five hours of sitting on the wooden kitchen chair, watching the drab street. Five hours of dank skies and drizzle, viewed through the curtains – lank and greasy with age – adding more shades of grey to the limited palette of the artist who had painted the scene.

"Jesus, this isn't what I joined the force for." He rubbed his forehead, eyes and cheeks with the palms of his hands, enjoying the noise and sensation the stubble produced. Once more, he shifted on the chair, the thin yellow cushion the owners had provided him with offering scant protection from the hard pine half an inch below. Beside him Lathers, looking annoyingly comfortable in the easy chair he'd secured in the name of experience flicked through his magazine noisily. Everything he did, he did noisily. Read, smoked, talked, pissed. He even breathed loudly. Doug was profoundly grateful that he would never witness him making love. Over the hours Doug attributed this need for noise, less and less to attention seeking and more to a fear of silence.

"Why did you join? Why did any of us join? Not to make the world a better place or any of that bollocks I can tell you now. There's worse jobs Dougy boy, there's worse jobs. And I can tell you that from real experience." Lathers closed his magazine – an out of date car one he'd taken from the lounge downstairs – tossed it onto the carpet behind them and reached for Doug's packet of cigarettes sat on the dresser between them.

"When I were a boy, fourteen, fifteen year old, I used to spend me summer holidays with me mam's sister and her bloke in Lincolnshire. Come the harvest I used to get up at five and cycle ten miles or so to this farm. For the next ten hours I'd be flat on me stomach in this low slung trailer being towed by a fucking tractor." He lit the cigarette, shook the match to extinguish the flame, inhaled noisily and winced. "Fuck knows how you can smoke these shitty things…"

"I reckon by the end of this shift you'll have a better idea though yeah? That's your fifth today, and I reckon you can make it to double figures by tonight, what do you reckon Lathers?"

Lathers eyed Doug, who was still staring straight ahead, not entirely sure, but not too concerned, if he was completely joking. "You suggesting I break the rules, and nip off to the Joe Dacky's round the corner to get some more fags Dougy? Very unprofessional. Dereliction of duty, that's what that's called." He paused, watching a mildly attractive woman pushing a pushchair along the street below them. "Very nice, very nice. You know what happened to them pricks down in Mary Street?"

Doug reached for a cigarette himself, "Aye." In what had rapidly become legend in surrounding forces, a D.C. and P.C. from a station across town were on an O.P. watching a pizza delivery firm. Mid-way through the evening they'd nipped across the road to the Jolly Gardeners for a couple of liveners only to return to the house they were using an hour later to find it had been broken into, their equipment and log book stolen.

"Anyway, where was I?"

"On some tractor in the fens."

"Oh aye. Yeah, so for ten hours solid with half an hour for your scran, you had to lie on your fucking stomach as they drove up and down these fields, pulling the spuds out of the ground. Some machine had already been and churned the ground up like, or got them half way up, but for some reason they didn't have one that would do the whole job, so it was left to pricks like me self, to pull 'em up proper like, you know?" he ground out the cigarette and checked his mug of tea was empty, "Your turn for brews Dougy, me mouths like Gandhi's bleeding sandal I tell ya. Its these fucking fags o' yours." He laughed, and put his mug closer to Doug's face.

"Anyways, that is a job for you. You wouldn't be complaining about this cushy number if you'd worked there, I can promise you that. It was so bloody dusty you'd end up looking like fucking… like… Lenny bloody Henry come home time."

They both watched as two men, one with a pronounced limp as if one leg was shorter than the other, passed along the street. One of them, the one with equal sized limbs took a final long gulp from a coke can before throwing it into the front yard of the house he was passing.

"Fucking litter lout. Anyways up, can't remember how much I got paid now, but it wouldn't be enough to keep you in jazz mags Dougy. That's a real job. Sat on your arse in a nice house all day is nothing I tell you, nothing compared with that. I've had others an' all just as bad."

Doug stood up, arching his back to stretch it, picked up the two mugs and headed for the door.

"Make sure you put two sugars in mine this time ya tight arse."

The kitchen was downstairs and overlooked a small garden. A square lawn was bordered by several shrubs and bushes, which would no doubt bloom into colour come the warmer months. A bird table in the form of a Swiss chalet stood at an angle in one corner, a half coconut shell hanging from one of its corners.

The house owners – a couple in their fifties – had been one of a number of residents approached about the possibility of letting a couple of officers use their upstairs room for a stake out operation on the squat opposite. Everyone had agreed, eager to do something that would bring about the eviction of those in it. Not willing, or too afraid to tackle the problem themselves many of the street had complained numerous times to the police and were glad that finally they seemed to be doing something about it. They needn't know that it was information from an on-going operation that had prompted the sudden interest in the squat. Besides, most of the residents were purely interested in the effect the place had on the prices of their own homes. They had chosen this house – not ideal as it was thirty yards along the road from the squat – as it was the only one that hadn't minded them smoking. So keen were they in fact for the police to use their home for the fortnight long operation that they had given them their bedroom, decamping into the smaller spare one for the duration of their stay.

He filled the kettle and took out two tea bags from another Swiss chalet. The couple's only daughter lived in Geneva. The lady of the house, an overweight, overbearing and over friendly woman who only seemed to dress in different coloured versions of the same shapeless dress, had filled them in on the complete history of not only her and her husband, but her daughter, her husband and both sets of extended family. Reading between the lines their daughter ("such a clever girl, she can speak five languages don't you know, five, Jack here" prodding her bored looking husband next to her, "didn't even know there were five languages did you pet?" and she descended into a fit of laughter that more often than not finished off her sentences) didn't get home that often, and they weren't able to make the journey over there ("not with Jack's ticker, won't let you up in a plane will they pet?"). As a substitute they had filled their house with mementoes of their daughter's European home. A cacophony of cuckoos welcomed every hour, making the couple of minutes around midday almost unbearable.

They arrived half an hour before she left for work and she would follow them around filling in and repeating details of their family life. Lathers had barred her from the op room – their bedroom – mentioning confidential files and had taken to hiding in there whenever she was in the house. That morning they had arrived to their usual bacon sandwiches ("it's so good cooking for someone who appreciates their food" - a sideways look at Jack pretending to read the paper on the settee) and she had a family album on the dining room table that she proceeded to go through, page by bloody page. Lathers had grabbed the thick white bread, tomato sauce just leaking from one side, mumbled something and gone upstairs, the sandwich clamped in his mouth. Doug politer, more conscious of other people's feelings felt obliged to stay, finally making it upstairs an hour and two albums later to be received by a grinning Lathers.

He stirred a heaped teaspoon of sugar into his mug and a half one into Lathers', returned the milk to the magnet laden fridge and carefully climbed the stairs. He returned to the unanswered question from before. It would have been easier for him now if he could point to one incident, or a series of incidents that had turned his thoughts to a life in the police force. Even if he could identify something that had inspired a sea change in his thinking and possible future it would help in moments of doubt. But there was nothing. And like Lathers had said it certainly wasn't down to any crusade to rid the streets and society of the scum; to help make the old and the vulnerable feel safer. He would have liked to feel that it was for good, if not heroic reasons, certainly for noble ones but if he was honest with himself he knew it wasn't. After thirteen years of second-rate education and mediocre results he hadn't been willing to extend it by a further three, and besides he had wanted to start earning some proper money - his Ford Escort needed fuel and there were girls needing drinks. The first week in September a fortnight before his nineteenth birthday he had had two interviews. One for the police, one for a large insurance firm with plush offices in the centre of town. He'd gone to both, and had decided that whoever offered him the job first would have his employment. The police won and Doug's career in the police force began three weeks later.

Once in, he had thrown himself into his new role, certainly more than he had ever done at school. He looked forward with something approaching enthusiasm, to the days when he would be man a mano with some notorious crime lord, or to when he would single-handedly decipher a set of seemingly baffling clues left by a genius but warped killer. It took about three years for it to dawn on him that those days wouldn't be coming. That the job he had chosen was very similar to the one he never got offered at the insurance firm, the main differences being he got a uniform and the offices weren't as expensive. Now eight years on, here he was, out of uniform, spending his days thumbing through photo albums of Swiss family bloody Robinson, making tea and listening to stories about farms in Lincolnshire. He knew it was a dangerous way of thinking, that as soon as you started to question if any of it was worth it anymore the bad guys had won, but it was getting harder and harder. Even now, in the wake of the first murder in their patch for three years, the first one that wasn't obviously a domestic for five, he had found it hard to get motivated. He would have minimal involvement. Administration. Canvassing. Criminals weren't so much as outwitted, or out-manoeuvred nowadays, they were simply slowly stifled by thousands of hours of filing, checking, cross checking, questioning, canvassing and administrating.

"Bingo." Lathers was writing in the black log book, glancing up and through the window. "Two twenty-three and matey boy is off on his rounds."

The surveillance team had determined the extent of these rounds, consisting of three regular drops around town and the bookies on Godiver Street. Small-time. Hopes were raised initially with the bookies, rumours and theories had surfaced that the shop was being used by the local dealers as a distribution point – a clever idea Doug had to admit – but it proved unfounded, the suspect was merely using it to place bets.

Doug put both mugs down on the stripped dressing table that sat in between the two chairs, reached for the camera, decided against it and sat down instead, his buttocks instantly feeling bruised once more.

Lathers returned the logbook to the dresser top. "Still no sign of our coloured friend." He took a swig of his tea and winced, "Jesus Christ, I'll make my own bloody tea next time."

This O.P. was part of an on-going operation to finally break a well-known drugs ring in the city. Two, three weeks of information gathering, putting more black and white photos into manila files, more cross checking, more feeding of the database. Then in a few weeks, months or maybe never they'd swoop to pick up those with the thickest files, and those with ones thick enough to use against them to squeeze more names out or to force them into turning Queens.

Sixty hours in and they hadn't come up with too much new. Shafeeq Bari who had led them to this particular address, was the only one worth them bothering with, the others in the squat would be caught up in the cross fire, but unless they were very unlucky or very stupid would be spat back out and onto the streets with nothing more than a slapped wrist and a fine.

Doug watched the figure on the pavement below. Rudy Ellis, twenty-five, five foot eleven, Caucasian, caught in possession of an eighth of marijuana when he was fourteen, cleared with a caution, clean record since, distinguishing marks – a small scar to the left of his left eyebrow, and a tattoo of two tears under his left eye. No known address. He watched as he hunched over slightly into the wind, and put the hood of his grey sweatshirt over his cropped head, his skinny jean clad legs taking him quickly along the pavement before disappearing out of sight behind the patterned pink curtains.

Spoon quickened his pace and put his hood up, more as protection from something unknown than from the persistent drizzle that hung in the air. Sat in the park two days before, the dream had started to mould itself into a plan, and since then had become more and more concrete. He was entering into what he thought of as his Lent. Half remembered stories from school assemblies about how Jesus had gone into the wilderness and how somehow this was symbolised by people not eating eggs was hardly the foundation for a life changing philosophy, but it was all he had, and he was going to run with it. He liked the analogy as well, seeing the squat, the life he had known, as the wilderness. There was temptation everywhere, and though he was pretty sure Jesus didn't go to Granada at the end of it he knew for sure that his would last a whole lot longer than the forty days. Forty days would be a walk in the park. Hey Jesus, try fourteen fucking years.

He had set himself two goals, both tough but achievable. He hadn't given himself any timescales, conscious that as soon as he felt himself slipping behind, his mental fragility would rear its ugly head, causing his own slightly better looking one to drop. He needed to save five thousand pounds. He had toyed long and hard with ways to do this. There was no doubt there were opportunities out there to do it in one or two deals. He knew people, or certainly knew people who knew people who could set him up. This was tempting, if only for the timescales involved. Now he had made up his mind of where he wanted, indeed needed to be, it had turned itself into an idealised paradise. Not an hour went passed when he didn't lose himself in imagined scenarios. None of them spectacular in themselves – meeting new friends in a street café; buying fresh bread from the small family run shop on the corner; getting his first job waiting tables at the tapas bar - the same tapas bar where he would meet the dark-haired girl who he would fall in love with and eventually move in with.

It was as if he was living a dual life, one surrounded in filth and peril, the other played out in front of the backdrop of the Sierra Nevada and the Alhambra.

And now that he could see the other life, he was impatient to say farewell to his present one and grab it. He also knew that it was that impatience that could very well destroy any hope he had of achieving it. He was sure as long as he could focus on that dream, he could hold the impatient, nagging voices at bay. There was also another, stronger reason he didn't want to go down that route. He didn't want his new world, sullied by his existing one. It was important that he should get there by proving he was worthy of his new life, and that if he forced his way there it would be like breaking into the wardrobe, stealing the looking glass, and the snow on the mountains would be a little less white, the air a little more polluted.

Five thousand pounds. He wasn't sure if it was going to be enough, or if he was being greedy, but it sounded the right amount for a new life. Five thousand pounds was not a massive amount - people spent and traded more than that every day, but in his current hand to mouth existence it may as well be twenty or three hundred thousand, and after turning down the easier quicker methods he knew he was going to have to make big sacrifices. Hence his Lent. Smoking, gambling and smack.

That was what Spoon needed to give up for Lent, and in the process he would purify himself for, and prove himself worthy of, the waiting paradise.

Smoking would be simple. Gambling came down to football accumulators two or three times a week. Not an addiction, not a problem, more of a hobby and originally a money making scheme. Three baron years had made a mockery of the latter, and though he was potentially cutting off a valuable resource he felt he needed to include that in his sacrifices. He didn't want to get to Granada by luck, but by hard work, conscientiousness and sacrifice. The three things that had been missing in his life up until now, and the reason he found himself in the situation he was in.

Heroin would be an altogether tougher animal. But what was sacrifice without pain? How much sweeter are the rewards when the path there has been long and tortuous? He was looking forward to the struggle, to the daily battle knowing he would win, and the hardship and horror ahead would only serve to remind him of his goal, and focus every fibre into achieving it. He knew many people who had come off it and almost without exception they told the same story, a different one than appeared in the popular press and government literature. It's like a cold. The worse fucking cold you've ever had, but a cold never the less. The only difference is that you are surrounded by people who have the cure. A wondrous, all embracing, instant cure.

He was going to take it steady as well. Granada wasn't built in a day. Wean himself off, cut back a bit each week, stretching the time in-between each hit. Like today, this wasn't so bad was it? Instead of sitting in the lounge under the warm, soothing duvet the opiate provided him with, he was out in the semi fresh air stretching his legs making his last trip to the bookies. OK yes, he was feeling anxious, and his skin didn't seem to fit him like it should today, his mouth and throat felt horribly dry and he was sweating a bit too much to be considered altogether healthy, but it was nothing he couldn't handle. He'd get some Valium, just to round off the corners. He pulled the hood further up around his head to shield him from the world outside and entered the bookies.

The air was thick with sweat and smoke, the smell the same week in week out regardless of the weather. He nodded to a few regulars and made for the counter his eyes ahead of him, searching through the fug to see if it would be Jeff – a weasel-faced balding man with a lazy eye and over active sweat glands, or Elaine – a short stocky brunette with bad skin and a large chest, who would conduct his last transaction.

"Alright Jeff, how's it going?" He reached into his back pocket to retrieve his folded coupon.

"Usual Spoon, usual. Can't complain, can't complain." His right eye had become so lazy now it couldn't be arsed to open.

Spoon as usual found himself thinking that this was a blatant lie, as Jeff spent very little time doing anything else but complain. In fact the only thing he did with equal fervour was sweat. He handed the crinkled form through the gap in the smudged glass window. "I think one of those is a winner Jeff, just check it for me would ya?"

Jeff licked his lips, and focused an eye on Spoon who seemed to be matching him sweat wise today pore for pore. He didn't move for a couple more seconds looking as if he'd just been asked to empty the contents of the safe into a proffered bag. Eventually he stirred himself and took the pink form laying on the counter, stood up and went to the open cabinet behind him, sighing. Spoon had been coming in for as long as Jeff could remember and he could count on the fingers of one of his greasy hands the times he'd claimed a win. He picked up a bundle of forms, licked his fingers and slowly and deliberately thumbed through them, thinking of the twenty or so unclaimed winning bets that Spoon had placed in the last year alone.

"Looks like your lucky day." He plucked the twin of the form in his hand from the bundle and slowly, begrudgingly walked to the till.

Spoon watched him, swallowing dryly. A win, was this a sign that he shouldn't give up? Was this the quickest legitimate route to Granada?

"Ten, twenty, thirty..." the notes were slapped down onto the counter, Jeff making a show of handing over the cash, as if this made up for the hundreds he'd effectively stolen off him over the preceding months, "Forty, fifty, sixty." His eye met Spoons' briefly, licked his lips and continued, "Sixty one, sixty two, sixty three," the pound coins clinked in time with his words, "Sixty three pounds twenty eight pence. Don't spend it all at once, you hear me." It sounded more like a command than an attempt at a joke, and a two pence piece tried to do its part to make the wish come true and rolled along the counter top and off onto the floor by Spoons feet, watched by all three eyes.

"Fantastic." He allowed himself a smile, stooped to retrieve the copper coin, before straightening up to see Jeff looking at him with either inquisitiveness or something not far from resentment. "Cheers…" He hesitated, feeling he should say something, some farewell, some words to indicate a chapter of his life closing, but instead he just pocketed the money, turned and strolled out, one more nod to an aging West Indian drawing on a spindly cigarette like a new born calf on its mother's teat.

After his moment of doubt earlier, he was confident once again that he was doing the right thing in leaving the bookmakers for the last time. If this win – a long time in coming – was a sign, then it was one telling him that he was on the right track. A long one, but one that lead eventually to a picturesque city in the southern reaches of Spain. Enthused once more, he set off towards the high street.

Twenty minutes later Spoon was as happy as he could remember being. He gripped the Spanish vocabulary book in his trembling hand, overjoyed by its solidity, its tangibility. Up until half an hour ago, everything had been in his head. He had spent hours and hours dreaming, plotting and preparing, but there was nothing he could actually point to, to hold. Now here he was, over fifty pounds in his pocket and everything he needed to achieve his second goal – learn Spanish. With something approaching a spring in his step he set off for the park.

He had decided another thing that would change when he got to Spain. He'd go back to being Rudy. His father, a huge Tottenham Hotspur fan had christened his son after their pacey Peruvian winger, at the time the darling of The Shelf. Before his smaller, pinker namesake had progressed out of nappies however, he had done the unthinkable and moved the mile or so up the road to Arsenal. Spoon knew it may be a simplistic way of looking at it, but it was at this time that his father ceased to take an interest in his son, as if he resented the constant reminder of his former hero's treachery. As it was he was left with the name that his father hated as much as him, and was the only white Rudy in England. In his early teens, one of his friends had claimed that Rudy looked like your reflection when looking in a spoon, and he spent two years as Spoon Face. Over time, it got shortened to Spoon, his face filled out and the origins of his second christening got lost in time. It had seemed the perfect way to wash his hands of his father and home life. He had achieved that. It had worked for him, but he no longer needed to hide behind a name. Besides, he doubted if Rudy would stick out as much in Spain as in the terraced streets of Britain. He reached the bench in the park overlooking the duck pond, the bench he had started to think of as his bench and sat down, rolling his future name around in his mouth, and decided he liked it.

His dry tongue flicked across his drier lips as he opened the book and rested it on his thighs, his eyes scanning the unfamiliar words.

"Hola, bienvenido a España" His heart quickened, thoughts of gambling, drugs and all temptation gone, "Welcome to Spain."

CHAPTER TWENTY-ONE

Back to basics. The phrase was dominating the political landscape, splashed across the pages of newspapers, and on the lips of everyone who took an interest in the former or read the latter. Mr Clarke did neither but the phrase was at the forefront of his thinking. If he had been aware that even as he was reorganising his shed, that very phrase was hastening the downfall of the Tory government it would not have moved himself or shifted his plan one iota.

Initial concerns over his plan had caused one of his Weak Moments and had in turn led to the uncovering of buried episodes, fears and frailties. Eventually, it had run its course, and the chart – his Prozac, his long walk in the country, his whispered encouragement from a loved one – had eased his concerns and massaged his throbbing temples.

His fears had stemmed from the failed hope that his plan – The Plan to restore equilibrium regarding number 101 on the chart – would be some magnificently intricate, brilliantly conceived scheme. When the idea had finally come, it hadn't felt like it was. Not what he had been expecting anyway. Still over the subsequent hours of self-inspection and recriminations, the plan's simplicity, it's downright bluntness began to feel right. Back to basics. The simpler the plan, the less there was to go wrong.

He straightened up to give his aching back a rest, his mind tirelessly going over and back over what he needed to do, a crying child's voice pleading for Jeff to come back going unnoticed. Monday the 16th. That was when he had decided D-Day would be. There was no particular significance with either the day or the date, but was the earliest that he could realistically put the plan together. That was another good thing about its simplicity. From its initiation, through the planning down to the actual carrying out of the plan, it could be done in under a week. Today would be a long and busy day however, and with this thought in mind, he kneaded his lower back briefly and continued rearranging the furniture in his shed to create enough storage for all he would need.

The plan was perfect in every way apart from a slight niggling doubt regarding the aftermath. Because of its scale, there would be repercussions. That would be unavoidable. No matter what precautions he took, however many safety measures he put in place there was inevitably going to be an element of risk, of danger. Of detection. But that was fine, he was prepared for that and could cope with it. Also, despite the absurdness of it, and the fact that it was the antithesis of his favourite ally logic, after what had happened after the incident in the Delta he half believed that there was someone, some force that would look out for him, and protect him. He was – he was absolutely certain of this – on the side of right, and despite all the filth, the vileness, whoredom and complete lack of morality that he saw in everyone and everything around him, he was confident that as long as he did right, he would be looked after. Number 101 was all of these things incarnate, so never before had he felt so confident that the guiding hand would nudge luck in his direction and divert any spoiling elements into the path of someone else. Many times he had pondered the existence of some huge worldwide equivalent of his chart, that not only had a column for Beechcroft Road and its environs, but for the whole world and every single person in it. The peaks and troughs would resemble the skyline of New York both in shape and scale. He cared little whose hand hovered over it, the car-sized eraser poised, whose head the eyes poring over the millions and millions of columns belonged to. He just knew that the one marked Mr Clarke was positive.

The one time in his life he had lost control, when the reins had slipped from between his white knuckled fingers – and also the last time he had touched alcohol – he should by all rights have been caught and punished, but events had conspired to give him another chance. He had, for one night certainly, and if he was harsh on himself for several weeks, allowed himself to be drawn into the murky underworld that the majority of people actively seek out and thrive in. He had for part of that winter become one of them, and look at what had happened. He had dipped his toe in and had been submerged in the filth and degradation that washed through the streets and lives of the public. He had become poisoned, both literally and metaphorically. In the lowest chapter of his life, culminating in the dank hotel room at the Delta Hotel, he had lost both control and the nearest thing to love Mr Clarke would ever manage. Even in his darkest moments however, with the trembling torch illuminating his innermost feelings and desires, though the first of these losses was almost freely admitted, the latter was never even touched upon.

The killing hit the radio and television the next day, and the local papers the following day. Debra Murphy was reportedly the victim of a crazed sex killer, and police were desperate to find the culprit before he inevitably struck again. According to the papers, the last known sighting had been in the Bluebell pub where several witnesses had come forward to say she had been drunk and had been ejected by the landlord. After that it was apparently a blank. Mr Clarke wasn't sure if this was the truth or if the police had reports of her with someone of his description but were holding their cards close to their chest in order to trap him. Three days after her rapidly cooling body had been found they pulled him in for "routine questioning". Mr Clarke and the D.I. – a brusque Glaswegian with a vulgar mouth and pock marked skin – instantly took a dislike to each other. The questioning was aggressive and repetitive and as far as Mr Clarke was concerned anything but routine. He responded with curtness and condescension, unsure what the actions of an innocent man would be, but unable to prevent his ire from rising or his blood from boiling. He was brought in a second time two days later, and though the questions were the same, there was a certain smugness about his interrogators that made him think that they were in possession of several pieces on information they weren't alluding to. His answers were the same, more monosyllabic, determined to give them no rope with which to hang him with. Yes he did know Debra slightly; no he hadn't seen her that night; no he had never been to the Delta Hotel; yes he had had plenty of girlfriends; no he didn't consider himself as odd; yes he would be very surprised if they had someone who had seen them walking to the hotel together that night; no he hadn't been in South Wales in July last year; no he hadn't got annoyed when Debra had turned down his advances and then stabbed her repeatedly.

He was released once again without charge, but they assured him they'd have him back in as soon as they had enough evidence. He knew it was partly an act, one that would be being played several times with different people in the co-starring role, but he also knew that his prints were bound to be in the room and surely it wouldn't be long before someone did come forward who had seen them together. For the first and only time in his life he had no idea what to do. Then the matter was taken even further from his hands.

A recently divorced local bank manager was found in his Ford Anglia the engine spluttering on the remains of its tank, a green and blue hosepipe wedged in the passenger window. A cryptic note back home on his dining room table mentioned among other things the fact that he had blood on his hands and also contained the phrase a Greek tragedy. To the police – more desperate to close the case than to get the actual man responsible – this was too good an opportunity to miss out on. They released pieces of the note to the press, seizing on the part about him having blood on his hands as a confession, and ascribing the Greek tragedy reference to the murder in the room of the Delta Hotel. The night porter was brought out and identified the picture of the bank manager as the person he now remembered seeing bringing Miss Murphy into the hotel in the early hours of the 15th February. Within days the case was both closed and swept under the carpet. The D.I. was praised for his quick work, and everyone went about their business ignoring the cries of injustice from the family of the accused.

The local journalist who had worked on a story two years earlier involving the same bank manager, a car accident, drunk driving and a dead pedestrian was told to shut his mouth by his editor who was scared of ruining the mutual back scratching agreement he had with the D.I.

Space in the shed cleared, Mr Clarke locked the padlock on its door and brushed dust, both imagined and real from his brown slacks and grey woollen jersey. He looked at his watch, quickly doing the arithmetic in his head. If he was quick he just had enough time for a cup of tea and a sandwich, but he had a busy day ahead of him yet. He had to go to the car auction, then three Halfords and five or six garages to visit. With a quicker than normal step he returned to his house.

CHAPTER TWENTY-TWO

Pulling the chemist's door closed behind him, Mike stood on the pavement, oblivious to the steady stream of pedestrians having to pass either side of him. He put the small white paper bag containing the shampoo into his coat pocket, buttoned it closed and considered his options. It was only now he realised he hadn't been remotely embarrassed explaining the situation to the lady behind the counter. In his current state of mind with the warring factions of fear, paranoia and looming depression on one side and his newfound hope, resolve and "fuck them before they can fuck you attitude" on the other, there was precious little space for anything else. Telling a middle-aged bleached blonde woman – and the two elderly women behind him in the queue - that he had pubic lice didn't even register on his personal Richter scale. In the same mood of enlightenment, the woman, resplendent in her crisp white smock – made to give the impression she was more of a nurse than a shop assistant – had retrieved some medicated shampoo with barely a bat of her heavily mascaraed eyelashes. His resolve was maybe starting to weaken when she started to explain that whereas this would, if used twice daily over the next three days kill all the lice, he would need to either shave all his pubic hair off or alternately he could purchase a special comb which would remove the eggs. He stopped her from fetching the comb, aware that everyone's attention in the small, overly warm shop was firmly on the little episode taking place at the counter, saying he would shave. He handed over the money and made for the door, the woman telling him he would need to use the shampoo on all areas of his body and that he would have to wash all his bedding as the lice could live and lay their eggs in sheets and duvets. He tried to catch the quickly averted eyes of his fellow customers as if to say "this is nothing, if you knew the half of it…"

Back on the street he considered his next move. He was still in his newfound mood of action, and was proud of his first success. New challenges faced him now however. It was all very well being determined to start fighting back, deciding to take circumstances by the scruff of the neck and start shaping them in your favour, but until you knew who to start fighting back against it was hard to know where to start. Whether it was nature or nurture, and standing outside the chemists in the rain – the miserable weather seemed to have accompanied Mike's dramatic fall from grace like a film soundtrack – was no place to start a philosophical debate about Mike Burley's personality traits, Mike's ideals, his personal codes of conduct that had been running along their own sweet way for the past twenty five years. It was going to be hard to reprogram all that in the space of one morning. When all this was over - and for the first time he allowed himself that wonderful thought that somewhere, there was light at the end of the tunnel, that yes it was all going to shit at the minute, but somewhere down the line he would get through this, maybe alone, maybe with the help of other as of yet unknown individuals, maybe, and this thought produced a surge of optimism that brought the hairs up on his neck and tears into his eyes, maybe with Rachel's help, once again the two of them side by side – when this was all over he would be a different person for it. A better, stronger person, one more capable of taking on the chin what life threw at him, and this time, if he didn't like what he was offered he would tell life to fuck itself and go away and bring back something that was to Mike Burley's liking. If he saw this as a perverted rites of passage it would be easier to deal with. The ones he had seen on countless American teenage films tended to deal with losing your virginity, the death of a parent, or usually the school prom, but if it had been decided that his would involve Ford Orions, pubic lice and slashed prostitutes, maybe the rewards would be all the sweeter. Whatever happened, gone was the Mike Burley of old. The one who had taken as his mantra "always leave them wanting more" and whereas that may work well in the theatre - in business, in the workplace, in life in general, it certainly didn't. For the first time in days he had started to think, to believe that he would get through this. At that precise moment, outside the chemists in the rain he wasn't sure exactly how, but believing he would, was a start. A bloody good start.

Defence. Defence and protection, that was the next step. If he was going to start fighting back he would need to start from a secure foundation. He would need to mentally reclaim his home, or certainly his bedroom. No more trembling at the sound of the post in the morning, jumping at his own footfalls on the landing. Logic told him that everything that the killer had done so far suggested that he was very unlikely to risk entering the house when Mike was in. That was all very well, logic could think what it liked, it wasn't the one cowering in bed, the only protection an 18-tog duvet. He had to know that if the house was breached while he was in, one, he would be aware of his presence and two, he would have the means to protect himself.

Almost four hours later Mike was in the Nag's Head once more. But this time it was different. This time he knew he would have one, maybe two pints – as a reward not as a crutch, or an anaesthetic, and then he'd return to his newly protected home. He'd even bought himself a steak, some frozen peas, oven chips and a large mushroom. Along with his personal hygiene, he had neglected his diet over the previous few days. He was amazed how his body no longer bothered to inform him it was hungry or indeed seemed to need food. He had been getting by on a couple of slices of toast every now and then. Two days earlier he'd attempted putting beans on top, but hadn't managed to finish half. Now though, his mouth was positively watering at the thought of the meat. He'd wash it down with some nice red wine – not too much mind, all the alarm systems in the world wouldn't save him if he was unconscious in an alcoholic stupor.

He looked around the horribly familiar pub interior. It even looked better in there today, less intimidating, threatening. Despite this being where it had all started – or was it, had it started in Jackson's office three hours earlier? He wasn't convinced the two incidents were at all connected – he had found he had come back to this pub, to this table in fact, time and time again. Whether it was to try and confront his nemesis; to see if he could spot something, some clue that he had missed the first time; or purely because in his state of mind, the stained walls and floors, the frayed settees and chairs seemed the most appropriate place in the world. Whatever the reason, he had found neither clues nor comfort, and if the owner of the voice on the tape was there, he was as inconspicuous as he had been on that Monday morning.

Almost two years ago, just after he and Rachel had finished university, Mike had embarked on a short-lived fitness regime. Two or three times a week for almost a month he had gone jogging, the three miles or so route in the park, in full view of the bridge where it had all started, or where it had all nearly failed to start. The initial enthusiasm waned, the envisaged dramatic effects on his body hadn't materialised and the regime was consigned to a locker marked with other people's names. While on his runs however, he had become aware that, dressed in sweaty T-shirt and shorts, his face red with either alcohol or exertion, he had gained membership to an exclusive club. Often on his lap of the park, he would pass other joggers going in the opposite direction, and more often or not there would be some form of communication between them, sometimes only a knowing look, but more often than not a smile or a wheezed "alright?". These were people Mike didn't know from Adam or Eve. If he had passed them in the street, in a pub or the supermarket he or they wouldn't have dreamed of acknowledging the other's presence. Once in the park though, dressed in the club's fatigues, it was a different matter.

This got him thinking what other clubs existed that he wasn't party to. Everywhere there may be people greeting each other with a nod, a slight upturning of the mouth. Looking around the smoky bar no one caught his eye. No one raised their eyebrows in furtive salutation. The membership of Mike's current club was exceptionally exclusive. "No one here been directed to a car with a murdered prostitute?" His eyes were saying, "No one else sitting there with a freshly shaved cock and balls to stave off a sexual disease? No one here having a couple of pints after booby trapping your home in an attempt to protect you from the sick fucker who's trying to ruin your life?" No takers. He drained the last of his pint, returned it to the bar and left, automatically checking to see if he was being followed or if anyone was taking an unusual interest in his actions. The rain had stopped as he walked home, his mind wondering what the dress code should be for his new club. The secret sign would be a trembling handshake and the permanent mask of fear worn by its members.

The bell he'd fixed to the inside of his front door jangled its tinny welcome, and inside all seemed as he had left it. Taking his Stanley knife from his pocket he quickly checked the downstairs rooms, before ensuring the strips of Plasticine were still intact on the stairs. The six-inch nails in the stairs below and above each of the three strips were also blood and shoe leather free. Upstairs was all clear, and retrieving his modified cricket bat from under the bed, he pocketed his knife and carefully returned downstairs to the kitchen, his red wine and his steak.

CHAPTER TWENTY-THREE

Out of everyone that Spoon had ever met, Terry was the easiest person to talk to. It wasn't just in dimensions that he resembled a psychiatrist's couch, and over the years that he'd known him he had told him things that he wouldn't have dreamed or dared to tell anyone else. He had told him things that he hadn't even been aware that he knew or thought. He knew that Terry didn't understand most of it, but that didn't seem to matter to either of them. Terry just absorbed all the words, the moans, the half-baked theories, gripes, plans and drunken ramblings like a huge sponge, occasionally nodding sagely as if it had been no surprise at all, this latest revelation.

The majority of conversations Terry was involved in were predominantly one way, but it had always been the case and he just assumed that was simply the way life was. For Spoon, Terry was the perfect valve for bleeding the pressure off. The ideal sounding board. He didn't ask him for advice or for his opinion on anything, he just found that by speaking to him, knowing he wouldn't be judged or get a smart retort, he more often than not would discover that he'd known the answer all along. Spoon often thought of his problems – his issues as they would probably be referred to in a real psychiatrist's office – as a tangled ball of wool (blue wool for some reason) and that by talking through all the different strands, airing them, he was able to detangle the ball. And it seemed better to talk to a twenty-two stone slab of uncomprehending flesh and muscle than to yourself.

"There's something I've been meaning to ask you Tel, did you know Danny before he started coming to the house?" They were walking slowly down the high street away from the house.

"Danny?" Terry spoke the word and chewed it over as if tasting an unfamiliar food. Spoon waited, there was a technique of talking with Terry, one that required time and patience.

"Yeah Danny, you know… Danny, the bearded guy in the house."

There was a pause while he digested this new piece of information, and then his face brightened, like the sun - albeit a fat, round, red one, coming from behind a bank of clouds. "Oh Danny." They walked on in silence for several seconds, before Spoon, realising he wasn't going to get the answer unless he reminded him of the question, prompted him again.

"Yeah Danny, did you know him before he started coming to the house?"

Terry brought his huge hand up to his head and scratched his thick blond thatch of hair. He was the only person Spoon had ever known who did actually scratch their head while in thought, and judging by the results produced, surmised it gave no benefit. His hand went down to his jeans pocket for the hundredth time that morning. To the little roll of money. His Granada fund. Originally he'd planned to keep it in his shoebox in the bedroom he'd claimed as his own. The box, complete with a small black lined drawing of the brogues that were its original occupants, lived in a gap between the floorboards and the ceiling of the kitchen below, access gained courtesy of a loose floorboard. In it he kept his drugs, and all his belongings that he considered to have any sort of value, be it sentimental or financial. It had never been bursting at the seams, and besides his stash, it was virtually empty. There was a picture of his mother. She was on her own, slightly left of centre, a dry stonewall directly behind her, a brown and white cow - decapitated by the side of the picture - in a field in the distance. His mother was wearing a familiar look, a weak, uncertain smile. One that suggested that she was trying to be happy, but that she wasn't sure if it was entirely appropriate. Her smiles always seemed, to Spoon anyway, simply a result of the tightening and moving of muscles as opposed to any outward show of internal joy, or even satisfaction. He didn't know where or when the photograph had been taken, or if he had taken it himself, and had no idea how he'd come to have it in his possession. When he had left home, he'd emptied his two drawers of junk into a holdall, and the photo must have been amongst it. Since then, the act of actually throwing it away seemed a lot more momentous or symbolic than just keeping it, so it had remained with him ever since.

Elsewhere in the box, were his passport, and a smooth pebble. Two inches long and half as wide, it had been given him by Ramona, a girl he'd met in Ibiza. She said the pebble – half pink and half a deep blue – symbolised their relationship, and as long as he had the stone, they would always be together, if not on the earth, but somewhere else, a deeper, spiritual place. Her name, she told him, meant protector and she promised him that that is what she would do. A couple of weeks after she had given him the pebble, she had had to return to the mainland, and he never saw or heard from her again. Occasionally he would sit and hold the pebble, turning its cool surface warm in his grip, and sometimes he would think of Ramona, and of her promise to him and wondered where she was, who she was protecting.

The shoebox was also the place where he would normally have kept his money. His Granada fund. Over the last few weeks, however, he had become more and more convinced that someone had been skimming off his smack. Only a little bit at a time, but he was sure it wasn't his paranoia. One of his customers had even accused him of selling him short. He placed hairs or threads of cotton on the loose floorboards, and these were always in place when he returned, but nevertheless he was convinced someone was not only aware of the hiding place but was going in and taking from it. He was slightly less certain who he thought could be doing it, but Danny was top of his accused list. He had no evidence, and half the time he was aware that it was probably more to do with the fact that Danny had been irritating him recently than anything else. There was one thing however, Danny had made a comment about Spoon's mother a few weeks back. It hadn't registered at the time as being of any significance, but recently Spoon had found himself wondering if the comment was prompted by the picture in the shoebox. Either way, he wasn't going to start accusing anyone, and when he thought about it with a clear, uncluttered head he became convinced that he was imagining the whole thing. Nevertheless, he'd decided to keep the money he saved on him at all times. At the minute, the fifty pounds hardly represented a problem but when the figure had grown to three, and then four figures he would have to reconsider what to do. For reasons he'd never been able to qualify, he didn't have a bank account, and maybe that was something he would have to reconsider, but that was something for the future. At the moment all his efforts were on growing the figure so it was big enough to become a problem.

"Dunno mate." Terry had stopped scratching his head and had actually stopped walking, turning around to face Spoon head on, his face screwed up by the effort of searching his memory. "I Don't think so."

"Never mind Tel, don't worry about it, it's nothing really." He started walking again. They continued in silence for several minutes, before Spoon spoke again, surprising himself as so often he did when talking with Terry, by spilling what he'd started to think about.

"There was this kid at my school Tel, Peter something or other, can't remember his last name, it don't matter anyway. Quiet lad, kept himself to himself like, but harmless enough. He lived down my road, so sometimes I'd walk to school with him, so I guess I knew him better than most. Anyway he had a phobia of spontaneous combustion," he glanced in Terry's direction certain he didn't know what that meant, but also knowing it didn't matter, half the time he doubted if Terry actually listened to half the stuff people talked to him about. Not through rudeness, he just doubted if he could cope with too much information at once, his ears filtering out the words, only letting ones through every now and then.

"Out of all the things to have a phobia about, that's got to be the worst." He shook his head, almost in disbelief at his own words. "If you're scared of heights, well, just don't go up on tall buildings or ladders, if you're scared of snakes, don't go in the fucking jungle, you know what I mean, but spontaneous combustion… well, that can get you at any time. Anywhere. To the casual observer, this phobia didn't affect his life, you know? But the casual observer, Terry, didn't see the long evenings in Peter's small dank bathroom where he'd lay immersed in tepid water for hour after hour. Every spare bit of time he'd spend it in the bath, just lying there. When he was in bed he'd just lay there shitting it that he was suddenly going to… well, burst into flames I suppose. Jesus, I haven't thought about him for years. Anyways, he was brilliant at swimming, obviously he loved it, it was, apart from his bath, the only place he felt safe. When I left school, I didn't hear anything else about him, and they moved house about that time too, so I never saw him again. Couple of years ago, though I heard what had happened to him." Spoon paused, for some reason desperate for Terry to hear and understand the story, not knowing why, but certain that it was somehow relevant to what was going on with his life at the moment. Terry slowed and looked at Spoon, who took this as encouragement. "Apparently, a couple of years after he left school, he was doing this charity swim across the Irish Sea I think, was going to be the youngest person to swim it." As he retold the story, he could picture the pale, slight teenager, and he was almost overcome with emotions that were far too strong and real than they should have been for someone who he had, in all reality, hardly known. His voice was growing thick, and he found he was having to swallow repeatedly. "He was raising money for the local burns unit at the hospital, and…" another swallow, "and he drowned." He stopped walking, no longer knowing or indeed caring if Terry had heard, not even convinced he'd said it loud enough to be heard. "He fucking drowned."

Spoon turned to face his friend, "I don't want to be like that Terry, so scared of something, of everything, of life, that it just rules your life,

224

making you run, hide, I don't know… fucking swim, anything, just to get away, to… save yourself. I don't want to be like that Terry…" His voice drifted off, then grew in strength again, his head shaking, "I just don't want to be like that."

The pause stretched into one, two, several seconds.

"What, you don't want to be a drowner?"

Spoon looked up into Terry's big earnest eyes, and nodded. "Yes, that's exactly it Terry, I don't want to be drowner."

***

The two walked on in silence for the next quarter of an hour or so, both lost in their own thoughts, their bodies going where their legs took them, their minds free to drift wherever. Eventually, Spoon realised they had come to a halt, and his eyes refocused on the shop window in front of him. It belonged to Gerard's, an establishment that despite changes in the world and to the market had stubbornly survived, refusing to adapt or modernise. It sat in the slightly uncomfortable niche between a junk and antique shop, and sold mainly the former masquerading as the latter. The window display, though Spoon doubted if it really deserved such a grand title, was merely an extension, an overspill of the cluttered wooden shop floor, as its contents spread to all corners of the small shop. The only thing that appeared to differentiate the ones crammed up against the large bay windows, was that they had mostly been turned around to face the street. As his eyes peered through the dirty window into the gloomy innards, they were met by those of a large rag doll, staring mournfully out onto the street, no doubt dreaming of escape. She was sat on a half size wooden chair, in front of which were piled a selection of old books mainly, from what he could just about make out, cookery books. On top of these, just within reach of the doll if she could have been bothered to lean over, were a dozen or so old medicine bottles and pillboxes. A huge frying pan hung above her head, swaying ever so slightly in some draft, while the ubiquitous brass warming pan was fixed to the wall on her left. For a minute Spoon considered if this was a clever pastiche on the lives of Victorian women, but then as his eyes quickly surveyed the rest of the window, he dismissed that idea as being over generous to the proprietors.

Terry, a couple of feet to his left, and, he realised the reason they had stopped, was stood, stock still, his fat snout-like nose touching the glass, the breath from his mouth forming an ever-increasing patch on the glass that threatened to soon obscure his view. Not for the first time in the couple of years they had been friends, Spoon studied his face. It was often easier to find out what he was thinking by simply reading the expression on his face as opposed to asking him to explain. His brain seemed to prefer to bypass his tongue with its limited vocabulary and go straight for the hundreds of muscles of the face to convey its messages. At that moment he was wearing a look that rapidly switched from wonderment to despair, on a continuous loop. Spoon tried to see what it was that could have been causing him so much concern. Directly in front of Terry was a battered chest of drawers, with an equally battered display of pottery and figures on top. What looked like a witch's broom leaned against it, while a pink, almost new child's bike hung from above, a fat teddy bear with one ear missing holding onto the handlebars for dear life.

He scanned the contents of the window, trying to see the direction Terry was gazing but gave up. "What ya looking at Tel?"

No response.

"Tel… Terry, what are you looking at, you alright mate?"

Slowly he turned his head in Spoon's direction, blinking, a look of bemusement on his face as if he had just returned from a reverie and didn't quite know where he had returned to. His big hand went to his big head, and rubbed his eyes and then his whole face. Standing there, twenty-two stones, arms that could twist your head full circle, fists that could crush every bone in your hand, he was the picture of vulnerability and Spoon had an almost irresistible urge to go and hug him. He went up to him and looked up into his eyes for the second time that day, but this time the pleading was all in the bigger man's eyes.

"What is it Terry?"

"Ahh, don't mind me Spoon, just me being my big old dumb self, that's all Spoon, come on."

"Bollocks, come on you can tell me man, what's wrong, what have you seen?" He gestured with his hand, sweeping the window display, desperately searching its contents once again, looking for a clue.

"It's just that donkey, Spoon…" he nodded his head towards the top of the chest of drawers and a porcelain horse's head that Spoon had dismissed twice.

"That?" He tried and failed to keep the shock from his voice, tried again, and managed to tone it down to mere surprise, "That horse Tel, yeah?

"Stupid, I know, it's just that I saw it weeks ago, and every time I come past here I can't help looking at it. You see it's just like this Donkey I went on all the time when me Mam took me on our holiday to Bridlington…" His smile lit up his huge face, and Spoon could see he was drifting back there, "It's just like him, can't remember his name, but me Mam took him on him every day. Lovely little feller. That was the best week of my life. Can't remember being that happy again. Only holiday we ever had."

Spoon studied the object more closely. It stood about eight inches from its square wooden base, and was of a horse's head, looking up, its scruffy dark brown mane, clinging untidily to its lighter brown hide. It's big off white eyes and gaping nostrils gave the impression of fear, but the mouth had an almost human aspect to it that made it look like the horse was smiling. This last trait owed more to the lack of the artist's skill, than to any duality of the horse's personality. It didn't look like any of the donkeys he'd seen at Southport and was glad there was no one else there that would have pointed this out.

"My Mam would love that statute. It would remind her of that week in Brid' an' all you see Spoon. That would make the old dear smile…"

They both stood there in silence looking at the horse's head.

"Why don't you get it then Terry, it can't… I bet it aint that much?"

"That's art Spoon, it's too expensive for me mate. I've been in twice to have a closer look like, and to see how much it was, and I can't afford it. Besides, the owner doesn't want me in the shop again without buying something, thinks I'm going to nick something. Or break sommat."

"Can't you save up or something…"? He leaned closer to try and read the small paper handwritten price tag stuck to the base, just managing to make out the £48 in faded blue biro.

"I'm skint Spoon, you know that, I owe Shafeeq all that money still, and the leccy bill is overdue, you know how it is." He sighed, completely steaming up the window, and turned back in the direction they were originally walking. "And anyway it's her birthday next week… It's not just that. It just gets me angry, gets me down that after all she's done for me, I can't even do that one thing back for her. That's just it… ignore me Spoon, just being my big stupid self, see?" It was the biggest speech Spoon, and probably anybody had ever seen Terry give.

"Bloody hell Tel, what are you like hey?" He watched him as he set off with his lumbering stride, patting his shoulder as he passed close by, enjoying as always the solid feel and sound it made. For five, ten seconds he watched his friend trudge off, knowing he was once more back in Bridlington. Feeling the roll of notes in his jeans pockets for the last time, he turned in the opposite direction, a few seconds later, a small bell announcing his entrance into the shop.

It was the first pint he had had for a while. The first since he'd started trying to save and cut down on his vices. It had been harder than he'd thought, but he was still determined and he supposed he was doing OK. He looked up at Terry at the bar ordering the drinks. He thought he was going to cry when he had handed over the horse to him, wrapped in a thick white paper bag. Instead he had slowly unwrapped it; his eyes full of joy, of wonder the like of which Spoon didn't even know existed outside the minds of children on Christmas mornings. And he knew then he had done the right thing. Spoon's mouth opened and closed, opened and closed, and then there had been an embarrassing moment when he had tried to hug him. Spoon - for some reason he wasn't entirely happy with himself about - not wanting to, not in the street. He had made Terry promise that he wouldn't mention it again, had told him that he knew he was grateful, but he deserved it, and that he'd had a big win on the footy, so it was really no big deal anyway. The only way he could silence him was to eventually agree to Terry buying him a drink, though Spoon had insisted they went to the Nag's, as Terry got free drinks as payment for his occasional bouncing duties.

Terry returned placing the two pints on the round table, the horse – carefully wrapped up again, wedged under his arm. Gently, lovingly, he placed it on the table next to his pint.

"Cheers Terry," he lifted his pint in salutation, "to your mum, Bridlington and our health"

Terry repeated the gesture. "And to good friends."

Spoon saw that Terry was going to launch into another barrage of thank you's so clumsily changed the subject. "I've been doing a lot of thinking recently Tel, looking at what I do, what I am, what I've done, what I'm going to be, what I'm going to do… you know, all that shit." He sighed, searching for the right phrase to some his conclusions up, settling in the end for "And it's all shit."

Terry's content smile crumpled in on itself as he digested this change of tact, something that once again, didn't make Spoon feel good about himself.

"Is this about that busking boy who drowned again Spoon?"

"No." Spoon took a long sip of his lager to hide his smile "Well, I suppose it is Tel, probably no coincidence I've been thinking about him at the same time. It's just that everything I do, is just trying to avoid something, to avoid actually doing something real, positive. It's always just a temporary little stopgap to keep the other shit, the real stuff away. I don't know, Jesus, I'm dying for a fag… I can't explain it, it's just that at the minute all I do is sit in the fucking house – no it's not a house it's a fucking squat Terry, that's not a home. What's a squat? It's an uncomfortable sitting position that's what it is, it's not somewhere to spend you're fucking life in." He took another swig of his drink, surprised where the sudden anger had come from, not wishing to ruin Terry's happy moment, but unable to stem the flow now the dam had been breached.

He took a deep breath. "It's just my entire life revolves around smack – taking it, selling it so that I can take some more – fucking football bets, and crappy stoned conversations in the fucking squat with people I… I don't even bloody know if I'm honest with myself. Al spends the entire day in some fucking coma, Shafeeq, well, he's a good man, but you know… he aint gonna be there for us all the time, he's got plans… Danny, Danny is doing my fucking head in at the minute… Oh fucking hell I don't know Terry, sorry, it's just I don't know what I'm going to do. I know I sound like some fucking teenager and I just need to grow up or something or take more smack, or less, I don't know." He stood up, slightly embarrassed, finished his pint and strode to the gents, cursing Terry for his ability to draw the poison from him with such unassuming ease.

He returned a couple of minutes later to see two fresh pints on the table, and Terry holding the horse's head in one hand and either stroking its mane or removing invisible particles of dust from it with the other.

"Sorry Tel, bit emotional today." He forced a smile.

Slowly Terry put down the head, wrapped it up once more and manoeuvred it slightly on the table top until it was in a position he was happy with. "That's OK Spoon, that's what friends are for."

"I guess so…" He took another big sip, licking the froth from his top lip. "I suppose it's the same for everyone, it's just that people use different methods to do it, but all I've been doing for the last… I don't know, five, six, ten years of my life, is trying to escape. Either literally to Ibiza, or else recently, just stuffing myself with pills, weed, smack, anything that will draw a veil over real life so I don't have to face up to the question of what I am actually supposed to be doing. What I'm actually going to do. Even betting at football… what's that all about? That's just another way of escaping, or trying to escape. The weird thing is, the only way to stop it all, to get out of the rut, the cycle, is to do it for real. Escape once and for all." He stopped, knowing where this was going. He had wanted to keep his plans secret, as if letting anyone else in on them would ruin them, expose them for what they really were, some half-baked fantasy that was never going to happen. But Terry was different, and he knew that he would feel better for it if he did tell someone, if only to hear his own voice spell it out.

"And that's what I'm going to do Tel, escape once and for all. I've been pissing around at it all these years, not knowing why, or where I wanted to escape to. I didn't have the balls, maybe I was never desperate enough to before but now, I've a plan, and I'm going to do it. It's not going to be soon, not this year, probably not next year, but do you know what Terry, I don't care, I know I'm going to go so that's all that matters. And I know where I'm going to go as well. To the most wonderful place in the world. Where no one knows me, knows who, what I am, what I've done before. Where no one knows I'm shit. To everyone there, I am what I tell them, and what I do, and I'm determined to do good things, to work hard. Proper work. To do things I'll have laughed at, scoffed at a few years, even months ago, but I think that's what I've always been trying to escape from, when really it's what I need to escape to."

He nodded to himself, happy that he had straightened things out in his head. Terry was unwrapping the paper from the horse's head again, and was inspecting it for damage, his sausage roll fingers moving with surprising delicacy over the folds and crevices of the mare's neck and mane.

"Look at that Terry, doesn't it look amazing?" He passed over the unfolded page from the magazine he had retrieved from his back pocket, smoothing it with the palm of his hand as he placed it down next to the horse's stand.

Terry turned his head, moved the page slightly so it no longer touched the wooden base and studied the photographs.

"It's Granada, Tel, in Spain. Look at that, and look around here. That's where I'm going to go. That's where I'm finally going to be OK, to be happy. I won't need to try to escape any more when I'm there, I'm sure of it."

"You really going away Spoon?" Terry's eyes were filled with sadness, tempering his enthusiasm. He had been surprised that he had actually been listening and taken it in. "Yes, I need to Tel. I need to."

There was a silence again, as Spoon took two long draughts of his pint, and Terry continued to scrutinise the pictures before returning his attention to the horse. "I don't know why anyone would want to leave... I like it here, we have friends, we're happy... why would you want to give that up Spoon?"

"You said earlier Tel, you have no money, you can't even afford a present for your mum. Nothing's going to change..." He stopped himself, the last thing he wanted to do was preach to Terry and tell him his life was shit. "It's just me Terry, I know what we have here is good, its special, people would kill for what we have. What worries have we got, hey? We've more mates than most people… I know, I know all that, but for some reason, for me it's not enough anymore, maybe I'm being unrealistic, but I know I'm going to have to do it. If it fucks up, well… so be it, I can live with that. What I can't live with is if I don't get off my arse and give it the best shot I possibly can." He finished his drink, and smiled again. "Don't worry Tel, you aren't going to get rid of me yet, I'll be around for a long time yet."

Terry had turned the head over and was running his finger over the grain in the untreated wood on the underneath of the base. "My old man had a Granada when I was a nipper. A dark green Granada."

CHAPTER TWENTY- FOUR

Saturday the sixteenth of November 1996 would be special for many people for almost as many reasons. People would remember it as their wedding day - after years of saving, months of planning, weeks of panicking and days of studying the weather forecasts it would eventually arrive. Others would remember it as the day when they began their final, long-term relationship; still others would have the day marked down as when theirs ended. Many, across the length and breadth of the United Kingdom would be born on that date and would celebrate it accordingly from then on. For Mr Clarke, that was the day he started making his bomb.

The previous two days had been spent driving hundreds of miles, buying, fetching and carrying, then assembling the materials, and as he stood in his rearranged shed that morning, he had pondered how far things had come. This was a step up, several steps up if he was honest with himself from killing cats and putting castor oil into bottles of milk. If he was that way inclined – which he most certainly was not - Mr Clarke would have been more than justified in thinking that he had entered the big time.

It was inevitable though, that from the moment he had first sat down and devised, then made the chart, that he would end here. In his shed surrounded by gallons of petrol, hundreds of Styrofoam cups and several wholesale size bags of flour. It had been a long and winding road, with many ups and downs. There had been blood lost, predominantly other peoples and usually vomited or shat out, and many tears spilt, but there was only ever going to be one destination, and here he was, hunched over the methodical hand-written notes he had made in the library two days earlier.

He had heard of the internet, but had never been on it before, and it had shocked him. Sat there in the stuffy, overheated room of his local library he had, for less than two pounds, been able to research exactly what he would need and how he would have to put the materials together to create a bomb. He had a slight working knowledge already, from several books on the subject purchased over the previous years – another indication that deep inside he had known where the road down which he was striding was going to end up. He knew that for accessibility of materials, ease of assembly and detonation, and overall destructive capability, he would be best off down the thermobaric route. What he wouldn't have known and what the books didn't detail was exactly how you would put the science and technical principals into practice. That was where the internet had stepped in, unveiling a myriad of ways in which to maim, poison, kill and destroy your fellow citizens.

The lunatics had finally been given the keys to the asylum. He had heard many ways spouted by as many experts on how the world was going to end. Some said that the polar ice caps would melt, sending mankind back into the seas from where they had appeared millions of years earlier, while others argued the deserts would spread and cover the earth's surface starving the booming population. Other theories revolved around the superpowers blowing each other off the face of the planet; while wilder ones included such elements as global terrorism, super viruses, sunspots and aliens.

Mr Clarke now knew that all those had been wrong. He had seen what would finally bring humankind to its knees after centuries of mixed success. He modified his earlier thoughts. The lunatics had been handed the keys to the asylum, but for good measure, they had also been told how they could arm themselves to the teeth, and where the best places to attack were. Why wait for external forces to come and destroy us when we could get off our arses and do it ourselves?

Straightening up to stretch his back, Mr Clarke rubbed his aching lower vertebrae, then his eyes and finally his temples. The poor light, his own aging eyesight and less than nimble fingers weren't ideal for the delicate work of stripping wires, dismantling clocks and all the other hundred and one things detailed on his A4 sheets. Despite the fatigue however, and the niggling pains, this was when he was at his happiest. For most people, putting the world to rights meant shouting their mouths off over a few pints at the local pub. That wasn't putting the world to rights, that was simply moaning. This was putting the world to rights. Changing those parts of it that were wrong. In the twenty or so years since the chart's conception it had, with Mr Clarke as its arms and legs, put many things right. And aching hand on rapidly beating heart, Mr Clarke could say that the world was a better place for it. It was important that everything was tackled, all those niggling, what some would deem as trivial occurrences needed to be righted, otherwise they would grow like waves in a pond – and there were enough people throwing stones.

If he had taken steps at the beginning with number 101, maybe it wouldn't have come to this, but hindsight was twenty twenty, and he could only do so much. If he had spent more time concentrating on that part of the chart, others would have grown out of control, and who was to say that they wouldn't now represent an even bigger problem than 101 did now. Surely it was better to have just one major negative bar than a whole swathe of them. The cancer that that specific column represented was about to be cut out, leaving the chart and hence his immediate neighbourhood in a very healthy state. And that would be all down to him. And the chart. Briefly, he allowed himself the pleasure of picturing himself in his bedroom, eraser poised over the chart, the act of destroying number 101 on the chart equally as satisfying as destroying the bricks and mortar and flesh and blood that it represented. It was something he had done only a handful of times over the previous years, most notably those of Potter and most satisfyingly that of his brother – completely removing them from the chart. Unfortunately there would always be someone else to come in to take over the space vacated.

Either in an attempt to prolong this self-congratulatory mood, or maybe it was just that when in such a frame of mind, he tended to think of his brother, it was to him that his thoughts turned, as he allowed himself the twenty-five minutes it would take to make and drink a cup of tea.

Mr. Clarke's brother, two years his senior had been the antithesis of his younger sibling. Despite the same stifling upbringing and home life, he had used it as motivation, and looked upon it as a constant reminder that if he didn't strive to better himself, to seek out, make and grab every opportunity, this is what his life would end up mirroring. This annoyed Mr Clarke. Maybe out of jealousy or bitterness that not only was he unable to spot these opportunities, but he didn't possess the qualities needed to grab and turn them to his advantage - certainly not until it was far too late, and there were too many other, younger hungrier people more than willing to take them. Maybe, it was because he saw it as a damming verdict on not only their shared childhood, but also on the life that Mr Clarke had unavoidably found himself steered down. Once he had matured past the inevitable petty squabbling and name calling, his brother, owner of a less studious but more agile mind, and finer but stronger features than his more puggy, younger kinsman, never criticised or made fun of him. Despite numerous opportunities, he never seized on them to belittle him, or highlight his awkwardness around women whenever he brought girls back to the flat. Something Mr Clarke never did. Over the years, as they grew older and more apart, their contact became more sporadic and formal. They would exchange Christmas cards, and every year Mr Clarke would be invited to his sister-in-law's cottage in the country for a weekend, which he would invariably decline.

Mr Clarke took the silence of his mid to late teenage years as contempt, and the latter invitations as his brother's way of teasing him, of flaunting everything he had, parading his intelligent, wealthy wife, the 14th century cottage in the Cotswolds that had been in her family for generations. He saw this all as a declaration of look at what you could have had if you weren't such a useless, awkward, socially inept individual. Of course none of this was ever spoken, but Mr Clarke knew it. He could read it in his brother's smug face; in-between the lines of the handmade Christmas cards; in the intonation of his messages on his answer machine; in the fact that he was always offered the grandest bedroom. The smoked salmon he received every

Christmas, may as well have come with the message, "Look what we eat, have a taste of this, so as to make the bland fare you are forced to live on, taste even more insipid."

Mr Clarke had taken all these slights, digs and insults and stored them. The chart recorded, year in year out the grandiose displays of affected happiness, and gradually the bar grew. It had been a constant source of irritation to Mr Clarke that his brother seemed to be untouchable. He was unable to contrive anything approaching a workable plan that would halt his column's progress. Despite himself, when dealing with his brother, or even attempting to deal with him he found he reverted back to the even more awkward, ineffectual person he had presented to the world in his teenage years. All his creativity, his methodical planning, everything he relied on became stifled, and it was this even more than his brother's actual actions that enraged him.

Then, in another piece of proof that maybe there was a bigger force guiding him, it was all resolved in one beautiful, perfect morning. Partly due to the fact that his brother's business had suddenly begun to struggle – something he referred to as black Wednesday had apparently cost him dear, and partly due to it not being a bad time to lay low after a successful, but ultimately dangerous couple of months working for the chart, he had consented to accept one of his brother's invitations. His parents had been there as well, and on his arrival, he had started to regret his decision. His brother showed no sign of his recent troubles, and if anything was even more upbeat, even more gregarious, offering Mr Clarke a month in his time share in France, almost begging him to take his Italian sports car for a ride. Through it all, Mr Clarke bit his tongue and inwardly fumed. His parents, delighting in and exaggerating the difference between their offspring made everything all the worse, and he was sat in his room thinking up an excuse that would allow him to return home without looking like he was running, when he heard the cries from downstairs. He tried to ignore them at first, until he realised that they were coming from his brother and also that it was something serious. He arrived downstairs to find his mother in tears, and his sister in law on the phone – apparently to the ambulance service. His brother, was on his back, half off the settee, his face a rictus of pain, arms folded and pressed against his stomach. Occasionally a strained choking sound would escape his gaping mouth, something that appeared to cause even more pain to the squirming figure.

An hour later and he was in the local hospital, preparing to have his appendix - that had suddenly and dramatically burst - removed, and forty-five minutes after that he was in the operating theatre, a scalpel easing its way through first his skin, then subcutaneous fat and finally muscle. Dr Stephenson, whose liver spotted hand had guided the scalpel, told the concerned relatives the following day that another hour, hour and a half at the most and it probably would have been too late.

There weren't many things that Mr Clarke felt obliged to do in his life, but the morning after he had seen his brother rushed into hospital, with his parents and sister in law gradually recovering from various levels of shock, mainly down to the assurances from Dr Stephenson that the patient was well on the road to recovery and was in no further danger, he had felt obliged to accompany them to see the recovering hero. It was with a heavy heart and indifferent mind that he entered ward eight on that dull October morning. The sister in charge of the ward, looking less than resplendent in her shapeless lime green overalls, had rigorously enforced the three visitors at any one time rule, and he had spent a miserable forty minutes in the waiting room. Eventually he was called, as his parents went looking for a place to sit down and have a cup of tea, now that they were convinced their first born wasn't about to die and they could finally think about themselves. He took his place besides his sister-in-law at the foot of his bed, for what promised to be an even more miserable forty minutes. His brother, in annoyingly good spirits, was more than happy to show his Dunkirk spirit, his ability to smile in the face of adversity, and the large white gauze covering the spot where the offending organ had been removed from his otherwise perfectly functioning body.

There was an article in the Sunday paper his brother was keen to read, but without his contact lenses in, he couldn't see his hand in front of his face not even if you painted it red and set it on fire, as he was keen to repeat ad nauseum to anyone who would care to listen when the issue of his eyesight came up.

He passed the paper to his wife to read, but after kissing him on the cheek – another blatant example of the couple mocking him, she left to go for a cigarette, leaving Mr Clarke to relay the latest predictions for the tiger economies over the forthcoming months and years. He contented himself with changing some of the hopefully more salient facts and figures, but was relieved when a surly nurse arrived, brusquely told them both that he would have to leave as she was going to check and dress the wound. She busily pulled the curtains around his brother's bed, told him to lie on his side and gave a look to Mr Clarke that implied that the wound on his brother's side would be nothing compared to the one he would receive if he didn't get out from under her feet. She didn't look like a person who was used to having to tell people anything once, never mind twice.

Pulling one of the heavy green curtains aside, he ducked slightly under its metal rail and closed it behind him, shutting his audibly wincing brother in with the muttering nurse. The other three beds on the ward were empty, their occupants either dead, back home or in the car park having a cigarette, Mr Clarke neither knew or cared which. A cheap vase sporting two chips and a self-conscious looking bunch of red carnations sat atop the high table that, before the almost violent attentions of the nurse had rested beside his brother's bed. Now it slouched on its casters, resting against the empty unmade bed to his left. Absently, his eyes wandered over the table top. The edges were raised slightly, to prevent the contents sliding off, and some water from the vase had pooled in one corner. The ubiquitous bunch of grapes – half eaten by various visitors - sat astride the equally so, in his brother's presence anyway, paperback extolling the efforts and theories by the latest self-made millionaire. The authors' smug face, smarming below his equally smug, thick, greased back jet-black hair, stared out of the creased cover, searching out the gaze of the next hopeful apprentice to divert some of his sparse funds into the already bloated bank account of the author, in the desperate attempt that maybe one day he too could wear the self-assured look of the self-made man. The only other two items on the table were a small off-white receptacle, which Mr Clarke assumed held his brother's contact lenses and a plastic bottle of bleach or cleaning solution the nurse must have placed on the table. A bright yellow jay cloth lay on the floor, almost hiding under the table.

The orange diamond shaped warning label on the bottle swam in and out of focus as Mr Clarke considered his options. He'd done his duty, unfortunately he would have to wait for the rest of the fawning family to get a lift home, but then that would be it and he'd be able to make some excuse up about his work – the fervour with which they followed the ups and downs of his brother's career left precious little energy to take much interest in Mr Clarke's mundane paid occupation, so no eyebrows would be raised. He would leave in better spirits than he thought possible, the weekend's twist of his brother being in hospital, being an unexpected bonus. He was just about to shout out that he was leaving to his brother when another option made itself known. Possibly a glorious one.

Glancing quickly over his shoulder, taking in the empty ward and equally empty corridor leading down behind and to the left of him, he strode forward, his legs making the distance to the table in two and a half paces. His eyes greedily took in the information on the plastic bottle's label, proclaiming the irritating nature of its contents. The bottle was crowned with a black plastic top, holding a thick semi translucent plastic tube-cum-straw which rose vertically for a couple of inches before describing a nearly perfect ninety-degree angle and pointing off out the Victorian sash window. The bottle felt both warmer and heavier in his hand than he had imagined, as in one quick, almost deft movement, he twisted, tilted and squeezed the tough grey plastic, sending a stream of colourless liquid into the receptacle containing the two glass contact lenses. A faint chemical smell rose from the table, before being devoured by the myriad of others that called Ward 8 home. The bottle glugged as it sucked up some air through the tube, but less than five seconds later, all was as it had been, Mr Clarke stood quietly on the other side of the bed idly flicking through a Sunday supplement that was on the stripped and naked bed opposite his brother's. The only noises were a hacking cough from some emphysema-blighted lungs further up the corridor and the occasional groan or swift intake of breath from behind the green curtains in front of him. He allowed himself a quick look over to the table, where the millionaire still gazed out. The bottle was as it had been before, the tube innocently pointing out to the car park. The only major difference in the room, was the beating of Mr Clarke's heart, as excitement and curiosity fought for top billing.

The green curtains were roughly yanked open, a stubborn curtain ring feeling the full force of firstly a stare and then a meaty freckled forearm. His brother, looking more dishevelled and paler than before the nurse's attentions smiled wanly up at his younger sibling who carefully closed the magazine and replaced it on the bed. The nurse gave Mr Clarke an accusatory look, commanded the bed bound Clarke not to touch or scratch the dressing and set off down the corridor. Her thick powerful legs had taken her almost out of site, before a loud tut that sounded like breaking glass announced her return and she strode back into the ward and picked up the cleaning bottle. Pink piggy eyes, darted and scanned the table top and then the surrounding area before locating the half-concealed jay cloth. Her body folded and it was snatched up between stout pink fingers, another accusing look, this time directed towards the older of the brothers, and then she was off again, with what she may have imagined was if not a sexy, a purposeful swagger, but unfortunately was more chaffing cowboy.

On the motorway two hours later, Mr Clarke's mind was playing over and over the possible effects the solution would have on the contact lenses, and more importantly his brother's corneas. He had hung around at his brother's bed, torn between not wanting to raise suspicions by practically forcing him to put the lenses in, and desperate to see what occurred. He had settled for complaining of a headache thereby ruling himself out of having to do any more reading, and mentioning the unfinished article he had started narrating to his brother and that the book on the bedside, which he now saw was called "Grab the Cash Cow By the Horns – How I made my first $10 million" looked interesting.

"Pompous twat."

Mr Clarke's eyes widened then hardened, and his chest began to inflate before he realised the comment had been aimed at the face on the book. His sister in law despised hearing her husband swear, and along with a long list of other measures he adopted in an attempt to keep hold of the only really continuous and reliable stream of income he had, he did as he was told. When he was on his own however, he would often dust off the now neglected bluer part of his vocabulary and give it full reign. To Mr Clarke, who hated vulgarity as much as his sister in law – but for better reasons than simply because of some assumed social standing and the behaviour expected therein – he just sounded like an errant schoolboy trying to impress his peers with some words he'd heard the older boys using.

"There's nothing he can tell me that I couldn't have told him ten years ago"

Despite his earlier reaction, Mr Clarke found himself siding with the face on the front of the paperback, and it was only the thought of the surprise patiently waiting in the ceramic pot that prevented him from comparing the two success rates.

Two hours after arriving back at his own home, the phone call had come. A tearful mother – my, she really had had a terrible weekend – related the story in between sobs and wails. He had grown impatient with her to hear all the details, and at the risk of showing his hand had questioned and questioned at first her, and then when it all became too much for his mother, his father, so that he could picture in his mind exactly the pain and suffering his brother had gone through and indeed, if his father's strangely emotionless predictions were correct, would continue to go through for the remainder of his life.

The three of them had returned to the hospital in the early evening, to at first find the patient asleep, and then when he woke, in high spirits. Apparently, he had been told that all things being well, he'd be out the next morning. They had stayed about an hour or so, and had said their farewells, his wife arranging a time for her to come and pick him up the next morning, unless she got a call to the contrary. Still insisting he was in fine fettle, and determined to show it to anyone who cared to listen or showed any interest in his wellbeing, he declared he was full of energy, would find it hard to sleep, after lying around on his backside all day, and would spend his time digesting the Sunday papers and picking holes in the book he'd bought in the mistaken belief of acquiring some tips on business acumen and strategy. He had asked his wife to pass his contact lenses, and then it had happened.

The screams had several effects. They woke the semi-conscious man in the bed opposite who until then hadn't fully come round from his operation to remove a kidney stone; they induced a similar screaming episode – though decidedly less heartfelt – from a four-year-old girl visiting her grandmother in the ward down the corridor; they brought shock, terror and finally tears to his wife and mother; they had caused first three nurses and then a passing doctor to come running down the corridor and into the ward; and they ripped the lining from Mr Clarke's brother's throat.

Under the guise of a concerned relative he had rung the hospital to discover the effects and likely cause. Apparently, a mistake must have been made with the cleaning solution that they had put his brother's contact lenses in before he had gone for his operation. They had subsequently checked the liquid in his brother's bottle and that appeared normal, so they were starting an exhaustive and intensive investigation. The solution that had mistakenly been used had left the lenses undamaged but had started eating into the corneas as soon as they had come into contact with them, and unfortunately this process had bound the lenses even tighter to the disintegrating tissue. In his frantic efforts to dislodge the burning lenses, his clawing fingers and nails had done almost as much damage as the solution itself. It had taken all three nurses, the doctor who eventually had to sedate him, and his father to restrain the screaming, writhing figure, and in the struggle his stitches from the appendix operation had come undone.

His brother had left hospital two weeks later completely blind in his right eye and almost entirely so in his left. On the same day Mr Clarke had taken his eraser to the column devoted to his brother and with a firm, even rubbing action had removed him for good.

***

The dregs in the bottom of the white china cup were cold. The few tealeaves that had managed to squeeze through the strainer were disturbed from where they had settled by Mr Clarke's hands, the rhythmical rotation creating a turmoil in the cup to mirror that inside his own head. During the short time it had taken to make and then sit down and drink his tea, his mood had changed. From congratulating himself on a good mornings work, to happy reminiscing of a joyous events, the chemicals and electrics in his brain had combined to bring a darker shade to his thoughts, covering everything – especially the lighter, brighter and shinier memories and images with a thick sticky tar-like substance that spread, clung and stank.

Why was he being bombarded with doubts and fears now? Now more than ever he needed to be strong, focused, to be able to commit all his energies and efforts into the task in front of him. The task that he had been heading towards - under his own steam but with the guiding and persistent hand of the chart pulling him along when he flagged and pushing him back on the right path when he erred - for the latter part of his life. His mind, usually so strong, so resolute, was beginning to weaken. Years of careful yet regimented and ordered training and restraining was beginning to unravel just when he needed it most. Was it merely a symptom of his aging, was it the pressure of being the sole representative of the chart, the only one who was able to do its bidding, or was it simply the added strain of the immense job in front of him, with its conclusion now so close he could feel its excited, feverish breath on his perspiring brow?

It was probably a combination of all three and many, many more, the roots of which drank from such deeply hidden desires and anxieties that even in his lowest, introspective and most soul-searching moments he wasn't able to unmask and confront their true identities.

When he felt the coming surge of these negative emotions he knew that the best thing he could do to avert, deflect or at least weaken it, was to go and spend some time with the chart. To draw strength from its solidity, its tangibility; to allow its ordered rows and columns to bring calm and reassurance to his tormented mind and weakening resolve. That was why he had created the chart in the first place, or why the chart had allowed him to give it a form, shape, texture and dimensions. In his darkest moment when it looked like he would lose everything, after he had allowed himself to be infiltrated by all the negative, disgusting and violent images, thoughts and urges that ruled the lives of the majority of the people in this world; when these desires and cravings had manifested themselves into human form – a human form in a denim skirt, white diaphanous blouse and soft, red, pouting, leering, saliva glistening lips – he had temporarily become submerged, drowning in the filth that the common man must breathe and call oxygen, imbibe and term nectar. It was then, that it had been born. Created out of the depth of despair and fear. A portal with which to channel his energies, his appetites and to shape them, redirect them. Control them.

He knew that was what he must do now - go to the chart, so he could see that everything, no matter how ethereal, could be represented by numbers, graphs, bars or figures. And once you could get it down on paper, or computer screen - even scratches in the dirt, once you could see it, touch it, you could face it, tackle it and destroy it. But he realised with dismay that he didn't have the energy to stand up, never mind climb the stairs. He sat and waited, cowering under the terrific weight of the thoughts pouring into his head.

CHAPTER TWENTY-FIVE

It wasn't too often that Doug was surprised nowadays. After eight years in the force he reckoned he had seen most things, so it was becoming more and more rare for something to make him stop and raise his untidy eyebrows. Eight years of picking up the pieces of relationships that had suddenly gone terribly and violently wrong; of seeing the culmination of alcohol fuelled benders and rucks, drug addled escapades and rapes; of just horrific and unprompted brutal violence. But also he had seen the other side of the coin. In his position on the front line he had seen more acts of heart wrenching kindness, heroism and instances of blind but ultimately rewarding faith, love and complete and utter compassion than anyone had a right to see in a lifetime.

Each year of the job which he very quickly discovered was one you worked twenty four hours a day, seven days a week on – you may take your uniform off at the end of the shift, or drive home and crack open a can of beer in front of the latest woefully formulaic sitcom, but you were still P.C. Spalding – had laid down another layer of the barrier which simultaneously protected him from, and trapped him within the outside world. The world outside. That was why the older guys in the force, those that had been there for getting on for thirty years were like they were. The barriers were so thick, so unscalable that not only did everything bounce off it, escaping into your own little space away from the overheard conversations, significant looks, double takes, and seemingly random exchanges in pubs became an impossibility. Off duty no longer existed.

Almost a decade of seeing the city stripped of its marketed veneer, meant it usually took something nigh on amazing to cut through it, and though the conversation he had had with the D.C.I. earlier that morning that had ended with him being instructed to come into the office, certainly couldn't be put into the category of amazing, shocking or even that far from the mundane, it had surprised Doug. In a good way. It had gone some way to recharge his batteries, to shake some of the layers of lethargy and ennui that had settled around him like cobwebs, especially during the last two weeks or so on the O.P. The telephone call, answered by his wife while he was in the shower, was just to inform him that they had decided to move on several targets tomorrow morning, including the squat he and Lathers had been watching. As he stood listening, dripping soapy water onto the carpet, listening to his planned day of a couple of pints at the Trafalgar, followed by roast beef and then a snooze in front of the TV and football go up in smoke, he almost became excited. Twenty minutes earlier, stepping into the shower after a long, but ultimately unfulfilling lovemaking session, he would have put his house on the fact that all the hours spent sat in that bedroom on Beechcroft Road peering through the strange smelling net curtains, all the subsequent hours that lay ahead of documenting and processing the information - scant though it had been, would ultimately end with nothing. No result, no arrest, certainly not one he would be involved with.

Now it seemed he had been wrong. He thanked the D.C.I. – said he'd be in earlier than the eleven o'clock meeting to ensure all the paperwork was up to date and replaced the receiver. Towelling off his body which he had let get a bit out of shape if he was honest, he started to think that maybe everything wasn't all lost, maybe he had started to give up on his career, the whole policing idea a bit prematurely. He decided there and then, watching his once flat and hard stomach, wobble slightly under the attentions of the bright blue bath towel, that he would start going to the gym regularly again.

Thirty minutes later, sat at his desk, four thick manila files in front of him, he felt the closest he had to enthusiasm in his role for several years, and he didn't know exactly why. He had made hundreds of arrests, some violent, some involving long chases on foot, car or both, so why had the thought of struggling with the dealers he had meticulously studied, photographed and had instructed to be followed; why did the chance to push their straining limbs and pock marked faces against the wall, read them their rights, as he deftly slipped on the cuffs, so arouse him? He knew why. Uncertainty.

That one word, he now realised was the answer to the question he had asked himself hundreds of times in as many days recently. Why had he joined the police? It was the uncertainty that had drawn him to it. The thought of turning up in the morning, and tackling whatever the job the streets, the world threw at you. You didn't get that in the insurance firm. That was why, when he had started to think that he had sussed it, that he now knew the routine, that the uncertainty had gone, that was why he had fallen out of love with the job. He supposed it was like a relationship, or marriage. When it starts out it is exciting, different to what has happened before. It is only when everything becomes a routine, predictable that it can turn stale and problems occur. People then start looking elsewhere for some excitement, something out of the ordinary.

Whether today's events would be enough to wipe off the previous couple of years was doubtful, but it was certainly a start, and if he was going to compare it to a relationship, then he was certainly happy to start the courting process all over again.

Doug's buoyant mood was matched by the atmosphere in the station. It was busy for a Sunday, and it wasn't just the promise of overtime that had created the buzz. There had been significant progress in the murdered prostitute case. Every room or corridor seemed to contain an excited exchange or overloud, backslapping laughter. This was the scene presented in a thousand and one television shows and films, and Doug found himself looking around half expecting to see someone discovering their drawer to be full of sand, condoms or tampons, the victim looking up at his guffawing colleagues with a look that said "You Guys!". A happy smile stretched Doug's lips, proud to be a part of it. This was why he had joined.

Lathers did his best to dampen his spirits. He had arrived at five past eleven stinking of last night's whisky and that morning's coffee and cigarettes. All three it seemed had been taken in excess. What had happened to the day of rest? he had wanted to know, displaying the first biblical leanings in the four years Doug had known him. Bloody hell, he saw more of Doug than he did of Cath his wife, though if the grim tales that he told relentlessly were even half the truth, Doug thought that that was a reason to celebrate. The other fuckers may not have anything to do on a weekend, but he certainly did. He'd had plans. Arrangements.

The briefing didn't get started until gone half past, the D.I. being delayed by the fast-moving developments in the murder case, which took priority. He was eager to stress the importance of their operation however. Drugs was the latest bandwagon the tabloids had jumped on and the government as usual wasn't far behind. The police had to be seen to be taking an even firmer and proactive stand on what was currently seen to be the greatest evil facing the country, so funds, men and press conferences were all being diverted into that, from the previous big issue. This week looked like it would be very good for the D.I. The public all loved a murder, especially if it was someone on the edge of society, someone who didn't mix in their own circles. It was like watching a film for them, one filmed in familiar places. Like Hollywood, but with uglier, less glamorous actors.

A murder always brought the police under the spotlight, and until then they had been struggling under its dazzling glare. Now it looked like it was coming together, and if these raids went smoothly tomorrow he could see some very good publicity coming his station's, and more importantly, his way. Promotion, and even honours weren't as far over the horizon as they had seemed this time last week. It had been in this frame of mood that he had delivered his briefing to the dozen men who would be taking part in the two simultaneous raids the following morning.

An hour later everyone knew their roles. Doug had given a brief talk on the people expected to be in the squat, with the help of blown up photos, stuck to a white board behind him. They expected there to be two in the house already, and were to wait until Shafeeq - the main target, arrived. Now, if he ran to form this would be at around 10 o'clock, but - and here Doug made a joke that no one laughed at regarding the unreliability of drug dealers - obviously this time wasn't set in stone so they would be ready to go from zero eight hundred hours and would remain so until they got either the order to roll or stand down. Lathers was to be in position in the house used for the O.P. and on his word to move, the rest of the unit would set off in two cars and meet at the squat. Two officers were to go to the back entrance, the other four, including Doug and Lathers would go through the front.

He had passed around copies of the photos.

"There may well be others in the premises we aren't aware of, but there will almost certainly be these two characters." He held up two photos, one of Spoon appearing to look right into the camera, another of Danny standing outside the squat in the process of either buttoning or unbuttoning his jacket.

"This one," he held Spoon's photo up in his right hand, "Rudy Ellis, twenty-five, small time dealer, mainly in heroin, though may also have amphetamines and pills. Practically clean jacket."

He returned the photo to the table in front of him and replaced it in the air with the one of Danny.

"No definite ID on this one, though maybe Dan or Danny. Doesn't appear to be into anything too deep, more a user as far as we can tell. The tails didn't unearth any dealing, though…" he flicked through a file in front of him, looking for some notes, before giving up, "…his behaviour was described as more odd than suspicious. Obviously, you don't need me to tell you that as he is a bit of an unknown we need to be on our guard…"

"Jesus fucking Christ…."

Lathers' grumbled complaint brought him back from his ramble, something he was prone to when speaking to a group, never knowing how much information to give, and usually opting for too much.

"Has he still got his beard?"

"As far as we know, this was taken over a week ago, but he was last observed…" once more he flicked through the notes, this time with more success, "Friday, and he had it then. No reason to believe he'd have shaved it off, but always the possibility."

A pause, and then another glossy photograph was held aloft. Shafeeq resplendent, even in the black and white image, in his white knee length coat.

"Shafeeq Bari. The grande fromage as far as we're concerned," he ignored the rolling eyes gesture from Lathers, "no previous but we've enough on him to send him down until well into the next century. He tends to be there for half an hour sometimes more, but as soon as he arrives we hit the place. Doubt if he'll get violent, probably too worried he'll ruin his threads, but will more than likely be carrying a blade."

"Finally there's this guy." The photo of Terry caused a murmur of conversation and some ironic laughter.

"It's your Mrs, Sniffer" More laughter, louder this time.

"Colin Murphy, but goes by the name of Terry." Most of you will have come across him at some stage. Does some bouncing work in town. Nice enough bloke, but thick as shit and built like the proverbial exterior khazi. We'd obviously like him not to be there, but we've got to assume the worse and that he will be."

The D.I. had gone over the ground rules as usual, stressing the importance of everybody's vigilance, and full concentration at all times. The briefing had fizzled out, pockets wandering off to the drinks machine, others organising a few drinks and roast down at the Lamb and Flag. Despite his assertions to Jackie that he'd come straight home, Doug didn't want to leave his colleagues, worried that once back in the familiar and trivial surroundings of home his enthusiasm would start to evaporate. He was hyped up now more than ever, and was even enjoying the banter with Lathers, who had perked up, now they were off to the pub. He'd go for a couple, but would make sure he was back. Jackie had said she'd do the roast for six, so he had plenty of time. Besides he didn't want to get wasted – big day tomorrow.

He returned the files to his draw, locked it, and quickly worked out in his head how many long before he would be back here in the morning. Eighteen hours.

CHAPTER TWENTY-SIX

Sundays are different. Special. Even now, as the weekdays had begun to encroach and eat up the peculiarities of the final day of the week, it still managed to retain its air of aloofness. Sunday was the day when you were expected to do nothing. You were actively encouraged to rest, to relax. With Rachel, Sundays had been fantastic. Her and Mike had always stayed in bed until the early afternoon. Talking, making love, laughing. Then they would rise, eat a quick breakfast before going for a stroll, which often began, certainly featured, and invariably ended up in one of several pubs that they had designated Sunday pubs.

That Sunday, Mike's bed partner was a cricket bat. Still in the positive frame of mind he had fastened around himself the day before - a mood that was strengthened by the memories of the previous evening, and the security his new bed partner gave him, the obvious differences in his life pre and pro tape didn't affect him. Or more truthfully, he didn't let them affect him anymore. He doubted there was much more damage that could be inflicted on his Dresden-like mind, and the thought of how he would be spending the day if things hadn't gone the way they had, barely registered.

He had cooked the steak to perfection, had had to wait slightly for the oven chips to cook through, and despite his reservations had enjoyed the whole bottle of wine, before retiring to his new secure bedroom for several hours of almost solid sleep. His small steps to recovery were sure and being planted in the right direction. Another positive day today and then tomorrow he had the meeting at work, and at last he was approaching the correct frame of mind to deal with that. At least that would be one mystery cleared up, and with the regular monotony of work once more filling his days, his life would start to take on a more normal appearance. As long as he didn't invite anyone home.

His fingers worked on the foreskin like rubber sheath on the cricket bat handle, rolling it down, exposing the tightly string bound wood, and then up over the top, where it overlapped by a couple of centimetres. The rubber smell filled his nostrils, and small black specks stuck to his hands. Sitting up in bed he hefted the bat, the carpet stays screwed to the treated willow caught the light that crawled in through the dusty window. It felt good in his hands and he was torn between the desire to put it to use on the face, torso and genitals of his tormentor, and the wish for all this new part of his life, the bodies, strange voices and weapons to dissolve away into the blandness of his former one. Using the bat would mean confrontation; that things had come to a head, and even despite his newfound confidence and attitude he still wasn't convinced he held enough of the cards at this moment. Still, it did feel good in his hands.

He didn't know how much actual damage it would inflict on its victim, mainly superficial he supposed. What he was sure of however was that it would hurt. A lot. He hadn't wanted to kill anyone, just inflict pain. What he had in his hands was the perfect device for it. It would slash. Slice. Hurt. His hefts gradually became more and more ferocious, and before he knew it, he was kneeling in his bed, swinging the bat this way then that, fending off attackers with great swipes of razor sharp metal and wood. Eventually he dropped it to the bed, his chest heaving, sweat beading on his forehead. Panting he took the bat with him to the bathroom, stripped out of his boxers, locked the door and turned the shower on.

When considering his weapon, he had narrowed it down to a shortlist of three, strangely enough all sports related. The simplest had simply been a golf club. That would need no modification – something that if it came to it would look more favourable in a court of law. It would strengthen any claim of self-defence, something that may be compromised by a purpose-built weapon. He doubted if he had enough room though to fully utilise the club's potential. He envisaged any struggle would take place on top of the stairs, where there was barely enough room to swing a punch never mind an oversized driver. This left a toss-up between the cricket bat and its American equivalent, the baseball bat. In his head, the best way to turn the baseball bat from piece of sporting equipment to something that would protect his house and person would be nails. If he could find long enough nails, and hammer them through the bottom few inches, so that they radiated in a circular pattern, he would have himself something that would potentially kill. The main stumbling block for this however – and at this point when he had been weighing up his options he had suddenly pulled himself up, once more amazed at the quick turn of events in his life that had resulted in him even having to consider such details – was that when he imagined himself using it, the nail would wedge into the attackers head, chest, eye – depending on how gruesome you wanted to be – thus rendering it a single use weapon. Despite the rage simmering in his mind and body, Mike seriously doubted if he had gone far enough down the road that he could see himself putting his foot on the chest of the screaming victim, while he calmly pulled the sticky nail from his eye, only to bring it down in a looping arc into his forehead.

He had settled on the cricket bat. A good, classic symbol of England, used to protect the traditional concept of an Englishman's home as his castle.

An hour later and he was downstairs in his castle, dressed in clean t-shirt, sweatshirt and jeans, halfway through a cup of tea. He had thought twice about watching the news, associating it with the bad days of paranoia and depression of only forty-eight hours or so ago, but had relented, if as much to see what was worrying the other people out there, as much as anything else. He had missed the headlines, and the shortened bulletin was hardly inspiring, the usual mixture of cabinet reshuffles, South American air crashes, and a human interest story thrown in for good measure at the end. The local news was heralded with a burst of music that had been the soundtrack to his life for a week. The sounds and imagery of the opening titles caused his heart to simultaneously expand and race while his stomach in sympathy decided to shrink and flip. His dry, bitter tasting mouth and throat reminded him, as if any were needed that he wasn't as far down the road to recovery as he had thought. He stood up to fetch the remote to turn it off, fearful any more exposure to something so wedged into the past would set him back, and push him off the course he had so recently yet steadfastly set out on, when the words the impossibly white-toothed, wide-mouthed newscaster was saying finally made themselves known to him.

His memory frantically scrabbled around for the rewind button, the words 'arrest', 'prostitute' and 'murder' bouncing around off each other in the room like balls in some 1980's arcade game. As the images on the screen changed to what looked like a press conference, the chief of police (his face burned into the back of his eyes forever from the hundreds of press conferences he had forced himself to sit through again and again) dressed in a dark brown suit, his tie not quite pulled up to the top of his white shirt, stood up from a long table covered in a white cloth, a bouquet of microphones jutting up from its centre.

Desperately Mike tried to recall if he had heard the word 'imminent'. Were they announcing that they now had a suspect and they would be making an arrest shortly? The cricket bat was in the bathroom, fucking hell, he'd been so wrapped up in his apparent recovery he had left the only means of defence upstairs while he swanned about downstairs drinking hot beverages. He whirled around to stare at the front door, just visible through the open lounge door, fancying he could hear them amassing outside even now to come and take him, and haul him in front of the cameras and baying press. Barely had this thought manifested itself than it was overtaken by the sobering one that if they had come for him, it would be the police, and whatever his thoughts were on the strength of his case of being innocent they wouldn't be improved if he went to work on the arresting officers with a modified cricket bat. A third train of thought then came, shouldering its predecessors out of the way. They would not be having a press conference to announce that they were about to arrest someone. No matter how hungry for developments the media were, how desperate to show progress the police were, such an episode would be counterproductive at best and ludicrous at worse.

All these thoughts coursed through his head in the time it took the man in the brown suit to stand up. Mike found that he had risen as well, and was now stood in the middle of the room, meeting the policeman's stare head on.

"I am here to inform you that at nine fifteen this morning, we arrested a twenty-nine-year-old man in connection with the murder of Lorraine Maddison." The clicking of cameras sounded like a football rattle and he waited for it to die down before continuing. "At this moment in time we are not at liberty to release any more details, but will keep you informed in due course. Thank you."

Two dozen questions were fired at him, drowning out another clatter of cameras. He waited for the cacophony to die down slightly, before repeating his last sentence and then looking to his left and then right, he thanked everyone for attending and strode swiftly to his left and out of camera shot. The image of the empty table was replaced by the serious looking, if slightly smug face of the newsreader as if trying to imply she was in some way responsible for the turn of events. She assured the viewers that they would keep them up to date with events as they transpired, before moving on to details about a proposed new road layout in the centre of town.

Mike did not, could not move for several seconds. While before, his mind had been capable of galloping along at tremendous speeds, hypothesising, formulating ideas, developing them and rejecting them all in the space of a couple seconds, now it seemed that it was wading through the mental equivalent of treacle. He couldn't assimilate all this new information. He was finding it impossible to even work out if this was good or terrible news. He stared around the room, seeking help from the cream walls and kitchen linoleum.

Gradually the enormity of this news sunk in and his confusion was replaced by elation. He hadn't been arrested. He hadn't been arrested. He didn't know what he shouted, or how long he shouted for. The house, so long a mausoleum, was filled with a maelstrom of movement and noise, tears eventually slowing his movements and forcing him first to his knees and eventually to the floor where he sat, sucking in great gulps of air, his body shaking uncontrollably as sobs turned to downright weeping. His voice was hoarse, his legs ached from running and jumping and his arms and shoulders throbbed, but he had never felt this good in his life. He slowly rose, taking in the room once more, even the walls seemed to shine with a luminescence. The walls of his home. His brain, now fully recovered and eager to take on and process any information it could, decided that he should go to the Nag's to celebrate. Treat himself to a Sunday roast and a few drinks, and then he doubted if he would ever go to that pub again. It seemed to be intrinsically tied in with the events of the last fourteen days. But he did need to go in there today. If he was in one of those American rites of passage films he would refer to it as needing closure on the place, but at that moment he didn't give a shit what term he gave it, he just knew that he needed to go there to go full circle. In another physical sign that he was leaving his current life behind and returning to the more comfortable one of old, he reached for the Stanley knife in his pocket and placed it in the draw in the sideboard. Quickly he found his shoes, fastened them, grabbed his keys and jacket and headed for the door.

***

The Bedford van looked at home in the small, shadowy garage. It was the type of vehicle that looked as if it preferred its own company, away from people's scrutiny and the hurly-burly of modern life. Its red paint had faded over the previous fifteen years, and was now the darkish pink that rises to an overweight man's cheeks as he struggles to catch the bus just about to pull away from his stop. Various parts of its bodywork had been touched up, though little consideration had been given to the choice of paint, and now it looked like a colour-blind artist had attempted to give it a camouflaged look.

There was an inch clearance between the roof and the naked light bulb that hung from the ceiling, casting dark shadows into the corners of the garage and under the van itself. Shadows that shrunk and grew as the bulb swung slightly in a draft, lending the walls and floor the appearance of a living, breathing, sleeping, creature.

Today the van was not alone though, and as the cool draft - spawned from the strong autumnal wind outside - nibbled at its uneven sides and worn tyres its new owner could be occasionally heard, scraping metal on metal, pouring liquid from a smaller vessel into a much larger one. As he moved around, or merely shifted his weight, the van would rock on its suspension, the old rusty springs groaning in protest before settling down once more. It sat heavier, and lower on its haunches than it had when Mr Clarke had driven it to its penultimate resting place three days earlier, the six drums of petrol that all but filled its rear, doubling its weight.

Officially the new owner was a Mr Stephen Calderwood, but it had been Mr Clarke who had handed over the £250 in cash at the auction the previous Saturday, and then driven it to its current location. It had taken two trips to transport the doctored petrol – hundreds of polystyrene cups dissolved in normal unleaded producing the nearest thing to napalm you could get without a chemistry masters and a laboratory – and several hours to siphon it into the drums. It was at these times that he had been so grateful for the drafts that poured in from above and below the large black metal garage door. The fumes still filled the enclosed space making his eyes sting and his throat and stomach burn. He'd resorted to breathing through a wet rag, but this only stretched the time he was able to work at it, before being forced to escape into the cold fresh air outside.

The garage, also rented in the name of Calderwood, was far from perfect, he would have liked something bigger, giving him more space to work, but it was private and in a remote part of town, so he had been content to take it, particularly as it was at such short notice. The hours spent in the garage and hunched over in the back of the van in particular had taken their toll on his aging frame, and this coupled with the close fiddly work and fetid atmosphere meant his eyes, lungs and head were coming out in sympathy with his cramping fingers, thighs and back. He knew there could be no shortcuts however, it wasn't something you have a trial run with, so everything had to be done exactly to the book and tested, again and again, and then when you were one hundred per cent confident it was all perfect, tested once more. This methodical, analytical approach, was meat and drink to Mr Clarke. The promised ends that were so close now that he could smell them in the petrol fumes and feel in the yards of copper wiring, meant the means went barely noticed. This was what he wanted to be doing, what he needed. What the chart needed him to be doing. He had left behind killing pets and maiming tramps, this was what he had been training for, for the last twenty or so years. Several times recently even he had started to feel that if not his resolve or will was fading, maybe his ability to carry out the chart's wishes was, but now he was more his old self, and a few aches and pains certainly were not going to deflect him from his task.

There had been many more bad moments recently. Thoughts and urges he had hoped were consigned to history were somehow gaining strength in the deeper parts of his psyche and making themselves known, trying to get a firmer foothold, but as so often was the case, he found that throwing himself into his work was the best way to keep them at bay. Not for the first time, a part of him wondered if this increase in the doubts was down to the fact that in twenty-four hours time, there would be very little work to be done on behalf of the chart. Yes, there were minor matters that needed sorting out, trifling concerns that would always need attending to, but was it maybe that he, the chart, needed more, bigger targets to satisfy its appetite.

He cut off this line of thought, only too aware of where it would lead and bent to his task in the back of the van. In another hour he reckoned it would all be completed, so that in the morning all he would need to do was to pick the van up and drive it and its deadly cargo to its final destination.

Outside, the dim light spilled out from under the metal door and onto the concrete driveway that it shared with five other garages. Occasionally a tang of petrol hung in the air before being whipped away by the eager wind. One by one, stars began appearing in the almost cloudless sky, like grains of sand thrown onto a jet-black floor. In the distance a dog barked, welcoming the blackness, before its voice too got snatched up by the wind.

***

Spoon hadn't moved for three hours. Al, the other occupant of the room wasn't much ahead of him in the movement stakes, but while he had stirred a couple of times, his eyes had remained firmly locked shut, while Spoons' were very much open. Not that he was taking in much of his surroundings. For most of those three hours, as the half-light in the room had gradually drained out leaving almost complete darkness, the muscles in his eyes had fixed his lenses so that if there had been an object a thousand yards away it would have been in perfect focus. The calm, almost lifeless exterior belied the struggle going on in his mind. It was thirty-seven hours since his last fix. His last fix. Ever. He was convinced of it, he just needed to be strong. One thing he had learnt over the last week was that being in the business he was in was the single hardest occupation when trying to quit. It was obvious looking back, but it hadn't entered his mind that selling the stuff to people equally as desperate for the hit as him, and then barely before the money was in his back pocket watching them relieve themselves of the craving, of the hunger, the yearning, knowing that absolutely nothing else in the whole fucking world would ever be as good as what they were feeling. Watching all this several times a day, knowing that it would be so so ridiculously quick and easy and he could be down there with them, sleeve rolled up, eyes rolled back, wrapped in the gorgeously, thick warm blanket of oblivion.

But he had resisted. Just. Twice he had had to physically flee. His throat had felt like it had become too thick to let air pass through into his lungs as he'd stumbled back out into the safety of the outside world. Once he had found himself in the pub down the road, ordering double whiskies. He had necked two, and was in the process of calling the greasy haired barman over for another, the acrid taste of need not even close to being purged, when he stopped himself. He wasn't a million miles away from caving in as it was, the last thing he needed was to take something that would lower his will power even more. He heaved himself away from the bar, which seemed to have developed its own gravity field, and trudged, head thumping, skin crawling back out onto the street again. That had been five hours ago. He'd returned to the squat, relieved to find Al on his own and also that whatever he was taking that particular day looked like it was already coursing through his bloodstream so he wouldn't have to witness it. Lucky lucky bastard. Spoon had sat down on the chair opposite the settee Al was sprawled out on, and hadn't moved since. He was half afraid, that if he did get up to move, his limbs would take over and propel him to places he didn't want to go, to make him do things he didn't want to do. Or didn't want to want to do. So he had locked his limbs in place, keeping them behind a wall of the mind's equivalent of white noise. He had desperately thought of anything, not wanting to fix on anything too long lest it be poisoned and transformed into a weapon that could be used against him. Random memories from childhood merged with snippets of conversations he had had over the last week, which in turn ran up against images of ducks on a small pond and a lone figure on a swing before these blurred and became imagined episodes in a café in Spain, snow-capped mountains on the horizon.

Now three hours later, he seemed to be getting slightly better. He had feared that he had been on the top of a steep slope, and what he was experiencing at the minute was only the gentle nursery slopes. At any minute now he'd plunge headlong down the black run, down and down, further and further, until he either bailed out, or eventually hours and hours, days and nights away there would be a tiny glimmer of light. But he was definitely feeling slightly better. The urge to run up to his room, to the box in the floorboards and to take just a tiny amount, for medicinal purposes only of course, was beginning to fade.

This allowed another train of thought to gain momentum. One that had been niggling and nagging away for a while, but had seized its opportunity, spotting that its prey was weak, and had enlisted the help of its buddy paranoia that was also making hay. For a while, how long? A week, three weeks, three months? he had been half convinced that someone had been helping themselves to his gear, just a little bit here and there, not enough to allow him to confront anyone, but just enough for him and his punters to notice.

He had already made up his mind who the prime suspect was too, and though he realised it was based wholly on instinct, prejudice and a haphazard process of elimination, he was convinced in his head, at that moment anyway, sat motionless in the dark, stinking room, that if there was someone stealing his property, rummaging through his belongings, then that someone was Danny.

While his mind was trying to keep other things at bay, it had quietly been doing its duty as judge and jury, and now he was almost prepared to have it out with him. Just to ask him, face to face, judge his reaction.

On arriving back, he had - admittedly in a state of agitation, quickly gone to put his remaining gear out of, if not mind certainly reach, in his safe box. Even in his fevered, frantic state there appeared to be something different in the arrangement of the floorboards. They weren't sitting as flush as they could, something that he always ensured before leaving the room. Underneath, the box all seemed to be in order, but he did fancy it was further towards the far wall than he had left it, but about that he could not be positive. He desperately tried to picture himself earlier that morning replacing the boards, to see if he had maybe, in his anxious state been slightly careless, but it was useless. It had come such a routine that his mind didn't even register doing it anymore.

It was then that he had noticed the radio. The nasal voice of the D.J. on the local station drifted in from the room next along the small dim landing, the room belonging to Danny. Not yet ready to confront anyone, or even to properly think about anything else apart from suppressing the urges that were hatching in his stomach, before slithering through his intestines, reaching his heart and entering his blood, making it itch, thinning it out, forcing it to rush faster and faster through his aching veins, arteries and capillaries, from where they infiltrated his muscles and skin, producing twitches and sweat and a ghostly pallor, he had nevertheless found himself walking to the wooden door that stood ajar. He had hesitated in the entrance, called out Danny's name, but could see that the room as empty. The D.J. was addressing only him, personally inviting him to spend the next hour with him, as they would be playing some soothing tracks to help that Sunday lunch go down. He had turned on his heels and slowly made his way down to the lounge, where he had taken up his position for the next three hours.

He knew it was because he was feeling shit, and that he really shouldn't start to think too deeply about anything, particularly anything that was of so much importance to him. Doubly particularly about the one thing he had pinned all his hopes on, his entire future, his life on, but he couldn't stop himself. Besides, sometimes when he was in one of these moods he was able to look at things from a more objective point of view. He was able to peer through the smoke screen of denial, lack of confidence and laziness that he had erected around most things of importance in his life. Sat there in the lounge, the soft but erratic breathing of Al - someone he called a friend, but barely knew – providing accompaniment to the wind outside, he started to think that his dream of Granada was just that, a dream. Did he really believe that he could save the sort of money that he would need? Did he really think that once he was out there he would be anything different than the person he was here, in a shit smelling squat in the middle of England?

He thought about these questions long and hard. And he felt tears form in his eyes - proper tears, ones formed from emotion as opposed to his body malfunctioning because he had denied it the poison it had grown dependent on – when he could answer yes to both questions.

As opposed to letting the surroundings, his life, the people he shared it with get him down, he would use them to motivate him. With the veil of heroin lifted he would see his surroundings for what they were. Yes, he would no longer have it to protect him from the horrors, the knocks, the downright ugliness of everyday life here, but it would also open his eyes to other opportunities that were waiting to be explored, exploited. He could get a proper job, work at a bar, anything. Anything to speed his escape away from here. From this.

In this newly found mood of vitality and action he discovered he had stood up. There was one thing he needed to get sorted out, if only for his own piece of mind. Slowly, but with a determination to his steps, he mounted the stairs, two at a time, his ears straining for any noise from outside announcing the arrival of Danny. Halfway up he was greeted by Elton John, his latest ballad floating down the stairs and drowning out anything from below. Spoon, with nothing more than a glance in the direction from which he had come, carried on until he reached the door he had stood in several hours ago. Dusk had robbed the room of all its light, a small green display on the radio at the far end of the room only managed to illuminate the couple of inches of the tea chest it sat on. His left hand groped along the wall for the light switch until eventually his fingers touched plastic and the room was filled with what light the 40 watt bulb could muster.

The room sprawled in front of him. It was bigger than his own, but just had the one window, standing opposite him, sacking and cardboard where glass had once been. Two double mattresses one on top of the other lay on the floor in the corner of the room to his left, a chair sporting a fake leather jacket and the tea chest the only other bits of furniture in the room. Above him a beam traversed the ceiling, and Spoon remembered how, when Danny had first moved in, he had gone on about getting a punch bag to hang from it, and that of course everyone could use it. He had never got the punch bag, and Spoon couldn't remember the last time he had been in the room.

If Danny comes in, he was just turning the radio off, that's all. He just wanted to satisfy himself and see if he could find any evidence that he could confront him with. That's all he was doing, looking to see if anything of his was here. That's all. His eyes settled on the tea chest and he entered the room.

***

The Nag's had been busy, full of middle-aged men getting out from under their other halves' feet while they cooked the Sunday dinner; and older men, those who no longer had an other half to cook for them. His normal seat, the one that he had come to think of as his own was taken, and it took him most of the first pint to get used to his new location, tucked in the corner to the right of the window. The mood was jovial, and hearty laughter rolled out sporadically over the smoky atmosphere. Mike noticed that people were dressed smarter than they would be if it had been a Saturday. They had made a little bit more effort and he was glad that he was in, maybe not smart, but at least clean clothes. It was strange to think that the concept of Sunday best was still not dead. It was dyed deep enough into the fabric of the country and those who represented it, to still hold some sway, albeit largely subconscious as they approached the end of the second millennium.

His roast beef came a third of the way down his third pint – lots of meat, slightly too well done for his liking, but the gravy made up for it, not enough roast potatoes – and despite a temporary lull as his memory taunted him with the memories of roast dinners he and Rachel had cooked as a couple, his mood remained very upbeat. It was definitely the right decision to come here. The hours he had spent there contemplating, barely treading water in the depths of despair, asking himself, his drink, the world in general, question after question that none would ever be able to answer, came back to him as he sat there on that Sunday. But instead of shaming him, or shrinking his smile, he saw them as badges of honour. No one could have gone through what he had and not have taken it badly. Many would have fared worse. A lot worse. He had taken everything and had survived. It wasn't over yet, he wasn't naïve enough to believe that but there was definitely light at the end of the tunnel, and you never know, it may even be Rachel holding it for him.

Something occurred to him as he was mopping up the last of his gravy with a potato he had saved for just that purpose. At the time, he was amazed it hadn't come to him before, but everything had been such a shock, his mood and life had been turned so completely upside down once again in his lounge earlier, that it shouldn't have been so surprising. The person arrested may be the owner of the voice on the tape. It stood to reason it would be, after all he was the guilty party. He wondered what he had done wrong, what clue or piece of evidence he had left. All of a sudden the enormity of the task of killing the woman and getting away with it became obvious. If he had thought about it more rationally in the preceding days and weeks it would have eased a lot of his fears. Killing someone wasn't easy. Or rather, killing someone was easy, doing it and getting away with it was incredibly hard. Someone would have seen him, maybe he had been hanging around for a few days choosing his victim. Also, the car. Yes it may be stolen, or under a false name but he would have been driving it around. He would have parked it somewhere. So many loose ends, so many what ifs, and maybes. The killer must have been going through a purgatory similar to his own this past seventeen days.

Of course, if he had been arrested he may try to implement Mike in it, but as he settled down with another drink, he couldn't see how he could do that. The worst that could happen would be if he got called in for questioning and what then? He would have to decide between telling the truth or just denying the whole thing. His prints may or may not be on the car, but his scarf was on the woman's body. That alone didn't make him guilty. Scarves go missing all the time. She was a hooker, he couldn't imagine she was too averse to picking up clothes she found in pubs, off the street. Jesus, some of the things she would force herself to do, she wouldn't even give that a second thought.

The other scenario would be that it wasn't the killer who had been arrested, some unfortunate who had been at the wrong place too many times, or maybe someone known to the police and someone they wanted shot of, and this looked like the perfect opportunity. He doubted the last idea, but if the last few weeks had told him anything it was that everything he thought he knew as fact could so easily be wrong.

This once again presented him with two scenarios. Firstly that this someone arrested was charged and found guilty, in which case there may be a slight wrestling of his conscience, but he doubted it would be anything more than a very slight grapple. Secondly, he was released. Which meant that they were back to square one. But he didn't want to dwell on that; in fact he didn't want to think about any of it for the next couple of hours. He couldn't remember the last time he had thought of anything that was normal, that didn't revolve around losing his job, his girlfriend, his sanity, his freedom or his life. Yes he could. Walking from the bus stop to work on that Monday morning, half a lifetime ago. What did he used to spend his time thinking about? He honestly couldn't answer that question.

The clientele had changed, gone were those who had just popped in for a couple, now the pub was filled with your more dedicated drinker. Most of these, either on their own or in small groups of two at the most three, were in it now for the long haul. Mike had managed to reclaim his old seat and had decided to stay for just a couple more. He was celebrating. What he had to make sure he did not do was overdo it and fuck it up for himself tomorrow. His meeting was ten thirty. He would dress assuming he would be taken straight back on, but hoped that they would set a date for a couple of days' time. He would look forward to a couple of days off work where he could actually try and relax. He knew that it was not a foregone conclusion that he would be taken back on, but he knew he was in the clear, he would be in a far better frame of mind to defend himself, and at the very, very least he would be able to get to the bottom of all this.

That left one remaining stone unturned. A beautiful stone, with long black hair and a smile that went up slightly more on the left. If after all this, he did get his job back, the person arrested was the killer, but he never got back with Rachel it would still all have been an absolute disaster. Now though, he could start to channel his energies into getting her back. They had a connection, they were soul mates, whatever that meant, and though he had gone about things the wrong way – something he couldn't be blamed for under the circumstances – now his head would be right, in order to get her back. It may take time. Months, years even, but he was willing to do anything he could. It was all he wanted in his life. He had been stripped down to his bare bones with all he had been through, and he now knew more than he ever had before what he wanted, needed to make him whole once again.

He dialled her number on his phone, praying that she hadn't changed her number. His thumb hit the green dial button and he suddenly panicked and almost pressed the red one next to it, convinced that he should have a speech planned. She would know he had been drinking, she wouldn't know that it was all ok now, that someone had been arrested so they could pick up their lives from where they had been unceremoniously dropped. Why hadn't he told her the truth from the start? It was that one decision he had made, sat at this table that had ruined everything. If he could have changed one thing it would have been that. The phone on the other end rang once and then went to voicemail. Too quick for Rachel to have heard it ringing and decide to cut him off and press the button.

Shit, he didn't want to leave a message, he hated leaving messages, he always rambled and said things he instantly regretted. It was easy to backtrack, make reparations in conversation. That was impossible if you left a message. He allowed her soft voice to torture him and cut it off just before the beep. His heart pounding, palms sweaty, he downed his drink and went to the bar, stumbling slightly.

"Hi, this is Rach, sorry but I'm on the phone or just ignoring you, so leave a message and maybe I'll give you a call back." There was silence for a second then a short electronic beep rang out.

"Hi Rachel, it's me… Mike… I… I hope you are Ok. Look, I don't want to leave a message, I just want to talk to you. Please give me a call. I love you Rach… Bye."

Shit, he hadn't been able to stop that horrible pleading tone enter his voice, and he should have left the pub before calling. Shit, shit. Still he'd try her later and talk to her.

The lights reflected back off the windows, the blackness of the night pressing down and cutting the pub off from the outside world. Over the hub of conversation and clinking glasses the wind tried to make itself heard, throwing itself against the large expanse of glass. Mike was drunk. He knew he was, so that was a crumb of comfort, at least he was enough in control to realise that he was in danger of losing control. He had phoned Rachel a dozen times in the last couple of hours and left one maybe two messages. He definitely wasn't going to leave another, that would definitely be the wrong thing to do, it would just make it look like nothing had changed, that he was still spending all his time drinking. But if only she knew. There was a massive difference. Now he was celebrating, and just wanted to share the good news with her that everything was going to be all right. That he was back. The old Mike, the one she had fallen in love with, who she had wanted to spend the rest of her life with, was ready to see her again. Oh why hadn't he told her everything from the start? He made a promise to himself there and then that if, when, they got back together, he would tell her absolutely everything, everything, my god he would treat her so, so well. She would want for nothing. But he needed to tell her this; she needed to know that everything had changed.

"…maybe I'll give you a call back."   Beeep.

"…Oh hi Rach, sorry if I keep leaving messages, I'm not trying to, erm, piss you off or… errrr stalk you like…" He gave a little laugh that he instantly worried sounded false, "look something has happened, and I really, really need to talk to you. Please just call me back. I love you so much. I just need to explain something, something terrible… but now it's all Ok, I… please Rach, just let me talk to you… Bye."

Shit.

The door opened, and a group of men entered, allowing a gust of chill wind to penetrate almost as far as the bar, before being eaten up and absorbed by the warm bodies and smoke. An argument erupted briefly in the bar area on the other side of the pub; a dog that had been asleep by the table next to Mike, stood up on four stiff legs, looked around and then up at his owner before yawning, licking his chops and settling down once more to dream about whatever dogs dream about.

CHAPTER TWENTY-SEVEN

Mike was dreaming. He was banging on a large wooden door with a huge fox's head knocker. It needed both hands to lift it on its rusted hinges and slam it into the wood, into a round dent made by similar visitors over the previous centuries. Behind him the path he must have just walked up stretched and snaked down to a black sea where waves, whisked up by the muscular wind, crashed into the headland on which the castle stood. Above him the night sky pressed down, only a child's handful of stars managing to break through the dark. Just as his arms and shoulders could barely lift the brass head anymore, the giant door swung silently inwards, offering him the sight of the huge candle-lit hallway. A chandelier hung almost to the floor, its hundreds of candles barely illuminating the air around it such was the thickness of the darkness. He could see tunnels or corridors leading off to the sides, burning torches fixed to the stone walls indicating the route like cat's eyes. But Mike knew that he must go up the staircase that stood opposite him, its grand sweeping design reminding him of the folds in a Victorian lady's dress. It was up there, up its thick, carpeted steps that he must ascend to find what he had come here for.

Skirting the chandelier that was at head height, he started the climb, torches similar to the ones in the corridors shone dimly in the distance, beckoning him onwards and upwards. The stairs, twenty feet wide, curved gracefully in on itself like a corkscrew, while the walls to the side were decorated with large, dark oil paintings, mainly of hunting scenes or large deserted houses sat in rolling countryside, but every now and then there would be people or places he recognised. His old headmaster had sat astride a horse in front of a ruined church, and an old man who was often sat alone with his tumbler of whisky in the Nag's had been playing cards on a Mediterranean veranda, his large cancerous nose unmistakable.

On and on Mike climbed, his pace quickening, only too aware that he had to hurry or it would all be too late. There was crashing and banging behind him, down from where he had come, but he ignored it, intent only on what was ahead, above him, waiting for him. Eventually the staircase came to a large square space with two corridors leading from it. The smell of human excrement hung in the air, but he barely gave it any attention, not caring what its source was, or even if it was his own. Ignoring the path to the left he jogged down the other one, knowing that he was getting close now. He tried to quicken his pace but couldn't, the very air seemed to be holding him back, forming thick sticky tendrils that clung to his pumping limbs, slowing him down more and more until he was barely moving. Still he drove on further and further along the corridor that had started becoming narrower and narrower. The roof was lowering as well, until he was forced to stoop, the awkward stance hindering his progress even more. Just as he thought he could go no further, that another step would see him wedged between the four wooden walls, he came out into a room and there she was.

She was stood at the window, her back to him. She was dressed in a white night shirt that hung down to the floor and seemed to give off a faint luminescence. There was no other lighting in the room, but he was able to see the four-poster bed on his right, and a garishly ornate wardrobe standing in the corner to his left. He stood statue still, not knowing what to do, what to say, now that he had reached his destination, found what he had been searching for, for so long. Hardly daring to breathe he waited for what could have been a minute, an afternoon, a fortnight – time he had spent drinking in the new image, studying the way her hair flowed like a waterfall down her neck, how the nightshirt swayed and shimmered in the breeze coming from the open window, the breeze that didn't reach him, stood just eight feet behind her. Eventually she turned to face him, her face just with a touch of make-up exactly as he remembered. She neither smiled nor spoke, but her eyes fixed on his and slowly she moved towards him. He tried to smile but the muscles on his face wouldn't let him, nor could he get his tongue to work to speak to her, to tell her that it was all Ok, he had found her. She continued to move towards him, her perfect blue eyes gazing into his; searching for the secrets he had tried to hide from her. He found his legs moving beneath him, retreating from her, and was powerless to arrest them.

Suddenly his calves banged into something solid and he sat down heavily in a chair he hadn't noticed when he had entered the room. Still she came closer and closer until the folds of her nightshirt touched his legs. Slowly she bent forward, her arms landing on his, holding them, securing them onto the wooden armrests. She was stronger than him, far stronger and he found he couldn't move, she was pinning him to the chair. She was moving her head closer and closer to his, and he realised she was going to kiss him. He opened his mouth to receive her, and she fastened her eager lips to his. Her tongue snaked into his gaping mouth, reaching further and further towards his throat. Her tongue was huge, its rough, dry surface filling every crevice of his mouth. He tried to push it out, using his own tongue to force the hideously tasting lump of flesh away from him, but he couldn't, he was powerless against her might. He struggled and squirmed beneath her massive weight as she threatened to suffocate him. Mike woke up.

Every one of his senses bombarded him with information, meaning his first few seconds of wakefulness were spent in confusion. This was quickly replaced by downright, raw panic. He was in a room he didn't recognise, even in the semi darkness he knew he hadn't been in it before. He couldn't move his arms or legs, and something seemed to be restricting his head, though he could turn it, and thrashed it wildly from side to side, trying to see if there was anything about him he recognised, anything at all that would give him a clue as to where he was. Breathing was hard, and as he swung his attention to that, he discovered there was something jammed into his mouth, some thick cloth that was forcing his tongue painfully into the back of his mouth making him feel like he needed to gag, but not being able to. What oxygen his thumping heart needed, was having to be sucked in through his nose, in big ragged snorts. His eyes, the only part of him that appeared to have unrestricted movement, tore around the room, as his head tried to filter and prioritise all the information being thrown at it. His legs were stuck, he couldn't move them at all, or his arms, they were stuck on top of his lap. No, he could move his arms he discovered, he could move them up and down but not apart, they seemed to be stuck together. He tried his legs again, in every direction, but they wouldn't budge. He could move his body, leaning forward at the waist he had a few inches of movement, but then the thing restricting his neck would stop him from going any further, forcing his sodden torso back onto the wooden chair.

He looked at his arms more carefully, and though the lack of light made it impossible to see with any clarity, his arms and wrists seemed to be huge, as if he was wearing one of those mufflers he had seen on Christmas cards depicting groups of Victorian women. He tried again to separate them but it was useless, he was sure his hands and wrists were actually touching each other, but he couldn't move them apart.

Desperately he tried once more to move his legs, but they were bound tight, probably around the chair legs. Whatever it was around his neck didn't allow him enough movement for him to see anything below his knees. He couldn't stand either, his feet fixed just off the floor, not allowing him any leverage.

He knew it would be useless, but he tried to shout, to force some sound past through the cloth filling his mouth. He managed to produce a high-pitched hum but that made him gag for real, and for several seconds he was convinced he would swallow his tongue, and all the questions his mind was screaming would go unanswered forever.

When he could discover no more about his person, he directed his attention to the room he was in. What light there was, was coming from his right, through some small cracks, and around what appeared to be a boarded-up window. There was little else he could make out; a darker shape in front of him may have been a chest of drawers, and what was probably a bed, maybe a futon lay in the corner to his left. Unless there was someone directly behind him he was alone.

The question of where the fuck was he? slowly turned into what the fuck had happened? He couldn't remember leaving the Nag's Head. Try as he might, he could not picture himself leaving the bar, either alone or with company. He would have to go back further, try to wade through the fog that had descended on the latter part of the afternoon and evening. He could remember ordering and eating a Sunday dinner, could remember moving from lager to Guinness, it getting dark outside. He could remember leaving a message, messages on Rachel's phone, he could remember... nothing else. His evening seemed to fade out into nothingness.

***

The van's engine whined its disapproval as Mr Clarke pressed down onto the accelerator, forcing the vibrating speedometer needle towards the thirty marker. He could not have cared less about the growing line of traffic behind him, the pairs of headlights shining in his rear-view mirror, but he was conscious he did not want to draw attention to himself and his van with its deadly cargo. It was almost as hard to get it to move off a straight line as it was to get it to quicken its pace, and as he pulled on the large black plastic wheel, his arms and shoulders sung out, the stiffness of two days of hard work giving way to pain.

The drive from his home to the lock up had taken him twenty minutes, but now in the slower van, and with the onset of rush hour he had allowed for an hour, and glancing at his watch it looked like he wasn't going to be far wrong. Two motorists saw their chance on a straight stretch of road and accelerated past, the first one making a point of looking into the cabin, seeing if he could make out who it was that had cost him an extra five minutes on his journey to work. Mr Clarke ignored him, behind his glasses and under his cap and scarf he was practically invisible, without looking out of place. The morning was cold, the biting wind forcing the temperature closer to zero than it had been for several months, and the heater in the van looked like it hadn't worked for years.

In his head he went over every minute part of the plan, mentally ticking off each task. Finally, as he turned the van into more familiar territory, he was happy that everything was prepared. He felt good. Very good. He guessed this was what excitement was, though there were nerves as well. He didn't want to let the chart down. He was convinced that he had done everything possible to ensure the smooth running of the plan, but there were always outside influences that could, even now derail everything. From parking up, to setting the timer, it would take twenty seconds. He had done it countless times the evening before. One of the reasons he had chosen this van was the fact that he could access the back from the driver's cabin. The timer was set for thirty seconds. He had agonised over the optimum length, and had settled on half a minute. He needed long enough to get out and away, but didn't want enough time for anyone to investigate what the van was doing or look into the back. It wouldn't take a genius to see what it was. If he was noticed leaving, the confusion the explosion would create would allow him to disappear, arriving back in his car later in the morning to survey the devastation. Dry mouthed, he depressed the clutch pedal, and after a momentary struggle with the gear stick pulled it back into the seven o'clock position and pulled down on the indicator, signalling his intention to turn left, into Beechcroft Road.

**

The twelve men filled the operation room, perched on tables, slumped on the plastic chairs or just leant against walls. A fog of cigarette smoke hung in the air gradually made its way towards the window that had just been opened, allowing the cool November air in. It was always like this before any operation, but particularly one where there was the possibility of trouble. By the sound of it the other property being targeted was much more likely to end in violence, but even at the squat Doug and the rest of the small team had to be prepared for the worst-case scenario.

He was hot under his stab proof vest, and he was glad for the open window. It was at times like this he really wished he smoked. If only for the opportunity to do something with one of his hands. He contented himself with drumming them on the Formica table in front of him. Beside him Sniffer pretended to be lost in the tabloid he had brought in, though Doug had noticed he had been on the same page for getting on ten minutes. Everyone was in the same boat, waiting. Waiting for the call from Lathers that would set both teams on their way. This is when the nerves, the excitement was at its worst. Once the call came in it was fine. The training took over everything meaning actions and even emotions were automatic. It wasn't until later, often hours later at the debriefing when the fear set in again, when the realisation that you had just been in very real danger hit home.

People handled the nerves differently. Some went into themselves, finding it virtually impossible to interact with their colleagues or even to hold down a proper conversation that didn't revolve around the coming operation. Others put on a show that everything was normal, that they were in no way effected by the thoughts of what could be about to transpire. This demonstrated itself in over exuberant displays of backslapping good humour, the members of this second group drifting together, gaining yet more bravado from the apparent good humour of those around them. Doug was very much in the first group and the raucous antics being played out in the middle of the room was beginning to irritate him.

He had stayed out longer than he had planned and hoped the day before, arriving home at closer to seven o'clock than six to a fuming Jackie and a deliberately burnt roast. He had eaten what could be salvaged while listening to his failings as a husband. Eventually he had snapped and gone to bed falling asleep an hour later, Andy McNab's Bravo Two Zero open on his chest.

The telephone rang, the shrill tone cutting through the conversation and bouncing off the walls. D.C. Davies, the nearest to it, grabbed the black receiver, aware twenty-four eyes bored into his forehead.

"OK, excellent... I'll tell the lads." He looked up, taking in the expectant faces, drawing out the moment. "Bacon sarnies are here lads."

A cheer went up from those standing in the middle, Sniffer went back to his tabloid and Doug continued to drum his fingers on the table.

CHAPTER TWENTY-EIGHT

His racing heart, panicking brain and bewildered senses meant it was almost impossible for Mike to judge how long he had been conscious for. The amount of light seeping through and around the boarded-up window to his right had gradually increased, and he could now make out the outline of a door to his left. He had discovered that the cloth in his mouth was being kept in place by another cloth, wrapped bandana-like around his head, tied at the back, while the thing restricting his head and neck was coarse and went up behind his head, fixing him in place like a dog on a leash. A poor return for all his brain's desperate questioning and his eyes' exploring. No sounds seemed to be coming from elsewhere in the house and he was now convinced he was alone in the room. Occasionally a car engine on the road below would drift up to his straining ears, but they always went on past oblivious to his situation only yards away. Twice more he had attempted to make his presence known, both attempts only resulting in a squeal that barely left the room while at the same time the resultant heaving and coughing sucked the thick cloth further into his throat.

Suddenly he was aware of a new noise, a muffled padding that seemed to be coming from below and to the left of him. He strained around in the chair, the coarse leash on his neck biting into his already raw skin. Someone was coming up the stairs. Towards him. The thought that maybe this person would be coming to his aid, to his rescue didn't even enter his throbbing brain. The steps were too deliberate, too steady. The owner of them knew exactly what was in this room. Despite his discomfort, the pain, at that moment Mike would have given anything to remain in that limbo forever. He no longer wanted answers to the questions his mind had been screaming to the empty room moments earlier. The footsteps came closer, the wood creaking under their owner's weight. The noise changed slightly as they reached the landing, but continued until they were outside the door. Mike's chest heaved, the combination of his thumping heart and snorted breaths now drowning out the noise from just the other side of the door. His eyes, locked on the light framed entrance tried to bore through the wood, desperate, but at the same time terrified to see the solid, real life manifestation of what he knew would be the owner of the voice on the tape.

He had paused outside but then, the door was pushed inwards towards Mike's seated, sweating body and a figure was silhouetted in the doorway. It wasn't as bright in the landing as Mike had thought, and it was impossible to make out anything of the figure other than it was a man, and he seemed to be about the same height as Mike. He could detect the tang of excrement now, over his own sweat, either carried in on the standing figure, or merely just from the house in general. The smell brought back a fleeting image of his dream, and he momentarily thought of castles and the crazy image of his headmaster flitted through his head.

The figure in the doorway hadn't moved, maybe letting his eyes get used to the semi darkness, then in one quick, smooth movement he lifted up a small black object and pointed it at Mike. The room was filled with light. White blinding light that seemed to be so complete, so overwhelming that it had its own sound, feel and smell. The light poured into his huge pupils, forcing his head back as far as the restraint would allow. Twice more the black object exploded with light, and Mike, convinced he had been shot welcomed the quick ending, relieved that there would be no more uncertainty, no more waiting. He almost relaxed, ready and waiting for the pain and oblivion that would surely come any micro second now. But didn't. Laughter filled the room instead, and just as he realised that he hadn't in fact been shot, he saw that the figure had moved. The doorway was empty but his eyes could see no more. His vision was filled with a hundred suns, each trying to outshine the others. Thankfully his ears came to his rescue, and he could hear the man behind him, still chuckling. Two more flashes in quick succession came from behind and then to his right and he realised the black object had been a camera. Snot, freed by the force of his breathing hung down in two bucking strings onto his chin, while his hands and feet clenched and unclenched uncontrollably, his bound tendons, ligaments and muscles trying to make up for their lack of freedom.

The figure seemed delighted by the display and was walking slowly around the chair, stopping occasionally to let out a chuckle or peer more closely at some part of his captive before continuing on his small circuit. He stopped at the dark object that could have been a chest of drawers and put down the camera.

"Oh Michael, if only you could see yourself." Another laugh, longer this time. "Come on man, pull yourself together, what would Rachel think?"

Though it was different in real life, it was unmistakably the same voice he had listened to in his bedroom, the voice that had told him he had a surprise for him.

Once again he set off, but this time he went to the wall next to the door he had entered a couple of minutes earlier and flicked the light switch. Once again light flooded into the room, but this time it was softer, less harsh. His eyes locked onto those of the man standing ten feet in front of him, and despite the beard and ten years of aging – ten years that could easily be twenty judging by the damage they had wrought – recognised him.

Danny, or Carl Baker to give him his real name, stood there, allowing his image, his identity to be wholly absorbed by Mike. Silence once again returned to the room, and Mike didn't know whether to be relieved or not. He thought seeing the face of his tormentor would be a good thing and had assumed knowing him and hence being able to categorise, pigeonhole him, would at least allow him an educated guess on what else he may be capable of, or even give Mike a clue on how he could defeat him. Seeing Carl Baker there however did nothing to help him. His jaw would have dropped if it hadn't had a cloth tied around it.

Carl looked pleased with himself. He just carried on looking at Mike, a smile fixed on his face, nodding slowly, either affirming questions being asked in his own head, or simply answering the question that was written all over Mike's contorted face – Carl Baker? Eventually he broke the silence, his voice coming in quick excited bursts.

"How are you Michael? You look like shit. Surprised to see me?" He resumed his pacing, round and around the chair, Mike trying to keep

298

him in his vision for as long as he could in one direction, before whipping his head around to the other side to follow him again.

"Cat got your tongue Michael?" Despite his grin the words were spat out, and the laugh sounded forced and false.

"Now we're going to have a little chat Michael, and what I'm going to do is take that cloth from around your mouth. What I don't want you to do is to try and do anything stupid. You can shout as much as you want, no one will hear you, there's just you and me in the house, and all that will happen is you will make me angry. And as you can see…" he stopped his pacing, stood still and spread his arms in a gesture that took in the whole situation, a smile - a more genuine one this time etched into his face. "…I'm holding all the cards, so…" The open arms turned into a shrug and he allowed the threat to tail off, continuing his procession and stopping when he reached the spot behind the chair. Mike could feel clumsy hands on the back of his head. This was good, this was definitely good. The initial blind terror had downgraded itself to good old-fashioned fear. Carl baker was no homicidal maniac. The evidence suggested he had gone slightly awry since they had known each other at school but that was all. A little chat he had said. He was going to scare him, teach him a lesson, get his own back for… he tried to dust off the parts of his memory where the file marked Carl baker was stored.

With a final tug the pressure around his mouth was eased and using his tongue he spat out the cloth from his mouth, sucking in great lungful's of fetid but beautiful air. Almost immediately he was yanked up, as the coarse leash around his throat rose and tightened slightly, lifting him and the chair a couple of inches off the ground before setting him down again so the front two chair legs just rested on the floor. The leash, which he now realised, was a rope sat under his chin, tight around the top of his neck and below his ears.

"Now Michael, as you can see, or rather feel, you've got a rope, a noose around your neck. All I need to do…"

The rope, coming down from the beam in the ceiling, where it was threaded through a hook and then down into the hands of Carl, lifted the chair once more off the floor, tilting with Mike's legs tied to it, forward. His mouth was slammed shut, a strangled cry escaping from between his straining lips. Instinctively his hands reached for his throat but the fingers were forced too tightly together for him to grip the rope. He hung there for two, three seconds, the rope eating into the soft flesh around his jaw, before the pressure was reduced and he slammed back down, first onto the front legs, then all four.

"…is pull slightly on this rope and… well you can see what happens. Just in case you feel like shouting."

Once again getting his breath back, Mike studied his arms. They were joined from the elbows to almost the end of his fingers, and seemed to be encased in a thick blue foam, the sort you would expect to be used to lag pipes. Around this foam, which was almost six inches thick, a thin black twine had been used to join the arms, hands and wrists together. Why go to such over complicated lengths was just one of a hundred questions that would have to join the back of an ever-increasing queue.

"Surprised to see it was me Michael?" The words, coming from behind his head, were spoken in a calm, almost conversational manner. Another question, shouted to be answered - was this good? Was it good he was calm, did that indicate madness, after all he had a man, an old friend for god's sake, tied up in a chair with a fucking noose round his neck. No sane person would be calm. On the other hand maybe calm was good, he was less likely to do something irrational like… like kill him. Yes calm was good he decided, just as he was jerked up once more, the skin from his Adam's apple being ripped off.

"I asked you a fucking question Michael, don't ignore me. Are you surprised to see it is me?" He let the rope slide through his hands, not noticing the burn, and Mike and the chair crashed to the floor, rocking for several seconds before settling on all four of its legs. Carl picked up the slack once more and put just enough pressure on the rope so that the noose slid up under Mike's chin.

"Yes, yes… very surprised Carl." Mike gasped, once more sucking in air, his hands, complete with twine and lagging, held out in front of him as if to ward of any further attacks.

"There, that's more like it, isn't it, a proper conversation. Like when we used to be at school. "

Not knowing if any response was expected of him, he nodded briskly.

"What would you like to talk about Michael?"

"I... I don't mind Carl"

"I don't mind Carl" Carl repeated it in a high-pitched mocking voice. "Jesus, you really are a pathetic fucker aren't you Michael? I get you sacked from your cushy little job; make your girlfriend despise you; make you the chief suspect in a particularly grisly murder; turn you into... turn you into a..."

Mike could actually hear his head and tongue struggling to find the right words.

"Look at yourself, you're just a pathetic little shit, look at yourself." Carl had let go of the rope now and was face to face with Mike, leaning forward, his face only inches from his captive's, imploring him to carry out some introspection. Mike's already frantic mind moved up another gear, as he spotted his chance. He could shout now, give it two maybe three good cries for help, and pray he was lucky before Carl could rush back round and pull the rope. Or, and this idea really tempted him, if he was to lunge forward, did he have enough freedom to reach the leering face in front of him? Could he get his teeth around his nose, bite down on the bone and gristle, maybe using his bound arms to twist his neck, break it, or just go on biting and eating away into his face until there was nothing left?

No sooner had the idea materialised than Carl had stood up and returned to his position behind the chair, the rope once more pulling up on Mike's chin and ears. Next time he thought, next time I'll bite the fucker. Just fail to stroke his ego enough for him to come around and take a look at his handiwork, just tempt him enough to put that face of his a little bit closer.

"OK, Carl. You obviously want me to ask you why you did it, or even how, so you could go on and describe just how fucking clever you are but I don't... unnnngggghhh"

The noose jerked up, three times lifting the chair off the floor. His head had started to boom, and something in his neck felt like it had snapped or torn.

"Don't be a clever cunt Michael. Look at yourself, I can do anything I want to you, absolutely anything, so don't even try to be... don't even start being a clever fucker." His voice was shaking in anger, this Monday morning was not going the way either of them had planned.

Despite his current situation, Mike found himself thinking that this latest turn of events would mean he would miss the meeting with Jackson at work, then something Carl had said came back to him. So, it was all linked – the job, the Ford Orion, even Rachel, and despite himself he did want to know what had happened. What he was accused of, how in the space of three short weeks Carl Baker had managed to ruin absolutely everything he held dear in his life.

"OK, OK, OK, how? How, no, what did you do? More importantly," He tried but failed to turn his head to look at the heavily breathing man behind him, to study his face, bore into his eyes, for... for what? Weakness? Guilt? He didn't know. "Why, Carl, why me?"

"WHY? WHY?" The words were screamed, each one accompanied by a pull on the rope. "You are fucking joking with me..."

"What the fuck have I done that..."

His head was yanked backwards once more but this time it was by his hair. He could feel Carl's hot erratic breaths on his scalp, and his anger meant he could barely pronounce his words.

"You ruin two people's lives… kill one person… and it doesn't even register… you're a bigger piece of shit than I thought." Mike's head was yanked up by the scalp in time with each of these last words, while inside it, his mind went back to the file marked Carl Baker, sweaty feverish hands desperately rummaging through it. They had been friendly without ever being friends. Carl had been just another average, awkward schoolboy just like the other hundred or so average, awkward schoolboys in that year. Maybe he had a few less friends, maybe he had been slightly more awkward in his own skin, more solemn than his peers, but it was very hard to look back without any impartiality now that he had him tied to a chair with a noose around his neck. But there was one thing, something that was starting to appear up through the thick smoke of time.

Carl was back in front of him now, facing him, incredulity struggling with anger for sole possession of his features, but this time he was standing two meters away, far too far for Mike to reach him. He would have to draw him near, risk taking a beating. His best chance, maybe his only one was to get him close enough for a strike and then just hope that six years of neglected dentistry could do the rest. At the same time he was desperately trying to blow away the smoke surrounding the niggling piece of information that he had about the bearded man stood with clenched fists in front of him. Then it came to him, in all its sickening clarity. Carl had slept with his own sister. Or had…

"Because of you Michael…" Each word, was delivered through tense, straining lips. He was having to control their release, let each one off the reigns individually, or there would have just been a torrent, a vile champagne cork explosion, a champagne that had sat and fizzed and rotted for years desperate to have its freedom. "Because of you… you and your disgusting little mind… meant I was fucked. My sister died because of you. I almost killed myself because of you. Because of you, I had people spitting at me in the street. Because of you…" The reigns were getting looser, the words coming quicker and louder, "No cushy little job for me Michael, no university degree for me, no girlfriend, no nice little terrace house in suburbia for Carl Baker. Because of you and your lies, your…your…your fucking lies Michael I was fucked. Because of you Michael, Lorna, she was only fourteen for fuck's sake had to read the graffiti about her on the walls by the park. She had to listen to the phone calls, see the letters, hear the abuse by people who she didn't even know. People who didn't even know her for fuck's sake." He was getting closer to Mike now, almost in touching, biting distance but Mike no longer was thinking about clamping his teeth around Carl's nose. He remembered perfectly now.

"Because of you Michael my childhood, my fucking life ended when I was sixteen. Lorna's when she was fourteen. We couldn't go out, we had each other and our family, sat in that house every day, every fucking night waiting to see if the phone would ring, waiting to see if some gang of boys, people who I had called my friends a year before, pissed up in a phone box decided to call us up to abuse us." He was quieter now, but tears were starting to flow down his cheeks, into the brown hair sprouting from above his grey lips.

"Because of you Michael my mother had a breakdown. She couldn't understand why people would do such things. Not to her two precious children. Why did they write such things, say such things? Was it something she'd done wrong? It was because of you Michael that Lorna ran away when she was fifteen. Why she ended up in a squat in Brighton fucking anyone who would smile at her, give her attention, show her that maybe for five minutes everyone wasn't a complete and utter bastard. Why she started injecting anything that she could get to block out the memories of the sneers, laughter and violence that she had done nothing, NOTHING to deserve. It is because of you Michael that three years ago she was so desperate to block them out she injected herself with a dirty, rusty, broken needle. Because of you she got septicaemia. It is because of you that she died Michael, and because of you she was left there in that dirty disgusting squat for two fucking weeks before she was discovered."

"That is why Michael. THAT is why."

Mike thought that over the last two weeks he had experienced every emotion, and he didn't think there was anything else in the bank. But he was wrong. Self-disgust was now wrapping itself around him, eating into his skin, his eyes, boring down through his stomach into his guts and entrails. This was worse than the fear, than the terror that he had lived with. Because this time he couldn't focus his rage on anything, anyone else apart from himself. He could remember it perfectly now, the rumour – the lies Mike, don't dress it up as rumour – he had started, he had told, for no reason other than… what? He couldn't even remember why he had told people that Carl Baker used to fuck his sister. He had said it, written it, laughed about it and then moved on with his life, hardly noticing the events that he had set in motion. He had left the town to continue with his life a year and a half later, completely unaware of the two that his words had ruined.

"Shit Carl... I'm... I am so so..."

"Sorry Michael? You're sorry. YOU'RE FUCKING SORRY?" His head was pressed against Mike's now, his eyes boring into those of the man he had tied to the chair, spit that had accompanied each and every word flecked on his captives crumpling face.

He stood up and walked away a couple of paces before turning around. "Well that's all Ok then isn't it? Michael Burley says he is sorry. It was all a bit of a laugh really and he didn't mean any of it. I tell you what, let's forget all about it and carry on where we left off shall we? NO. We can't do that because my life is screwed and Lorna... Lorna hasn't got one anymore."

Silence filled the room once more, stretching out into each corner, every little nook, dent and scratch on the walls. Mike sat there, the pain in his neck, the pins and needles in his arms and feet forgotten. He was back at school, back where all this had started. He had thought it had all begun in Jackson's office that Monday morning. It hadn't. It had begun outside the physics lab fourteen years ago. He could see Carl now, alone in the classroom, the question "Why?" "Why him?" permanently on his face. Dreading the breaks, the lunch hours, the times when the loners, the victims, those that for some reason had been chosen and singled out as different could no longer hide. While everyone else surrounded themselves with the safety of their peers, wearing their cloaks of normality with pride, they cowered, yearning for a time when they too could dissolve into the background and become like those that mocked them. Become normal.

"I don't know what to say Carl."

"Do you know how long I've been waiting for this moment? How many nights I've dreamed about this? While you've been out getting university degrees, having girlfriends, worrying about what tie goes with which shirt so you wouldn't stick out at work... while you've been living Michael, I've just been dreaming about this moment. I used to go into your house and sit there. Sit in your lounge, on your settee watching your television drinking tea from your mug. Then I'd have to leave, because that wasn't my life Michael, that was yours. And I would come back to this... this shithole. I didn't think I could get any more angry. I thought that what I'd been going through for the last fourteen years was as bad as it would get. But I was wrong. Seeing what you had, what your life was like, compared to what was left of mine... I knew then that I was right. That whatever I did to you, however much I fucked you up it wouldn't be enough."

Mike sat there taking this all in, his heart, despite himself going out to the man who, for the last three weeks he had wanted to grind his face into the floor with his foot. He had to pull himself out of this. The recriminations could come later, what he had to do was to ensure that there was a later. He had to get back that anger, use it to get him out of this room, to kill if necessary the man in front of him. The man who had killed an innocent woman, slashed her stomach and bundled her into the boot of a rusting car. It wasn't hard. He forced the images, the recollections imagined and real back down. He could beat himself up with those when he was free, after he had got out of this house and into a police station.

"Whatever you do now Carl it isn't going to bring your sister back. It isn't going to bring the last ten years back. It's just going to mean that you'll never be able to live a normal life. To do what I've done. You can't go around killing people Carl for fucks sake. There is no way in the world you're gonna get away with it and then you're in prison. Is that what you want? What you need is to put all this..."

"Don't you tell me what I need to do." The words were yelled at Mike, and were followed by his fists, first his left then his right catching him on both cheeks. The chair with Mike on it toppled backwards under the force, and the rope, loose on the floor couldn't stop it crashing onto the thin-carpeted floor. Standing over him he glared down into the red face staring back up. "Don't you ever tell me what I can and can't do."

"What about the woman you killed? She was somebody's sister, somebody's daughter."

"Do you think I give a shit about her, about some cheap whore, about anyone? I don't even care about myself Michael. The only person, thing, in this whole world that concerns me is you, and how I can cause you as much pain, of how I can destroy every little part of you. To completely ruin you and your life and everything that everyone has ever thought about you. Do you know how I'm going to do that Michael? Go on have a guess."

From this angle, looking up into Carl Baker's face, he changed his mind about him. He looked every inch the homicidal maniac. He didn't want to know what was going to happen. He didn't want to guess. He just wanted to close his eyes and for everything to disappear. To wake up three weeks ago. Fourteen years ago.

He waited and opened his eyes, but he was still there. Still in the house that smelled of excrement. Still tied to a chair, on his back staring into the manic face of Carl Baker, someone he had gone to school with. Someone whose life he had ruined, and whose sister he had as good as killed. His next chance, maybe his last one, was going to be when Carl lifted him back onto the chair legs. He'll get him to right him; he seemed to want to talk to him, describe how clever he had been and to justify to both of them the things he had done. That is something that was best done with him sat on the chair resembling something approaching a normal human being, as opposed to like this – a beetle dying on his back. As he pulled on his arms and hands, he would use his weight, the chair's weight, to pull him back onto him and bite him, eat him. He no longer cared if he had to devour his whole fucking head - he had to get out of this house in one piece. Alive, he'd settle for alive.

"I asked you a question Michael. What do you think is going to happen? Come on, all your university degrees, all your... friends, your girlfriend," a smile slithered across his face, a smile formed of malice not humour, "sorry your ex-girlfriend, none of them can help you now Michael. Just you and me, so come on have a guess."

"Come on Carl, I can hardly fucking breathe like this, pull me up and we'll talk." He waved his big blue hands in the air. He could see Carl looking at him, through him, deciding what to do. Eventually, he stepped aside and picked up the rope, lying forgotten to Mike's left. It snaked up to the beam directly above his head before leading back down, down to and around his neck.

Like a man in a tug of war match Carl pulled on the inch thick rope, pulling with one hand then the other, the strain pulling Mike, chair, lagging, booming head, thrashing heart and straining neck and all, up, up, up until the chair was on its back legs, then as he eased the pressure it toppled down onto all four. The rope, leaving an impression of itself under Mike's chin and in the softer flesh of his upper neck, settled back down resting on his bobbing Adam's apple. Mike fought back the tide of unconsciousness that he could feel surrounding him, like a thick black cloud just over the horizon. The muffled cry that had squeezed from him, echoed in his ears, joining the drummer's heartbeat rhythm that had set up shop inside his head.

"This is fantastic, everyone should have one of these in their homes. Man on a rope. Shit on a rope." His hollow laugh filled the room, as he moved to the side of Mike, still holding the rope loosely in his hand. Mike breathing hard, tried to move his head and shoulders to restore some circulation to them; tried to ignore the screams for attention from his hands, wrists, arms, legs, ankles and feet.

"It's weird how easy it is to completely ruin someone's life. I mean I don't have to tell you that Michael do I? You're the master of it, you managed to do it, ruin two people's lives with just a few words. I wasn't that lucky, I had to try a bit harder, work at a few more things, but still, in the face of it, it was still pretty bloody easy. You see I didn't want to just destroy your life now I… I had to destroy everything that people think, thought about you. Rewrite the history for Michael Burley. Ask anyone who went to our school about me and they'll say one thing. Slept with his sister. Sister shagger. No matter what I had gone on to do, cure cancer, world peace, heavyweight champion of the fucking world, yeah not bad they would say, but he still shags his sister."

"That's what I'm going to do to you. Get rid of this nice bland boy image you think you've got of yourself, and replace it with a new one. One that isn't so nice. One that will have those people who had called you a friend, a lover, a son, look at themselves with disgust, feel like they need to cleanse themselves from your presence. And do you know what Michael? It's easier than you think."

"Five years ago I went to jail, not for long, almost a year. I take it you've never been to prison Michael?"

Mike found himself shaking his head.

"It's not that bad, no worse than this shit hole and the pathetic fuckers who live here. It's amazing what you learn in there. It's like the fucking boy scouts in there, except everyone is trying to fuck you not just the scoutmaster. Those eleven months taught me so many things Michael. How to kill people, maim people, blind people. There are so many things you can do with, to the human body Michael you'd be amazed. It taught me how to break into a building, escape from a building, blow up, burn a building. Break into a car, blow up a car, crash a car to kill your passenger and yet walk away unharmed. It's like the boy fucking scouts for the real world. I came out feeling like I was in the SAS, but there was only one war I needed to fight, and that was the other thing I learned in there. Twenty-two hours in your cell gives you time to think Michael. Properly think. When I went in, I hated you, of course, but I had no idea what to do with that hate. I didn't know where you were, where you'd gone, if you were even in the same fucking country. I had some vague plan of finding you and just beating the shit out of you, I don't know blinding you or something, but that was it, nothing more solid than that.

"Those eleven months, go on Michael, you've got the fucking degree you can work out how many hours that is… I decided what I needed to do. I planned it all, in that shitty cell, listening to my nigger cellmate farting and snoring and threatening to break my fucking legs if I didn't massage his shoulders every evening. Down to every little detail. I had so many back up plans, so many plan b's, c's down to fucking plan zeds. All I had to do was to find you, track you down, and then follow you around, get to know you, what you did, how you lived. And then I would strike." A laugh, a genuine one burst from his mouth, "Oh and how I struck Michael." He walked around behind Mike and stood on the other side, wanting to pace, but not wanting to let go of the rope. "Tell me one thing, what did your work say to you when they sacked you? Did they spit at you Michael, shout at you?"

"No… why, what the fuck did you do?"

"Just some pictures, hundreds of pictures over a couple of weeks, from three different email accounts. Pictures you had obviously requested, paid for, to feed your disgusting needs."

"Pictures… what sort of pictures…?" But as he asked the question Mike was starting to guess exactly what type of pictures. The scene in Jackson's office came sharply back into focus.

"Young girls, Michael, very young, and boys. Doing the type of things that you would have done to the lovely Rachel on that big bed of yours with the stripy blue duvet."

Mike was only half listening now; his head was whirling, as missing jigsaw pieces slotted into place.

"It was obviously all meant to be Michael, because everything worked like clockwork. I was thinking I was going to have to post the tape through your door, because obviously the timing was crucial, we couldn't leave poor Lorraine all alone in that car boot for long could we? Or someone else might discover her first. But you were so, so predictable Michael, and into the Nag's Head it was, wasn't it? Do you know what the hardest thing was?" The words were pouring out unchecked now, his hands were flexing on the rope, his eyes roaming all over the face of the man in front of him. This was the best moment of his entire life.

"The hardest thing was to get some disease from the whores that I could give to the lovely Rachel. British whores aren't as pox-ridden as the tabloids would have you believe Michael, let me tell you. But eventually I found someone, dirty enough, filthy enough and as a reward I slit her stomach for her. But of course, that was you wasn't it Michael, you murdered the poor girl, only on the streets to pay for the shit she pumped into her arms, though I suppose she would have moved away from her arms years ago, she'd be onto her thighs by now. Or maybe her groin.

"I wasn't sure if it would work, it wasn't essential that the lice, the crabs whatever they are survived long enough in the clothes, the sheets I spread them on. If it did work it was the icing on the cake so to speak. I saw you coming out of the pub one day scratching yourself like some sort of mangy dog, and I knew that I could do no wrong. Everything I did turned to gold. I doubt if there is a god Michael, after what he let you do to me, to Lorna, but if there is, then maybe he feels guilty for what he let happen and he's certainly helping me right the wrongs now. My only regret is that I couldn't witness the arguments, the screaming, the tears. I was hoping for a more public break up Michael, but I suppose we are English aren't we and we don't like to wash our dirty washing in public.

"Even when they arrested some poor fucker yesterday it worked out perfectly. The final part of the plan, Michael… all this," the rope still gripped in his left hand he spread his arms, indicating the room, the chair, Mike, everything, "I thought this would be the hardest part. I thought I was going to have to get this thick twat Terry I have to deal with sometimes, to help me get you to the house. It's not even his real name Michael. No one in this shithole has a real name, it's as if they're ashamed of who they are and just make up a new name. That's probably why I fitted in so well. You see I'm Danny here Michael. This is Danny's room. These are Danny's hands on this rope around your neck. But you can be sure of one thing. It is Carl Baker who is going to end all of this."

He walked around to the other side of the chair again, Mike's head snapping around to follow him. "But no, even that was all so so easy. When I heard yesterday they'd arrested someone, my first thought was that it may have been you. I watched your house, and then saw you coming out, looking very proud with yourself. What were you doing

Michael, celebrating? Celebrating that this nasty little affair was all over and that someone else was going to go down for the murder that you had done?"

Panic was making it almost impossible for him to take in any of what Carl was saying, he was able to get snippets, but his brain seemed to be working on a different timescale than the room he was in. Thousands of thoughts were entering his head every second, and he was having to sort through all of them in an attempt to come up with some way, some plan of how the fuck he was going to get out of this. He had heard that in times of great stress, the human body is capable of incredible feats of strength. There were cases of mothers lifting crashed cars all on their own to save their child trapped underneath. He didn't have to lift any vehicles; he just needed to break some string. He strained every possible inch of muscle, of tendon and ligament, pulling on every drop of energy, blood and will in his cramping body, concentrating on first his arms, then his legs then everywhere. He pulled and strained until he was convinced his eyes were going to fly out of his head, that the blood vessels in his face, in his neck would burst, decorating the room with his thick oxygenated blood, or that his limbs would simply break and come apart, leaving the lagging and twine in position, but still he carried on. But nothing happened. He was still tied to the chair, his arms still sat uselessly on his lap.

"All I had to do was wait for you to get pissed. At one point Michael I was standing about ten feet away from you watching you speaking on the phone. God you sounded pathetic." He put on a whining voice, "Please Rachel, I love you Rachel, I need to speak with you, something big has happened. "I couldn't have scripted it better. If you had turned around you would have seen me, and we would have had a chat like old school buddies. I thought that was what I was going to have to do, but you leaving your drink on the table every time you went for a piss meant I didn't even have to lower myself to talk to you. One of the advantages of living with these wankers is that it's like living in a fucking chemists. Every time you went for a piss, I just borrowed your ashtray and put just enough shit in your drink to make you pass out at the table. People pass out in that place every night, you were just another sad bastard trying to find an answer, some happiness at the bottom of a glass.

"They'll find you today, maybe tomorrow hanging in this room, having decided to end your pathetic life. They'll also find some injection marks on your arms, but that will just be one other small part of your life, of Michael Burley, that no one knew existed. It won't be hard to piece together what happened. Finally your perversions, your tastes that will never sit at ease in a normal society caught up with you. Your relationship had ended as well, so you turned to harder drugs. Rumours will spread I'll imagine that it was something you had been hiding for a while, after all, look at what else you had managed to conceal from your parents, from Rachel. Maybe it was all these things, maybe it was guilt about the poor street worker you butchered, no one will know for sure, but after a while, do you know what Michael?" His face was getting closer now to Mike's, he could feel and smell his breath on his face, and see how the hair of his beard moved as his lips formed the words, the words that despite everything else going on inside his head were clear, each one registering like a huge flashing neon sign.

"No one will care. I give you two weeks, three weeks at the most, then everyone will forget about you. All the memories they have of you will start to become coloured, by the real Michael that they never knew. When they speak of you in a year's time, you'll be a sad little paedophile who killed some whore then topped yourself. Even Rachel will draw a line over the time she had spent here with you, remembering little things that maybe had existed maybe hadn't, and she'll beat herself up about not noticing what you really were. But then even she will just get on with her new life, find a new man, a real man…"

"YOU LITTLE FUCKING, HELP, SOMEONE GET ME HHHUUUUGGGNNN"

His whole body jerked up under the force of the taught rope, his two sets of teeth slamming shut slicing off the end two centimetres of his tongue. His mouth filled with the thick hot liquid, some trickling down his chin, managing to squeeze through his clamped lips.

***

Mr Clarke heaved on the steering wheel and the red van, its dim headlights barely visible in the dull November morning, turned across the damp tarmac. Going faster than he had intended, he guided the creaking, whining vehicle up over the path and down the drive that ran by the side of 101. The drums behind him bounced, putting more strain on the already stretched suspension, and a scream of metal on concrete shot out into the brittle air along with a small shower of sparks. The front door slid out of view through the driver's window and he slammed his left foot on the break and pulled on the large handbrake. In one smooth almost athletic movement that belied his years, he unbuckled his seatbelt, clicked on the interior light and squeezed through the gap between the front seats. The six drums sat in front of him, the liquid sloshing noisily inside.

The theory, the physics, the chemistry, all that was fine. It had been written by hundreds of professors, physicists and engineers. It had been studied by thousands more, but it was one thing recreating it in equations and even in the laboratory, another thing entirely doing it with trembling sweaty hands in the back of a creaking Bedford van. The crucial part was the first explosion, the small one that would fill the air with the first load of the doctored petrol. A second later this would be ignited creating a second much larger explosion as it greedily sucked up the oxygen inside the van and its immediate surroundings. In turn this would ignite the remaining fuel, creating the third explosion. The big one. The one that would eradicate 101 Beechcroft Road and more importantly the corresponding bar from the chart. It was going to be perfect, beautiful, and not for the first time Mr Clarke regretted that he would be unable to witness the spectacle in its entirety. He would hear it all, and that would be enough, and he would have the coming days to watch and revel in what he had done. What he had created. Destroyed.

Putting these thoughts aside, he ran through the checks, the same checks he had run through the previous afternoon in the fume filled garage, dozens and dozens of times. That was when he saw it and froze, the air in his throat and lungs suddenly becoming like lead, forcing him down towards the dirty metal floor of the van. The copper wire connecting the timer to the smaller drum was sticking up, pointing and waving at the ceiling. His eyes, then his fingers went to the spot it should have been, and it was obvious what had happened. The wire had sheared off where it went onto the timer. The movement in the van on the journey here must have put too much strain onto it and it had snapped off. Aware that time was rushing along, that he should be by now setting the timer to go and be making his way out of the van he knew he had to think and act fast. If the wire had snapped anywhere else he could have simply twisted the two ends together, but it had snapped at the end, leaving nothing to connect it to. It would need to be soldered, or the whole mechanism taken apart. Anger and frustration overwhelmed him, there was nothing he could do, he would have to abandon the whole thing. He knew the thing to do was to get behind the wheel and leave, get out before anyone saw him, before he raised any suspicions, then maybe, just maybe he could come back later in the week, tomorrow when he'd fixed the timer. But he couldn't move. Why had he been so stupid, so unprepared. All the preparation, the infinitesimal attention to detail had all been for nothing because he had failed to secure the barrels in place. Because he had failed.

An image of the chart flashed into his mind, its rigidity, its simplicity, its perfection mocking his pathetic attempt to do its bidding. Almost a minute had gone since he had brought the van to a halt and with a monumental effort he forced his limbs to lift him up and turn so he could get back into the driver's seat and back to the garage, where he would try and salvage what he could from the shambles he had created. It was just as he thought he saw movement in the rear-view mirror that another thought came to him. An alternative plan of action - one that would make everything all right. It took less than two seconds for him to make up his mind, and his mind and body, galvanised with renewed energy, he quickly checked the rest of the equipment. The image of the chart was still there but now it wasn't mocking him, now it was guiding him, its straight lines and angles calming him, steadying his hands and regulating his breathing. Yes, this was the right way forward; this was how it should have been from the start. That wire was designed to break off, and he was just grateful that he had realised in time the path he needed to take.

Slight alterations made, the checks complete, he leant back against the metal side of the van taking stock not only of the huge bomb in front of him, but also of the bigger picture, of everything he had achieved so far, of everything that he and the chart had accomplished, would accomplish in the next half minute. This was where it had all been leading to; this was where it was all supposed to end. Nothing had ever felt so right in his entire life. Images of people, wounded people; dying people; screaming people all flicked through his mind, all people that had been touched by his hand, that had had their lives their destinies shaped, moulded, and destroyed by the chart.

Putting the disconnected timer onto the floor between his feet, he took a deep breath, leaned forward and flicked the homemade switch on top of the smallest drum.

CHAPTER TWENTY-NINE

Doug had just drunk the last of the tea when the first explosion went off. Powerful enough to remove most of Mr Clarke's fingers and face, it sounded to Doug, and the rest of the officers waiting in the operation room more like a loud pop than a bang, and the chatter hadn't died down by the time the second blast, this one a proper roar accompanied by tearing metal and breaking glass, ripped through the red van just outside the police station. This second explosion instantly killed Mr Clarke, shattering his body and sending it out through the dustbin lid sized hole ripped in the van's side. Limbless and headless, his burning torso flipped over twice before settling down, next to a sign stating that unauthorised vehicles would be removed.

The air was filled with the angry screams of alarms from within the building just as the rest of the fuel in the remaining five drums erupted with another, louder all-consuming roar. The van disintegrated, just an inferno of doctored fuel, sat on a bubbling, whistling metal and plastic stand with four burning wheels where it had stood waiting for its fate only five seconds earlier. The very front of the cabin, with an old AA badge attached to its radiator looked out unharmed, unaware of the carnage behind it. Metal tore through the air, slicing through the bushes and a tree, gouging into the soft earth that lay to the right of the driveway and small car park; bouncing off the walls and concrete. Flames shot up into the air chasing shards of metal, ten, twenty, thirty feet high. The roar, competing with the alarms, was punctuated by the falling metal and glass as it careered back to the earth. All eight windows on that side of the building were gone, the station staring agog through its glassless eyes at the destruction being wrought upon it.

Two floors up Doug threw himself to the floor as shards of glass showered down around him. Over the cacophony outside and the alarm wailing on the wall above and to his right he could hear people screaming in another room and someone next to him was shouting about the IRA. Turning onto his back he quickly checked himself, discovered that he was unharmed and surveyed the chaotic scene around him. People were yelling and running down the corridor behind him, and through the small part of what had been the window he could see thick black smoke, penetrated here and there by brilliant orange tongues of flame. Pieces of metal were starting to fall, raining down onto the ground below adding their staccato rhythm to the pandemonium. The room was filled with the acrid smell of burnt rubber and metal and what he hoped wasn't flesh, and even from his position under the table, twelve feet from the jagged framework of the window he could feel the heat. His hair and shirt were buffeted by a strong breeze, as the inferno sucked up what oxygen it could. A hand shook his calf and he spun round narrowly missing his head on the table top, to see D.C. Davies' face inches from his.

"You Ok?" The question was bellowed into his face and was backed up by a clenched fist with a protruding thumb pointing to the ceiling. Doug nodded and returned the sign. Behind him, someone was asking for the sodding alarm to be turned off, while someone else was shouting that they had something sticking out of their fucking eye. D.C. Davies was pulling at his leg again, and this time his thumb was pointing to the door. Quickly he crawled towards the door, around the table legs and chairs, over the glass covering the carpet like confetti at a crazy wedding. Through the foul smelling hot air. The breeze had lessened but this had allowed more of the thick hot smoke to enter the room, and he could see it sliding down the walls in poisonous curls. It obliterated the ceiling and as it reached the floor it was spreading across the floor consuming the crawling, swearing figures. Coughing and spluttering was added to the recipe, and then the sound of tables and chairs being thrown aside, as panic started to seep into the atmosphere.

Doug reached the corridor and stood up brushing off the glass that had managed to embed itself in his knees, elbows and palms. People were running along the corridor to his left while, behind him his colleagues, only minutes earlier waiting for the telephone to send them on a raid across town emerged one by one. In all the chaos, all the shouting, the panic, the smell and the heat he was surprised at what image was most prevalent in his mind. Surprised but happy that at this moment, when his life was in very real danger, that it was Jackie, his wife, that his thoughts turned to.

The attack on the police station, 101 Beechcroft Road, carried out by a Mr Terrence Clarke, at 8:34 am on the morning of 18th November 1996 resulted in just one fatality. The list of injuries was long but thankfully most were not serious, and though D.C. Galbraith did lose the site in his right eye, the force could count itself as fortunate. A Mrs Philappoussis, who had been walking on the footpath behind where the bomb had been detonated, was the only member of the public to be hurt. She sustained minor cuts caused by flying metal but thankfully her four-year-old son who she was taking to playschool was unhurt.

It would take the authorities three weeks to discover who the burnt remains in the car park belonged to.

CHAPTER THIRTY

Almost a mile across town, only the third explosion managed to make itself heard to the occupants of the largest bedroom in the squat. Mike, with the blood spilling from his mouth, down his chin onto his dark blue sweater, down his throat, threatening to drown him, ignored it. There was not enough room left in his head, he had no spare senses to dedicate to the noise that may have been a car backfiring, may have been a car crash, a plane crash – the way the world had been behaving, it could have been a nuclear bomb.

The sirens that abruptly sprung out through the crisp autumn air, first one then two, then half a dozen, multiplying like feral cats, briefly took Carl's attention away from the figure in front of him, and even Mike allowed himself to begin to start to think that maybe they were coming to save him, rescue him, but almost as quickly it became obvious that the sirens weren't coming nearer, and if anything were going away from his first floor dungeon.

Reading his thoughts, Carl sneered. "No one's coming for you Michael. No one's going to save you." He was pulling on the rope, just keeping it tight enough to keep Mike's bloody chin tilting towards the ceiling, making every swallow, every sucked in breath, an effort. The rope in his hand, he walked back around behind the chair, so he was standing with his back to the window, facing Mike sideways on. Mike's eyes peered at him through the corners of their sockets, the tension on the rope preventing him from moving his head.

"You're probably wondering why I went to the trouble of using the blue foam on your arms and legs Michael. Do you know why? Hey? Do you know why?" Each word was accompanied by a tug on the rope, each question mark by a bigger one.

Mike wanted to shout, to scream, that he couldn't give a fuck about anything he had done any more, that he didn't want to hear another word about dead prostitutes, child porn, heroin addiction, prison, septicaemia, S.T.D.'s, police investigations… anything. Sat there his tongue pumping blood, tied to a wooden chair in a shit smelling house, a noose around his neck – a noose held by someone he had gone to school with but hadn't seen since, he didn't want to hear anything. He didn't have the energy to fight anymore. He had endured one false dawn, but he could take no more. He didn't even know if he was scared any more. He wanted to yell all this to Carl, to tell him, that whatever he had planned, he didn't care, stripping him of his final victory. But he didn't. He couldn't. He just stared at him through bloodshot eyes, down his nose and into the gleaming ones in Carl's grinning head.

"When you're dead Michael, your neck stretched, your tongue," a giggle escaped his excited mouth, as his eyes sought out and found the small chunk of tongue lying between Mike's trainers, "your tongue black, you're eyes bulging, I'm going to take off your restraints, cut through the string, remove the foam, and all you will be able to see are the puncture marks where you had obviously been injecting yourself That'll explain the crap in your body as well. No one is going to believe its suicide if you've got rope marks on your wrists and ankles are they?"

The blood had slowed down to a trickle now, but with his jaws still clamped shut, Mike was forced to swallow the thick warm contents of his mouth.

"You see I've thought of absolutely everything. They can say what they want about our prison system Michael, but it's the best thing that ever happened to me. Without that, well we wouldn't be here Michael, and you know what?" he moved within kissing distance of Mike's rouged lips, "I wouldn't have missed this for the fucking world."

Holding onto the rope with his left hand he stretched as far as he could with his other and just managed to get a grip on the camera sat on the chest. "Shall we have one more picture for the album Michael?" Clumsily he rotated the camera in his hand so it was pointing the right way, and so that his index finger hovered over the button. "Smile."

The flash filled the room once more and then again. "There, good boy Michael. Though, you really should have made more of an effort you know." He laughed as he tossed the camera onto the mattress in the corner, then his face became serious once more like a cloud moving across the sun. "My only regret is that Lorna will never see these Michael. So she could see that the world isn't as fucked up as she thought, that bad things do happen to bad people not just the innocent."

"You haven't got long left now Michael, and I want you to spend your remaining few minutes thinking about a couple of things. First of all, get rid of any thoughts that this isn't going to happen Michael. No one is going to save you, no one knows you are here, and I am certainly not going to let you off. This isn't my plan to scare you Michael, and we

328

both know I've killed before. You are going to die in a very few minutes. Right, now you understand that, I want to tell you what I'll be doing for the rest of my life. Just in case you were worried." A laugh escaped him again, and he moved round to the other side, his back to the closed door, his face inches from the blood that was starting to dry on his chin.

"After you're dead and I've cut you off the chair, and got rid of the foam and everything. I'm going on a little trip. A holiday. You see I've been saving up Michael, but when you're like me, when you're like the sort of person you made me, you just can't get a job, open a bank account, go to the fucking cash machine Michael and withdraw a hundred pounds here, a hundred quid there. We have to use other… banks, other accounts. An off license here, old woman with her pension there. They are some more people you can add to the list of your victims Michael. Tens more lives you've screwed."

"It's not a fortune, but as you can see," he gestured to the room, "I'm a man of simple means. I don't need much. And it's enough for a start. A good start. By lunchtime today, I'll be in the air Michael, heading for America. For a new life. Start again, find myself a pretty young Yank girl, and live the life that you had all planned with Rachel before… before I came and ruined it all.

"And that brings me to the other thing I want you to think about as the rope tightens and your neck stretches. Rachel. In a couple of years, probably less she'll be with a new man, saying to him all the things that you thought were special for you. Doing all the things in bed that you thought were purely for Michael Burley. Planning the rooms in their new house together, their next holiday, what they are cooking for dinner that day. Someone is walking around out there now," he gestured to the bordered up window, grey light from its edges struggling to make its presence felt in the room, "will see that face, that body, every morning he wakes up."

Carl stood up, feasting his eyes on the face in front of him. Mike just sat there, tears rolling down his face, mixing with the sweat and blood. No one moved for a couple of minutes. Mike, convinced now that everything Carl had said was true, that there wasn't any more hope for him, tortured himself with the images Carl had placed there. Rachel's smiling, happy face stared back over a glass of wine; from the dressing table as she applied just a dab of make up; above a plate of food, her long slender fingers fanning the food in her mouth as she struggled with the too hot food.

He closed his eyes, not wanting her image to escape through his huge gaping pupils, hoping to lock it inside with him. Carl walked round to the back of the chair, that had started to shake with the sobs of the man in it, and pulled on the rope. Pulling one straining arm over the other, he leaned back, his eyes never leaving the face of Michael Burley as he was lifted towards the beam in the ceiling. A short series of grunts accompanied his slow ascension, the chair once it became free of the floor, hung loose, still tied to the shins of the hanging man. The figure started to rotate, and Carl saw that his eyes were still clamped shut. There was one more, louder grunt, then the noise as Mike's neck finally broke and then the room was filled with silence. Only Carl's laboured breathing and the gentle creaking of the rope breaking it.

CHAPTER THIRTY-ONE

The vast space was filled with people. Excited people, irritated people. People struggling with bags - some on tiny wheels, others having to be carried. Families dressed in t-shirts, shorts and flip-flops despite the cold November weather outside, mixed with others in thick coats and jeans. Some were holding up handmade signs bearing the names of family members others displaying the glossy logo of travel firms. In the middle of it all Spoon stood, taking it all in, somehow feeling that he didn't belong, that he was looking at it all, all the other people from the outside. For the twentieth time since arriving at the airport his hand went to his back pocket and felt the comforting thickness of what it contained. Content, it crawled spider like to his other back pocket and patted the stiffness of his passport, mercifully still in date. His other hand clutched a bright yellow carrier bag that contained the rest of his possessions. These amounted to a small assortment of clothes and a pebble. A smooth pebble, one half blue one half pink. At one stage the bag had also contained a photograph of a woman. A woman standing self-consciously in front of a stone wall, with half a cow in the background. At the train station where he caught the train that had brought him to the airport he had taken the photo out and gently kissed it before folding it and placing it in a waste bin.

He hadn't slept now for twenty-four hours but he had never felt so awake. From the moment he had entered Danny's room the evening before, it was as if had stepped onto an escalator. He had killed Elton John, and had gone to the tea chest, lifting up the creaking wooden lid covered with stickers, doodles and graffiti. Inside it was a lot more ordered than he had expected, neat piles of what looked like mostly junk. The usual assortment of pornographic magazines, some neatly folded clothes, some pictures of what could have been a younger beardless Danny and younger girl. There were what seemed to be a random selection of newspapers, both in style and date. Just as Spoon was beginning to wonder what the hell he was actually expecting to find, next to an open roll of cloth displaying several delicate tools - small hammers, screwdrivers and many long, thin pieces he had no idea what to call, he saw a red Swiss army knife. His Swiss Army knife. The one with R E scratched into its side. The one that he had kept in his box and that until seeing it then had not been aware it had moved.

He had picked it up, turning it over and over in his hands. He no longer cared if he was caught. He started systematically going through the remainder of the chest, pausing briefly when he uncovered what looked to be some files and parole card belonging to a Carl Baker. He had almost given up finding anything else when his hands gripped a large jiffy bag that was lying under a pile of boxer shorts. He almost ignored it, but something had made him go back to it and retrieve it. Inside wrapped in more newspaper cuttings he had discovered his future. Thousands of pounds in neat elastic-band tied bundles. Every denomination from fives up to fifties. Spoon didn't need to count it to know there were at least three or four thousand pounds, probably more. The sight of it, row after row of the queen's stately head looked up at him asking him what he was going to do. He was many things, he knew that, but until then he didn't think he was a thief. The money stared up at him, feeling at the same time glorious but so very heavy in his sweating fingers. He couldn't stop himself casting nervous glances over his shoulder, knowing that whatever happened now he had overstepped a line. He knew he would have to leave the squat now for good whatever happened. There was no way he could stay knowing that in the chest, in the room mere feet from where he slept was the answer to all his problems. He either took the money and went to Spain, or he put it back in the chest, took his knife and… and what? Start again in another squat, in another provincial town. He could see the image of the snow-capped mountains that had briefly flared so brightly only seconds before, fading. There was one other object lying on top of the money that he had ignored until then, the sight of the money obliterating everything else. He forced his hands to let go of a bundle of fifties he had been squeezing and opened the deep red passport. It looked brand new, and he could smell the leather as he prised the pages open. Danny's face peered out from the inside of the back cover. Next to it the name Carl Baker swam in front of his eyes, the same name he now recalled that had been on some documents elsewhere in the chest.

Spoon didn't need to know any more. He didn't want to know. They all had secrets, hidden lives, tales of woe and misfortune. That was why they had all ended here in a squat, existing on the outside of society. But Spoon's instinct – an instinct that wasn't called upon very often but when it was, rarely let him down – told him that Danny's story, Carl's story was different. Dangerous. His mind made up, he put down the passport and grabbed up the money. Ten minutes later he had left the squat for the last time.

Two trains had brought him to the airport and after brief enquiries, he had bought a ticket for the next flight to Malaga. He had spent the night on one of the many chairs watching the people come and go, eavesdropping the excited chatter about faraway places and had dreamed about his future, about the scenes in the photographs. The photographs that had joined the one of his Mother in the station bin. This time when he pictured the scenes however, the walls of the houses looked more solid, like he could almost touch them, and the people in the streets and café appeared to be smiling and looking at him.

A voice over the Tannoy brought him back from his reveries. He took one final look around, checked his money and passport, and headed for the large yellow sign that said departures.

Printed in Poland
by Amazon Fulfillment
Poland Sp. z o.o., Wrocław